Praise for Kate Cary's **BLOODLINE**

"An interesting blend of mystery, horror, and romance, and readers who love vampire novels will find it a refreshing twist to the classic story."

—*School Library Journal*

"Intriguing reinterpretation of a classic."

—*Kirkus*

"[F]ans of gothic fiction in general and Van Helsing in particular will want to get their hands on this latest incarnation of the Dracula mythos."

—*Bulletin of the Center for Children's Books*

Also by Kate Cary

Bloodline Book Two: Reckoning

BLOODLINE

A NOVEL BY
KATE CARY

razor
bill

Bloodline

RAZORBILL

Published by the Penguin Group
Penguin Young Readers Group
345 Hudson Street, New York, New York 10014, U.S.A.
Penguin Group (USA) Inc., 375 Hudson Street, New York, New York 10014, U.S.A.
Penguin Group (Canada), 90 Eglington Avenue East, Suite 700, Toronto,
Ontario, Canada M4P 2Y3 (a division of Pearson Penguin Canada Inc.)
Penguin Books Ltd, 80 Strand, London WC2R 0RL, England
Penguin Ireland, 25 St Stephen's Green, Dublin 2, Ireland
(a division of Penguin Books Ltd)
Penguin Group (Australia), 250 Camberwell Road, Camberwell,
Victoria 3124, Australia (a division of Pearson Australia Group Pty Ltd)
Penguin Books India Pvt Ltd, 11 Community Centre, Panchsheel Park,
New Delhi - 110 017, India
Penguin Group (NZ), Cnr Airborne and Rosedale Roads, Albany,
Auckland 1310, New Zealand (a division of Pearson New Zealand Ltd)
Penguin Books (South Africa) (Pty) Ltd, 24 Sturdee Avenue,
Rosebank, Johannesburg 2196, South Africa

Penguin Books Ltd, Registered Offices: 80 Strand, London WC2R 0RL, England

10 9 8 7 6

Interior design by Christopher Grassi

THE LIBRARY OF CONGRESS HAS CATALOGED THE HARDCOVER EDITION AS FOLLOWS:
Cary, Kate.
  Bloodline : a novel / by Kate Cary.
    p. cm.
  Summary: In this story told through journal entries, letters, and other primary sources, a
British soldier in World War I makes the horrifying discovery that his regiment command-
er is descended from Count Dracula.
  ISBN 1-59514-012-3 (hardcover)
  [1. Vampires—Fiction. 2. World War, 1914–1918—Fiction. 3. Diaries—Fiction.
4. Horror stories.] I. Title.

  PZ7.C2629Bl 2005
  [Fic]—dc22
                                                            2004026078
Razorbill paperback ISBN: 978-1-59514-078-4

Printed in the United States of America

For Deborah Smith

BLOODLINE

PROLOGUE

Journal of
Captain Quincey Harker

13TH JULY 1916

Blood from last night's raid has hardly dried on my uniform. Still the familiar craving builds in my belly and I long to wield my sword.

I can almost feel the blade slicing through air, then skin, then flesh, then bone, blood spraying the wooden walls of the enemy trench, the smell of it suffusing the air so sweetly.

I feel my mouth moisten as I drag the enemy soldier, screaming, into the shadowy recess of his trench. I snap back his head and bury my teeth into the succulent flesh of his neck. Fear makes the pitiful creature's blood pulse so fiercely through his veins that at first piercing, I have to swallow greedily so as not to gag.

I revel at the thought of the killing to come and, with it, the feasting—so different from the sly, quiet stalking of prey

1

in days before the world was at war. Here in battle, no such artifice is necessary. I take my victims how I please, so long as they wear the uniform of the enemy.

Outside I hear the steady thump of the artillery and closer, the clatter of my men; they will be fixing bayonets to their rifles and inspecting their battle gear one last time, their sodden boots slipping in the mud that covers the floor of the trench.

Even in my dugout I can smell their delicious fear mingled with the evening mist that rolls in from the corpse-strewn craters of no-man's-land. My lust for blood rages inside me.

Enough. I must tend to my own weapons—not that I have any need of them. Why waste the tearing of flesh on a senseless bullet when it is so pleasurable to drain a life away personally?

It is time to prepare for battle.

CHAPTER 1

*Letter from Lieutenant John Shaw
to Miss Lily Shaw*

NORTHERN FRANCE
13TH JULY 1916

Dearest Lily,

Just a few short lines to let you know I've arrived at the front. I am told I will report to my new commanding officer—one Captain Quincey Harker—first thing tomorrow.

Captain Harker has become something of a hero to the men here, it seems. I just hope that I shall prove a worthy aide and fulfill my duties as communications officer to his satisfaction.

Your parcel containing the new red leather journal was waiting for me when I arrived. It was such a comfort to be welcomed by something from home. Thanks. You've been a darling, as ever—the best sister a chap could have. All those blank pages to fill will be a boon, for I'm told there is little else to do here in the trenches when one is not on duty.

Worry not, Lily. With such a well-regarded commander as Captain Harker, I am certain to return to you safe and sound.

I'll write more when I've settled in.

Your loving brother,

John

*Journal of
Mary Seward*

30TH AUGUST 1916

It has been nearly seven weeks now since the town of Purfleet sent over a hundred of its men to fight in the Great War. A convoy returned fifteen of them to the sanatorium late this afternoon—as casualties.

Some have lost limbs; others have been gassed, eyes blinded and lungs so burned that it pains them even to breathe. Their suffering has been made worse, no doubt, by the long journey from France. We only managed to find room for them by moving some of the more recovered onto camp beds in the corridors.

The number of wounded in this war seems endless. Each

of my new cases stirs a longing inside me—a fervent wish for this horrible conflict to be ended.

This morning, Sister sent me to help with one of the new arrivals—a young lieutenant. His eyes were closed and his dark lashes looked like coal smudges against his smooth, pale skin. As the two orderlies laid him on his bed he remained still, almost rigid, clasping a red leather-bound book to his chest.

"A quiet one, this," one orderly commented, gathering up the stretcher.

"Makes a change," answered the other grimly. "They usually start yellin' as soon as we move 'em. Times are I want to stuff a rag in each of their mouths."

Their coarse words didn't shock me. I knew it was their way of coping with the daily horrors we see here at the sanatorium. Low moans of pain and fear seep from every ward, float down every corridor—just as they did before the war, when the sanatorium was run by my father as a hospital for lunatics.

As a child I used to visit him in his office with Mother. She'd hold my hand as we walked down the wide corridors lined with bolted doors, urging me to pity the poor raving souls contained within.

"Here's his chart." One of the orderlies handed me a grubby envelope. "Lucky bugger, by all accounts—carried back from the front line by his commanding officer."

I slipped the card out from inside to read the notes on the lieutenant's injuries. Bayonet wound to the shoulder, healing well, but brought down by an uncommonly virulent strain of trench fever.

I looked at the soldier's name—John Shaw. It was familiar. Did I know this poor soul? I examined the soldier's face more carefully.

Yes! With a start I realized that this man was indeed John Shaw from Carfax Hall, the estate adjoining Purfleet Sanatorium.

I'd met him and his sister, Lily, only once, in the summer after I turned fourteen. They arrived quite unexpectedly with their rather stern-looking nanny at a neighbor's garden party. I had spent the whole afternoon sighing over this very same John Shaw, then a tall, handsome boy with a lazy smile, on holiday from Eton. He never spoke to me. Nonetheless, our eyes met several times. And for the next week I kept a secret book in which I inscribed his name and mine over and over again, the letters entwined like wild roses.

That was before the war began. Another life. Another world.

I took one of Lieutenant Shaw's mud-covered hands in my own. His flesh was cold, so icy I feared he might be dead. Aghast, I turned my head to call a doctor, but at that moment he drew a deep, rattling breath. He did not seem to know I was there, just lay there stiffly, seemingly untouched by the noises of the ward around him.

Remembering my duties, I left him to fetch soap and water. Then gently, I eased the red book from his grasp, smelling the earthy odor of its leather over the sterile tang of the ward. From the way he'd clutched it to his chest, all the way from the battlefields of France, the volume was clearly precious to him.

I opened its cover and saw it was his journal. Page after page, written in a strong hand. There were also letters and a sprig of lilac between its leaves.

I closed it and put it safely to one side as I got on with washing the filth from John Shaw's chilled flesh. Except for the tremors that shook his body from time to time, he did not stir.

My heart ached. How different was this homecoming from the one he'd had just a few summers ago!

"Has he spoken yet, Seward?"

Sister's commanding voice startled me. She was standing at the foot of the bed.

"No," I replied. "Not to me, at least. But this man and his sister live in Carfax Hall, just beyond the sanatorium grounds."

She glanced at John Shaw's notes. "Someone should let Miss Shaw know of her brother's whereabouts," she said. "But not until tomorrow. He seems to be at no immediate risk, and we need to get all these men washed and settled."

"I would be happy to call upon Miss Shaw," I offered. "I do not know her well. She and Lieutenant Shaw came to Purfleet after their parents were killed, and they have always lived very privately. But I'm sure I could break the news more gently than a telegram."

"Thank you, Mary," Sister replied. "That would be most kind of you."

For the next several hours, Sister kept me busy as ever tending to the wounded. I had barely time to think. But in spite of myself, my eyes kept wandering to the still form with the red leather book by its side.

By the end of my shift, John Shaw had not stirred. I stood at his bedside, looking down at his pale, unresponsive face. Where was his spirit? What might I do to help him?

Then my eye was caught by his journal. Might words from his own life draw him back into the world?

I picked it up and began reading to him. "'This journal is to be a record of my experiences while fighting for King and Country. It has been sent to me by my dear sister, Lily, back in Purfleet.'"

I glanced at his face. He remained utterly still. I wasn't sure he could hear me, but I read on. And then I heard a low, tortured groan.

I looked up. He was lifting his head slowly toward me. His eyes opened, a beautiful blue, looking into mine. There was such anguish in their depths—as if the bayonet had pierced his very soul.

He rasped out one agonized word. "Stop."

With trembling hands I shut the book.

His head sank wearily back onto his pillow.

I sat there, heart racing. Had I done wrong? Had my reading harmed him somehow?

As I watched, his hands began to do a curious, wandering dance in the air, as if he were batting away invisible insects. Without thinking, I reached out and clasped his fingers in mine. "Hush," I whispered. "Be easy, sir."

His answering grip, sudden and tight, made me wince. His eyes opened once more and fastened upon my face. His gaze widened.

"Angel," he said. His voice was no more than a sigh. "Save me."

He brought my hand up to pillow his cheek. I sat there, not daring to move, as his breathing deepened. The lines of strain in his face eased and I realized with a sort of wonder that he was sleeping naturally. At last, I gently pulled my hand away.

What had he gone through at the front? What hideous memories tormented him so? Again I found myself thinking of his journal. If I knew what he had endured, wasn't it possible that I could use that knowledge somehow to reach him in his darkness?

There was only one way to find out. Without allowing myself to think about it, I slipped the journal into the large front pocket of my apron.

As I write in my own journal, here at home, Lieutenant Shaw's sits unopened on my desk. I wrestle with my conscience. Should I read its words uninvited? It draws my eye like a living creature, clasping between its pages the letters and articles he has saved. How can I ignore what might give a clue to what tortures him?

Or am I simply making an excuse to pry? Am I hoping to recapture the twined roses and summer smiles of that day we met?

No. I want to help him if I can!

Enough. Enough.

I shall read it.

CHAPTER 2

War Journal of
Lieutenant John Shaw

NORTHERN FRANCE
13TH JULY 1916

This journal is to be a record of my experiences while fighting for King and Country. It has been sent to me by my dear sister, Lily, back in Purfleet, keeping the home fires burning.

She has pressed a lilac from our garden between the pages of this book to remind me of the beauty and peace of England—that very thing I have come to the battlefront to protect.

There is something delicious in beginning a new book, even in such circumstances: the creak of the spine bent back for the first time; the pure, fresh whiteness of the topmost page. Only my ink shall stain it. What stories might it contain by its end?

I arrived here at the front just after sunset. The march

from the train was hard, through a weary landscape, burnt and battle scarred. The constant drizzle had thickened into rain as our party approached the trenches and the roads turned to mud by the constant traffic of lorries and horses. My boots are still caked in the stuff and the smell of it is foul.

A sergeant arrived to lead me to the division I was to join. I followed him to a dark world of narrow alleyways—the trenches.

The earth walls rose eight feet on either side of me as I climbed down into the huge trough. For a moment, I wondered if this must be what it is like descending into one's own grave.

My boots touched down on the uneven trench floor, made of sandbags with duckboards running along the ground. The surface of the wood was slimy with mud.

What a labyrinth it seemed! The tunnels snaked for miles, twisting and turning and dividing until I felt I was in a rabbit warren. The air was rank with the filthy odors of humanity. I fought down the urge to retch.

Soldiers littered the walkways, shuffling about their business. In the darkness, I could distinguish them from the mud only by their movements.

"We're here. Front line," the sergeant told me. "This is Corporal Jenkins. He'll take you from here."

I could just make out a stocky man, whose face wore a look of resignation. "Ah, our new communications officer," he said, saluting.

I returned the greeting and fought off another wave of nausea.

Jenkins noticed the look of disgust on my face. "You'll get used to the smell, sir," he told me as the sergeant withdrew. He pointed up to the darkening sky overhead. "We're just grateful they haven't roofed the place over. We'd probably choke from the fumes."

Jenkins let out a weary chuckle that was echoed by men at their posts beside us. They stood on the fire step, peering over the top of the wall, looking out for enemy activity. Their rifles were trained on the charred fields of no-man's-land.

Looking down the trench, I could see two soldiers crouched beneath a sheet of corrugated iron. They appeared to be brewing tea on a small charcoal burner.

"Where do you all sleep and eat?" I asked.

"No canteen and dormitories here, sir," Jenkins grunted. "I'm afraid this is it. We cook and sleep where we are." He gestured toward a small muddy alcove carved out of the trench wall. It was only big enough for a man to squat in. "That's where I'll sleep tonight," he told me.

I raised my eyebrows in disbelief. How could a man find comfort and rest in such cramped quarters?

"It's not so bad really, sir," Jenkins continued without a trace of resentment in his voice. "We'll move back to the supply trench in a few weeks; there's more room there. Or if we're lucky, they'll give us a couple of days leave. Then we can go to the nearest French village and borrow a barn off the locals. A bit of soft hay and shelter for a couple of nights always does us a world of good."

I was about to reply when a shrieking whine pierced the air. A flash like lightning burst fifty feet from the trench. I ducked as an explosion set the planks shuddering beneath my feet. Great chunks of earth rained down on my tin helmet.

"Looks like Fritz has finished his tea and decided to shift his fire," Jenkins commented. "That's the nearest shelling we've had from the Germans in an hour. Come on, sir, I'll show you your dugout. I think you'll find—"

Another explosion drowned out the rest of his words. Jenkins turned and, crouching as he ran, led me along the trench.

I hurried after him and felt guilty relief when he stopped beside a sturdy wooden door in the trench wall. "Here we go, sir. These'll be your barracks." He pulled the door open. A heavy curtain of tarpaulin lay behind it, which Jenkins tugged aside. "Keeps out the mustard gas," he explained. "Just a bit of it burns your skin like the dickens." He let the tarpaulin drop behind us as we stepped inside.

The room was dark and rich with the musty odor of earth and boots. There was a small, dirty window, but the moonlight hardly penetrated it. I waited while Jenkins lit an oil lamp. It illuminated a small space, maybe ten foot by ten foot, with a narrow bunk and a table—and a ceiling so low I felt I should stoop lest I bump my head.

"Safe from shrapnel in here, sir," Jenkins informed me. "Though if it's a direct hit, you don't stand any more chance than those of us outside."

"Quite right, Jenkins," I said, shaking the man's hand. "I guess we're all in the same boat, then."

I scolded myself for thinking poorly of my accommodations. Jenkins and his compatriots didn't even have a roof over their heads. At least here there was a ceiling, shelter from the elements, and some privacy.

I gazed once more around the room and noticed a parcel on the table. I picked it up and saw my beloved sister's handwriting. "Thank you, Jenkins," I said, keen to discover the package's contents. "I'll be all right from here."

Jenkins didn't need more than a hint. "Yes, sir," he said. "I'll leave you to get some rest. Captain Harker will probably want to see you first thing tomorrow. He'll be preparing to go off on one of his night raids at present. Seems he's more at home in the dark."

"A creature of the night, eh?" I joked. "Something a bit unsettling about that, isn't there, Jenkins?"

He didn't smile. "Captain Harker is a fine commander. No one I'd rather follow into battle. You've never seen a man so fearless. He gives us all courage. I think we would follow him to hell if he asked us." Jenkins paused. "But he's a strange one, too. Sometimes takes off on those night raids all on his own. Says it keeps him sharp . . . as if he needs to be any sharper." He nodded then and took his leave.

I stood there for a few seconds, considering what Jenkins had said. I couldn't help feeling awed at the prospect of meeting Captain Harker—a man brave enough to face the enemy on his own.

A moment later, I remembered my parcel; I picked it up and eagerly ripped off the wrapping. Inside, to my delight, was this handsome journal.

Before I sleep, I shall write darling Lily my heartfelt thanks.

14TH JULY 1916

I was roused from my bunk this morning by Jenkins. "Lieutenant Shaw!" he shouted. "Captain Harker wants to see you, sir!"

I pulled on my boots, then hurried along the trench to my new commanding officer's dugout. I reached his door, straightened my collar, and finally knocked.

"Come!" a voice called in response.

Swallowing the nervous lump that pressed at my throat, I opened the door. I pushed my way past the gas curtain and entered into a room dimly illuminated by the artificial light of an oil lamp. Curiously, the small window in the room was covered. Not even a glimmer of sunlight filtered through.

The shadowy form of Captain Harker was seated at his desk, leaned over a pile of papers. He did not look up.

As I waited, I stared with unease at his shadow, outlined on the wall beside him.

The shadow's profile, distorted by the flickering lamplight, appeared to belong to some stooping, murderous demon, illuminated on a church fresco.

I stared harder and imagined the demon's muscles taut— ready to strike.

Then, without warning, the demon spread its wings and lurched forth.

For an instant, my heart trembled. Then I realized that the captain was now standing, his movement the thing that had caused the shadow to change form.

I felt a foolish relief and chided myself for my childish imaginings.

As the captain stepped forward, I could at last see his face.

The grotesque form of his shadow had done him a great injustice. His towering height and sharp features would be considered quite handsome, I believe.

He regarded me closely for a few seconds. I could not distinguish the color of his eyes in the half-light, but they seemed to burn into me with disconcerting intensity.

At last, he held out his hand. "Lieutenant Shaw," he said genially. "I've so looked forward to meeting you."

His smile was astonishing—so full of warmth and charm that it had the effect of putting me quite at ease. "Thank you, sir," I responded.

"We've been facing the same enemy division for months now," the captain told me. "The monotony of trench life seems to sap the men's bloodlust. It will be good for morale to have a fresh soul around the place, not weary or jaded like the rest. And I trust you'll also prove good company for me."

"I shall do my best," I replied.

"I know you will." Harker's eyes seemed to glow. He did seem genuinely pleased at my arrival.

"Sit," he invited, "and tell me about yourself."

"Where should I begin?" I answered, pulling up a rough wooden chair.

"Begin with explaining how a young man educated at Eton should come to speak Romanian as well as English and German." He glanced at a file that I assumed must contain my records. "They certainly didn't teach it when I was there."

"You were at Eton too, sir?" I asked, pleased at the thought that we must share similar memories.

The captain nodded. "I left in 1905. A while before you arrived, I imagine."

I quickly calculated that he must be twenty-nine—ten years older than myself. Yet he could easily have been mistaken for one of my contemporaries. I had seen soldiers my own age already emaciated and gaunt from war. Remarkably, Captain Harker's smooth, fine features betrayed no hardship.

"We lived in Romania with my parents until I was nine," I explained. "My father was a diplomat."

"We?"

"Myself and my sister, Lily," I answered him. "She's a year younger than I. We returned to England with our Romanian guardian after our parents were killed in an accident."

"How terrible," Captain Harker murmured.

The tender subject made it hard to sustain his intense gaze. I looked away awkwardly. "It was harder for Lily than it was for me," I continued. "I was quickly dispatched to board at prep school, while she was left to grieve in a strange old house that our father had purchased in England. At the time I feared the grief might kill her. . . ."

I glanced back at Harker. The curiosity in his expression compelled me to go on. "Lily has always been such a sensitive soul," I explained. "But Antanasia, our nurse, never left her side. I believe that Antanasia's ministrations are the sole reason that Lily pulled through."

Harker nodded. "Have you no other relatives?"

"No," I replied. I forced a smile. "Death seems to have followed our family closely, but I am determined to outwit him until I am very old."

Harker's eyes burned through me with that same intense stare. "I have no doubt you shall get your wish, John."

I couldn't imagine why he was so certain. The battle-weary soldiers I'd encountered yesterday had, in a single day, made me horribly aware of how raw and inexperienced I am in this dark place. Yet his eyes held such conviction that it was easy to believe his words.

Harker returned to his chair. He slid open a desk drawer and took out a bottle of whiskey. "You will be surprised to learn just how much we have in common, Lieutenant," he said, smiling again. "But such a story deserves a drink." He poured a measure into each of the two tumblers that sat beside his lamp.

"My father, Jonathan Harker, died shortly after my first birthday," he began, handing me a glass. "My mother, Mina, was comforted by Count Tepes, a family friend and Romanian nobleman. They fell in love, and she and I went with him to his native Romania, where they married."

I took a sip of whiskey and found it rather strong. "So you too grew up in Romania?" I asked, stifling a cough as my throat burned.

Harker nodded. "Until I returned to England—for Eton—at thirteen."

"You are the first person I have met outside Romania who speaks the language," I remarked, gratified. "Apart from Antanasia and Lily, of course. Whereabouts did you live, sir?"

"Our home is a castle in the Carpathian Mountains. Transylvania," answered the captain. "Very close to a town named Bistritz. I suppose you lived in Bucharest?"

"Yes," I confirmed. "But we often traveled around the country. We may have visited Transylvania, when I was too young to remember. My parents loved the Romanian people; they found them warm and full of charm. If a little superstitious . . ."

"Ah, yes." Harker smiled. "And what did your parents make of Romanian folklore?" he asked.

I felt the heat of the whiskey reach my belly. "They tried to shield us from the peasants' dark stories," I replied. "They thought them too frightening for children."

Harker laughed. "But one should never shield children from darkness. For darkness will find them anyway. And all the more easily if they are not prepared." He swallowed his drink in one gulp and placed the glass back down on his desk.

"Did *you* believe the superstitions, sir?" I asked him curiously.

Captain Harker raised a sardonic black brow. "I still do," he said with a smile.

CHAPTER 3

War Journal of
Lieutenant John Shaw

17TH JULY 1916

As a communications officer, I take no part in active battle. It is a strange role I play, sitting in my small office, pad and pencil in hand, while the other men are shooting, shelling, fighting, and dying.

Lieutenant Butler, my counterpart in the communications office, assures me that our mission, eavesdropping on German radio communications, is vital. And yet . . .

Yet I wish to take a larger role in all of this—especially after what I have just seen.

Today I witnessed something of why Captain Harker is so revered.

The men had gathered in the trench at dusk, tense as they prepared for the next assault. While they awaited Captain Harker's arrival, they adjusted their bayonets with trembling fingers.

Then Harker strode toward them. He was something to behold, with the commanding stature of an emperor—at once an awe-inspiring and heartening sight. He flashed a confident smile. As his gaze swept over them the men snapped to attention, seeming to grow taller themselves, their mouths hardening with purpose.

Giving the command, Captain Harker mounted the ladder. In an almost superhuman feat, he leapt up and over the top of the trench. The men followed close behind him.

Despite the peril, I could not help but watch from the fire step as they marched into battle.

At once, they were spotted and our men were amongst the flash and roar. Harker raised his sword in defiance of the barrage that met them. The ground exploded as the enemy's well-aimed shells ripped into it. Some men fell swiftly. I felt the force of the blast that took them; earth splattered into the trench. I could smell the iron odor of blood mingled with cordite hanging heavily in the air.

But Captain Harker pressed on, head up, facing the enemy as if death would not dare touch him. Tin helmets tipped forward against the onslaught of both bullets and hardening rain. The men followed, advancing toward the enemy line.

Who is this man? I wondered. What about him allows him to sneer at death? I do not know, but I long to join him in the fray—to bring glory to my country and this regiment.

I was on early shift today. "Been busy?" I asked Lieutenant Butler as I entered the communications dugout to relieve him.

Butler nodded wearily. The desk was chaotic with paper. "Translating what I heard from the listening saps last night," he told me.

"Picked up anything interesting from the enemy lines?" I asked.

"Just the same old chatter. The poor sods sound more terrified than we do."

I picked up a German newspaper that lay on the desk. The crumpled news sheet felt brittle in my hand—as though it had once been sodden. "Where was this found?"

Butler rubbed his eyes, which were red from fatigue. "Someone picked it up when they flushed the enemy out of the eastern trench."

"Excellent! A victory! And we captured their newspaper," I commented wryly.

"For what it's worth." Butler shook his head. "Read it; it's utter piffle."

As I flicked through the pages, one of the headlines caught

my eye. *Dämon der Gräben.* "Demon of the Trenches," I translated. I read out the article beneath the lurid headline:

Speculation and rumors concerning a so-called demon of the trenches continue to grow. More soldiers have died at their posts, their bodies torn and bloody as if mauled by some animal. One soldier, however, claimed it was no ordinary animal that has been savaging our men. When interviewed, Lieutenant Klinsmann said:

"On the 12th July, I was patrolling my trench. The moon was bright that evening, so it was easy to see. Rounding a corner, I came upon a scene I will not forget for as long as I live. The bodies of my men lay slumped together, the floor of the trench awash with their blood. Beyond them I saw more men, stunned like rabbits in the headlights of a car, unable to defend themselves as a devilish black-pelted creature with eyes burning red as embers savaged each of them in turn. I shot at this demon with my pistol, but my bullets did not harm him."

Though the attack was real, with fifteen casualties recorded that night, no one else survived who could corroborate Lieutenant Klinsmann's story. Lieutenant Klinsmann has since been recalled to the Fatherland.

I tossed the paper back onto the cluttered desk and chuckled. "I'm surprised their newspapers are printing rot like this. It can't be good for morale."

Butler shrugged. "My guess is that our intelligence lads started the rumor to spook them. And they seem to have swallowed it hook, line, and sinker."

"This poor Klinsmann chap certainly did," I agreed.

Butler shook his head. "This war is as bad for the mind as it is for the body. In the fog of combat, we aren't always able to see things for what they really are."

29TH JULY 1916

Private Smith, who spends part of his day stationed outside the communications dugout, received news from home that he's going to be a father. Everyone is jolly pleased for him. He's well liked among the men, being such a good-humored chap.

I spent the day inside, listening to the saps, but when Butler relieved me at sundown, I decided to find Smith and pass on my good wishes to him. Corporal Jenkins told me he was on sentry duty.

I made my way along the trench and found Smith standing on the fire step, his rifle resting on the parapet in front of him. "I hear congratulations are in order," I said, keeping my voice low and giving him a gentle slap on the back.

"Yes, sir. Thank you, sir," he answered quietly, keeping

his eyes fixed on the darkening horizon ahead of him. The guns for once were silent, and only the low murmurings of the men disturbed the quiet evening.

"You must be pleased," I went on. "Is it your first?"

Smith nodded. "Honeymoon baby, I think they call it, sir." He turned momentarily to give me a quick smile. "We was wed five days before I left to come out here." He paused. "When all this is over, I'll be goin' home to me little chap."

"Chap?" I chuckled. "But Smith, how do you know it will be a boy?"

"It will be, sir." The private gave me a shy grin. "I just know it will."

He gazed down at me, and I noticed that his eyes were clouded with tears.

"Is everything all right?" I asked quietly, concerned now.

"Sorry, sir," Smith said, quickly wiping his eyes with his sleeve. "It's just, I didn't mind what happened to me before. I was scared, of course, but I knew that if I copped it, my Elsie could find herself another bloke to take care of her, and she'd remember me with pride . . . but now there's a little 'un on the way. If I die out here, my lad will grow up never knowing his dad. . . ."

I felt my own throat tighten, moved by his heartfelt words. But there was little comfort I could offer. I gripped his arm and gave it an encouraging shake. "Chin up. Why don't you write Elsie a letter?"

"I never got round to much schooling, Lieutenant," Smith admitted.

"That's all right. I can write it for you." I reached for the crumpled notepaper I always carried with me. "You keep your watch and tell me what to write. I'll make sure to get every word to Elsie, safe and sound."

So while Smith kept guard, I scribbled down his mumbled words of affection to Elsie, speaking of his delight and of how he couldn't wait to get home to her and the nipper. It gave Smith some peace of mind, and I was glad to have been the one to provide it.

1ST AUGUST 1916

I was awoken in the early hours by a massive explosion that shook me from my bunk. My heart hammered in the darkness. Had my dugout been buried under a direct hit?

I pulled on my boots and groped for the door. It opened easily.

Emerging, I saw the sky lit up by explosions—flash upon flash—shells landing all round us. I crouched down, cowering in the doorway. The sound and the flame transformed the scene before me into a depiction of hell itself.

"Move! Move!" Sergeant O'Reilly yelled. Soldiers hurried past carrying empty stretchers. I saw O'Reilly's mouth open and close as more flickering shellburst lit up his face and drowned out his voice.

It was hard to keep my balance there in the doorway as the passing soldiers buffeted me. Then I shook myself. What was I doing huddled here? I had duties to attend to.

My first instinct was to help the wounded among us. I stumbled toward the newly formed crater in the trench and tripped on a lump that lay in the broken earth. Fearing I had trodden on one of the wounded, I looked down.

Nobody was there, just an arm, bloody and outstretched as if to greet me. Tendons and muscles dangled from its end as it oozed a sickly red into the mud.

My vision blurred. The horror of the sight threatened to overwhelm me. But I fought against it. I had to be strong. I swallowed hard and staggered on.

In the area of the blast, there were hundreds of writhing, screaming bodies. It was impossible to know which of the injured to attend to first. I felt a hand grasp my ankle and forced my gaze downward. A young private curled like a kitten on the ground was shrieking up at me in agony.

I knelt to help him up, putting one arm around his shoulders and another on his belly.

A warm, oily substance covered my hand. I glanced down and found a gaping wound in the soldier's belly. His intestines and other organs threatened to spill out of him.

I grasped what skin I could and did my best to hold his guts inside. "Stretcher! Bring a stretcher!" I shouted. But no stretcher came.

The soldier had no strength in his legs, so I did the only thing I could think of. I tipped him over my shoulder, carrying him like a sack of coal.

"Holy mother of God! Holy mother of God!"

I tried to block my ears against his tortured screams and ignore the warm dampness of his blood spreading across my shoulder.

I delivered him to the medic and returned to the crater. I carried back another man and another until I grew numb to their agonized cries. I thought only of where I headed, putting one foot before the other and struggling to keep my balance beneath their writhing weight.

Afterward I crouched, exhausted, against the side of the trench. The shelling had eased, or at least moved farther down the line. An hour or so later, as dawn light began to seep into the shadows, the distant hammering fell away into silence.

"Sir? Are you all right?" Jenkins's voice sounded beside me.

I looked wearily into his filthy face. "Jenkins. You're not injured?"

"No, Lieutenant," he growled. "We live to fight another day." His tone was heavy with irony.

LATER

I was called to Captain Harker's office a short while ago.

"Your bravery during our last attack has proved you

worthy of your officer status, Lieutenant Shaw," he told me, looking pleased.

"Thank you, Captain," I replied, though I wondered how he knew about my actions. Try as I might, I could not recall seeing Captain Harker during the day's chaos.

Harker waved his hand toward the chair in front of his desk. "Sit down, Lieutenant."

I did so.

"How have you settled in?" he asked me. "Enjoying life at the front?"

I was getting used to caustic trench humor now. "Surviving so far, sir," I answered.

"If I were you, I'd feel somewhat helpless stuck here in the trenches," Harker suggested.

I stared at him, taken aback by his insight. The pull to have a more active role in battle had been growing steadily in me ever since I arrived.

"You want to be out there," finished Harker. "In the thick of it."

"I want to *fight* for my king and country," I declared.

"And you shall, John." Harker smiled. "Fear not, your orders will come soon. Then you and I will do our work together—under the cover of night."

I stared at him. Excitement and fear mingled inside me. A night raid! Did Harker plan to take me on one of his solitary assaults? I pictured myself climbing over the top of the trench, exacting revenge on those who had harmed our fallen comrades.

I returned to my dugout with my mind racing, my pulse pounding with excitement. When will I get the command?

I must close now to go and relieve Butler.

4TH AUGUST 1916

I will not write much for I am weary to the bone. The enemy raided the trench last night. We were taken by surprise; no one had raised the alarm.

They threw a grenade into the trench ahead of their arrival. A stupid strategy. Though we lost two men in the explosion, we'd have lost a lot more if the enemy had slipped in silently and slit all our throats.

As the impact from the explosion woke me I scrambled from my bed, reaching for my sword and pistol in one movement.

"The Hun are attacking!" Jenkins roared as I burst from my dugout. "We've got them pinned down in no-man's-land, but they're not retreating!"

With gun and grenade, we held them off as best we could. Jenkins and I stood side by side on the fire step, shooting at whatever shadow moved in the darkness ahead of us.

A wave of satisfaction washed over me whenever my bullet struck its target.

"Breach! They've breached the trench!" a voice bleated in the darkness.

"Hold your positions!" Harker's voice called above the sound of gunfire. Then screams, horrible bloodcurdling screams—from the same direction.

I prayed it was not our own men who uttered such anguished cries.

Jenkins and I continued to fight, but soon we were out of ammunition. "Damn," Jenkins muttered. "We're sitting ducks."

"Not for long," I told him. I scurried down the trench to the dugout, where the boxes of ammunition were stored. I was about to enter when, out of the corner of my eye, I saw Captain Harker, locked in combat with an enemy soldier.

I straightened, ready to defend my commander with my sword. But then, in the darkness, Captain Harker grabbed the soldier by the throat. I watched as he lifted him in the air—with only one hand!

The solider struggled to break Harker's grip, but try as he might, he could not. He flailed desperately.

The captain's face contorted into an expression of utter hatred. The German let out a squeal of terror, but the sound was cut short by a sick crack. The soldier went limp. Harker must have crushed the bones in his neck.

When the man was still, Harker gave a shudder. Then he dragged the soldier's lifeless body to a dark recess of the trench.

I blinked once. Twice. Had I really witnessed this incredible display of strength? It seemed wholly unreal and Harker the creature of another world.

"Lieutenant!" Jenkins yelled from our position. "We have to hold 'em!"

I raced back to the fire step to rejoin Jenkins in battle.

When the all clear was finally given, I helped transport the corpses of our fallen enemy back into no-man's-land. My limbs have little strength left after the effort.

German blood now adorns the walls of our trench—a grim reminder that we must remain ever vigilant, ever ready to face the enemy. With Captain Harker to guide us, I have no doubt that we shall remain strong.

5TH AUGUST 1916

Early this morning, despite our hunger and fatigue, Captain Harker ordered the remains of our division to assemble. We stood there, shivering in the cold pre-dawn.

"I wonder what he wants at this time of the morning?" Jenkins asked. He searched my face for a hint of Harker's motive.

I shrugged, having no idea what Harker wanted.

"Captain's coming!" Sergeant O'Reilly announced. We all straightened our backs and stood to attention.

Harker strode down the trench, his gaze strafing each and every man like artillery fire. We all stiffened, sensing his obvious rage.

"Last night the trench was breached!" he barked. "The enemy reached our door while we slept peacefully on." He paused, drawing a steadying breath to control his temper. "We *cannot* afford to fall into a stupor! *You* are all that stands between your families and hell, and yet some of you shuffle around these trenches like ghosts—as though you are already dead and there is nothing left to fight for! Are you going to let the enemy march right over you and on to England, to murder your wives and butcher your children?"

Some of the men shuffled uncomfortably. I couldn't help but feel a sense of indignation on their behalf. In the short time I'd been here, I'd witnessed the daily hardships they faced and been amazed by their resilience. Did they not bristle with the same sense of injustice?

Harker paused. "Private Smith was found asleep at his post last night."

The allegation was rich with menace. It took me by surprise. Nearby, the color drained from Private Smith's face.

"His negligence is what let the enemy slip into our midst," Harker snarled. "They might have killed every one of you."

Smith began to sputter an explanation. "But—but Captain, I—"

"O'Reilly! Jenkins!" Harker barked, cutting him off.

The sergeant and corporal stepped hesitantly forward. "Yes, sir?" O'Reilly responded.

"Take Smith to that wagon over there." Harker pointed over the top of the trench to an overturned wagon in no-man's-land. "Tie him to one of the wheels."

I heard a muted gasp from the men. Jenkins and O'Reilly looked at each other, their faces rigid with disbelief.

"But there is no protection there. He'll be blown to bits!" I exclaimed.

The men turned fearful gazes on me as I questioned Harker's decision.

Slowly, the captain faced me. The sun was beginning to rise over the horizon behind him, and he seemed ringed with fire. "The enemy raiding party was not spotted until it had reached the barbed wire," he told me, his voice calm and cold. "Smith's forty winks might have cost us forty lives."

I could not deny it. Harker was right. Yet I did not know how he could order such a thing. Smith was not yet twenty, and a father-to-be.

"No, sir!" Smith shouted as Jenkins and O'Reilly approached him. "I won't do it again, sir. I promise!" He cowered as Jenkins reluctantly reached out to take his arm. O'Reilly grasped the other, and Smith tried to pull away. "No!" he cried, his eyes frenzied. This time his words came as a shriek.

Harker said nothing.

"Please!" Smith cried the word again and again, his screams growing wilder as Jenkins and O'Reilly hauled him up one of the ladders and over the top of the trench.

The three men stumbled over the uneven soil toward the wagon. Smith kicked and flailed. Jenkins and O'Reilly were forced to drag him.

Harker ordered us all to watch while Jenkins and O'Reilly tied Smith at wrist and ankle, spread-eagled on the cartwheel like a martyred saint.

"That is what happens to fools," he growled. "And anyone thinking of untying that rope will find himself in similar circumstances." Then he strode away to the dark seclusion of his quarters.

When they'd finished, Jenkins and O'Reilly scurried back to the trench, leaving Smith alone and helpless in the rising dawn light.

"Harker," Jenkins spat.

"What's that? You often say you'd follow Captain Harker to hell if he asked you," O'Reilly grunted.

"Yes. But I didn't think he'd make me one of his demons," the corporal replied bitterly.

Journal of
Mary Seward

30TH AUGUST 1916

I have read only a small portion of Lieutenant Shaw's journal and I no longer wonder at the horrors that addle his mind. The cruelties he has witnessed and the conduct of his commander, Captain Harker, are so unspeakable as to drive even the sanest of men insensible. Indeed, it is all described so vividly that I fear I shall see Harker's face in my nightmares.

I want to close this journal forever. I wish to burn it so Lieutenant Shaw need never look upon its terrible passages again.

Still, I have not yet found a way to reach him. To show him that the horrors of war are behind him and that he is safe again. I do not want to, but I must read on. I only wonder what terrors await me.

CHAPTER 4

War Journal of
Lieutenant John Shaw

7TH AUGUST 1916

Harker went on another of his solitary raids last night. The men busied themselves once he had left, brewing tea or writing home. Trying to distract themselves, I suppose. But I know that like me, they were keeping one ear pricked for the sickening screams that would inevitably drift back from the enemy trenches. Screams the likes of which I have not heard—unless Harker is involved in battle.

As dawn neared and the other men slept, I stood alone in the moonlight awaiting Harker's return. I hoped to speak to him about Private Smith. Surely he had served his penalty and could be brought back into the trench before it was too late.

I heard a rustling above me and looked up with a start. The silhouette of Captain Harker towered on the brink of the trench. He stood there, in perfect stillness, his greatcoat flapping at his legs. He did not see me.

I strained to glimpse his face. It was dark and shiny in the moonlight. I squinted, then realized with horror that it was stained with thick red blood.

Harker licked his lips clean of the stuff and gave a satisfied sigh.

My own blood chilled at the sight. What kind of perversion was this?

As the sun began to redden the horizon, Harker jumped down into the trench. He landed easily, nearly floating to the duckboards—as if it were a three-foot drop rather than an eight-foot one. He turned and strode away toward his quarters.

For the first time, a hideous thought entered my mind: Captain Harker, so respected, so revered in battle, actually took a sick pleasure in his killing.

If that were true, we were in the command of a madman.

LATER

Jenkins came to tell me that they'd brought Smith down.

I jerked my head up incredulously. "You mean he's survived?"

"No. But his widow will be able to make a decent burial," Jenkins informed me flatly.

The news hit me hard. I wanted to weep. Because Smith

was dead—because his unborn child was already orphaned—and because my hope that he'd survived was so childish, so senseless.

"I've been wonderin' what it was that got him," Jenkins continued. "He had no wounds—none that I could see. But his color—it was beyond pale. And the look on his face was utter terror. Like he'd seen the face of the devil himself."

I turned away, wondering if Smith had simply died of fear—hanging there on that wheel while the earth around him exploded.

If so, I thought bitterly, it is Harker who killed him—just as much as that German solider in our trench or any of the others he's slaughtered. Smith's blood is on his hands. May God have mercy on him for it.

LATER

Smith's death has affected me badly. My body feels drained and my heart seems to lie heavy in my chest. To me, death in action had always been a thing of honor. Until now.

The brutality of which Harker is capable shocks me. It seems vicious and cruel beyond belief, utterly unconnected with the world I have known.

I wonder how I will be able to return to that world when all of this is over.

Jenkins showed me a somewhat primitive way to kill lice today.

"See!" He held the candle flame against the fabric of the jacket dangling from his other hand. "Run the flame along the seams 'cause that's where the buggers breed. Move it slow enough to roast 'em but not long enough to singe your shirt."

"Is that the only way to get rid of the infuriating blood-suckers?" I asked incredulously.

"It's the only way the army knows." Jenkins grinned.

The constant itching I experienced since coming to the trench had grown more and more unbearable as every piece of clothing I owned became infested with lice.

I followed Jenkins's example and took a candle to my own jacket. "I can hear their bodies crackling!" I declared, reveling in the sound of victory.

"There'll be more to replace 'em tomorrow," Jenkins replied wryly.

No matter. Today I'd be free of the lice. I ran my candle up and down each seam, killing and killing.

Over the stink of burning insects, the smell of roasted meat filled my nostrils. I looked along the trench. Murray and Allen had caught a rat and skinned it. They were grilling it over their burner.

My stomach churned. The unending diet of tinned slop had left us all craving meat, but to feast on the animals who fed off our fallen comrades? I wondered if Murray and Allen would detect the flavor of their brethren inside the bodies of the rodents.

13TH AUGUST 1916

I was on a day shift today. The line crackled as I listened in to the German communications coming in from the saps. It was almost time for Butler to relieve me when I heard a rap on the door.

"About time, you lazy . . ." My words trailed off as Captain Harker entered the dugout. I tensed, now undeniably uneasy in his company.

"Anything of interest on the saps today, Lieutenant?" Harker asked, sitting on the edge of my desk.

"Not so far, sir," I said.

Harker glanced around the small dugout. "This is a tiny office they've holed you up in," he observed. He fixed his intense dark gaze on me. "You look like a dog in need of a run. I shall take you on a raid this evening. I promised you'd see some action."

"Me, sir?" I answered, my heart beginning to race. Just days ago I had yearned for the opportunity to join Captain Harker behind enemy lines. Now I feared not only the enemy but Harker himself. What barbarity might he be capable of on such a raid?

He drew a map from his pocket and spread it on my desk, covering the notepads and pens that lay there already. It was a rough sketch of no-man's-land and the nearby enemy trenches. "There's an enemy gun dug in here." Harker jabbed the map with a long finger. "A nest of snipers." He flashed me a brief grin, then went on, deadly serious. "We are going to destroy it."

"Just us, sir?" I asked, hoping for the comfort of at least another soul during our journey.

"Of course," Harker answered easily. "A smaller attack assures us the element of surprise."

A rivulet of sweat crept down my back at the prospect.

Harker's eyes gleamed with anticipation. "Prepare yourself well, Lieutenant Shaw. Seeing your enemy face-to-face is quite something."

LATER

News that the captain is taking another officer—and an inexperienced one at that—on one of his night raids has not gone without comment amongst the men. I myself am really none the wiser to Harker's reasons.

"You're goin' over the top at dusk?" Jenkins asked.

I nodded.

A louse leapt from the seam of my jacket. I caught the fleeing creature between a thumb and finger and stared for a while at the tiny squirming parasite that had caused me so much discomfort.

Then I crushed it. The pop, as I extinguished its life, filled me with some small satisfaction.

I examined the collapsed body stuck to my fingertip, stained red by the blood that it had sucked from me—blood that I had claimed back. "How many lice would it take to suck all the blood from a man, do you think?" I asked Jenkins. I showed him the dark red smear on my fingertip.

Jenkins looked at the squashed louse, then at me, a look of concern clouding his face. "You seem tired, sir. Perhaps you'd better try and get an hour's kip before your raid with Captain Harker. Don't worry, I'll wake you in good time."

But of course, I can't sleep. How can I rest knowing what lies ahead of me?

I have checked my equipment repeatedly. There is nothing left but to sit and wait.

Though fear pulses through me like a fever, I am determined to see this through. I must be strong enough to face the enemy—as well as my commander.

Dear Lily, I do this for you and for England. May God bless you and protect me so that I might return safely.

There is Jenkins's knock. I must go.

It is one in the morning, but I cannot sleep; my wound pains me, and my legs and back both ache with a fury. I returned to the trench today after two days in the field hospital. At least I can now distract myself by writing in my journal. I shall record the events that led to my injury during the night raid.

I watched the evening mist drifting through no-man's-land as I waited for Captain Harker at the agreed location. Around me the men squatted in the trench, brewing tea and burning lice from their uniforms in their customary way. The wind carried mustard gas and my eyes stung and watered. I wrapped a scarf around my mouth and nose in a futile effort to keep the gas from my lungs.

The rattle of enemy guns sounded in the distance. Then suddenly, there was the familiar burst of noise as a screaming tornado of lead flew overhead, missing the trench by a great margin.

"Bloody shells," swore Sergeant O'Reilly.

I stared down. The hated rats scuttled over my boots.

"No damned respect," Corporal Jenkins spat. He put down his cup, reached for his rifle, then speared one of them with his bayonet.

Its squeal startled some of the men farther down the trench. They spun round expectantly, some fumbling for their rifles.

Jenkins held up the impaled, still-struggling creature, its engorged body shimmering in the half-light. Grim half smiles spread through the men.

"Ready, Lieutenant?"

Captain Harker's voice startled me. I hadn't heard his approach. I turned sharply to see his figure, tall and obscure in the dim light, face hidden beneath the shadow of his helmet.

"Yes, sir!" I replied.

The captain looked hard at me. "Very good," he said. Then he turned and began to climb effortlessly up the wooden ladder.

Heart pounding, I heaved myself up after him. The parapet scraped against my jacket as I dragged myself over the edge. I stumbled onto the battlefield, body braced for the sudden hail of bullets that might burst it wide open.

I tried to slow my quickening breath while crawling after the captain, pressing my belly into the mud as he surveyed the ground ahead.

Meanwhile, my thoughts nagged at me. *Can you trust him? Can you trust the man who ordered the killing of Private Smith?*

Even if I could, what about the enemy? How many Germans were in the gun entrenchment? What would the next hour bring?

Harker pointed to a gap in the enemy's barbed wire where our guns had managed to pierce the deadly web.

We slithered forward like worms over the cratered earth, keeping low, trying to melt out of sight of the snipers. The mud seeped into my uniform and I felt it squelch against my skin.

We crawled over brush and the bodies of the dead. The corpses did not even bend beneath my weight as I followed the captain's route.

"Don't fall behind," Harker ordered as I struggled to keep up.

Before us, the wall of barbed wire rose high above our heads. Harker thrust through the gap.

As I pushed through the wire after him, sharp metal barbs reached out and grabbed me, tearing first my sodden uniform and then my flesh. I yelped instinctively—and a jolt of panic shot through me. Who knew how many Germans guarded that gun? Had any of them heard my cry?

I stared at Harker, waiting for his reproach, but his eyes were fixed on the silhouette of the gun emplacement. Like a predator observing its prey.

Utterly fearless, he moved on, weaving his way through the blood-soaked mud. "Stay close!" he ordered over his shoulder.

We slid down into the shallow shelter of a shell crater a few yards in front of the emplacement. I could now see the barrel of the gun jutting out from its iron shielding, silent and unmoving. I held my pistol tight in my hand, trying not to tremble as I prepared myself for action.

Harker crawled over the edge of the crater. He drew his sword and slipped, silent as a shadow, into the hollow where the gun was embedded. I followed.

For a moment all was silent.

Then three screaming soldiers rushed at us. Five more behind them.

Harker lifted his sword and slashed those nearest, tearing flesh and muscle as easily as soft butter. The soldiers' blood sprayed the wooden walls. They fell, the butchered flesh of their fallen bodies convulsing beneath their torn uniforms.

The others backed away, barely able to raise their rifles. Harker let out a cry and lunged at them.

I didn't see the hand catch hold of my foot—just felt it yank me down.

I crashed onto the duckboards, sliding on my back in the stinking mud that coated them. An enemy soldier loomed over me and lifted his rifle. He aimed the gleaming blade of his bayonet at my throat.

He glared at me, his face full of hatred. He tightened his grip on the gun barrel and thrust the blade downward.

I rolled hard to my right to avoid the fatal wound. Pain seared through my shoulder instead as the metal forced its way deep into my flesh.

My fear numbed me to the agony. I scrambled to my feet and charged into the soldier, unbalancing him. He staggered for a second, giving me enough time to lift my pistol and fire. Surprise flitted across his face as the bullet opened his chest. A red stain blossomed outward from the wound, coloring his uniform. He gazed down, then dropped to his knees.

I breathed hard as my mind struggled with scene before me. I had faced the enemy and won. I knew I should be happy. But my victory was short-lived.

The cold barrel of a rifle pressed against my temple. It was another enemy soldier, and this time, I could gain no advantage on him.

I turned to face my executioner. His boyish looks, blue eyes and the white-blond hair of a child, seemed bizarre to me. I did not expect death to be delivered by one who looked so innocent. He struggled to steady his shaking hands and prepared to squeeze the trigger—

His rifle barrel suddenly fell away. I watched silently as he fell facedown into the mud.

Captain Harker was standing behind him, his sword gleaming with blood.

Harker had saved me! Saved me from certain death.

My vision grew blurry as the pain from my wound washed over me. I sagged against the side of the trench, struggling to keep my footing.

Harker turned from me. He stared down at the thick red

that pulsed from the wound he had sliced into the boy's throat. His teeth glinted like daggers as he contemplated his latest victim. His eyes glowed with a furious light.

As my vision dimmed, I saw Harker pull the boy up by his uniform. He leaned in close to the spurting gash he had inflicted.

Then darkness overtook me.

CHAPTER 5

*War Journal of
Lieutenant John Shaw*

When I came to in the field hospital, the morning light flooding through the open flaps of the sprawling tent made my skin smart. I knew I was still scorched from the mustard gas. A doctor was fetched.

"How's the shoulder?" he asked, peeling away the dressing to reveal the torn flesh beneath.

"Not bad," I lied.

"Can't see any infection," he announced, pressing the bandage back into place. I winced with pain as he went on. "You're a lucky chap, you know. Your captain carried you back from the enemy lines himself. Ordered me to get you back to your unit as soon as possible. Clearly thinks you're too good to do without."

I was hit by nightmarish images of the raid. Some of my

memories were undeniably real. But others . . . others I could not be sure of. I felt myself break into a sweat.

"Looks like you've picked up a touch of fever," the doctor said, his eyes narrowing. "Pain in your back and legs?"

I nodded.

He fetched me a twist of paper, a physic of some sort.

I took it from him, nodding my thanks.

The powder made me sleep but gave me no peace. My dreams were filled with soldiers torn apart by shell fire, bayonet, and knife; howling in pain and terror; drowning in pools of mud, desperately scrabbling to get out. But most of all, my mind returned to the image of Captain Harker—his eyes glowing like a demon's—reveling in our enemy's blood.

Now that I am back in my trench, among the stench and shadows, my dreams have taken a more surreal turn: blood, gallons of it, coursing down into the trenches; teeth mutilating soft flesh; eyes shining red in the shadows—dark, terrible images that haunt me. They seem so real—as if called back by memory.

Is it the fever making me insane?

What frightens me most is that I have no answer.

18TH AUGUST 1916

I awoke last night, drenched in sweat, to hear a loud knock at my door.

"Lieutenant?"

I recognized Jenkins's voice. "Come in," I muttered. I gritted my teeth against the pain that burned in my shoulder.

"Lieutenant Butler asked if you're up to relieving him, sir," Jenkins said apologetically. "He's on his knees, doing continuous shifts these last few days."

"Of course." I forced a smile. "I'll be there in a moment."

"There's a bloody big moon out there," Jenkins commented. "The battlefield's lit up like the Crystal Palace. There'll be no one out there tonight."

"Except Harker, I suppose," I muttered.

Jenkins nodded. "I suspect so, sir."

I dressed and relieved Butler and, trying to ignore the increasing pain in my back and legs, I sat and listened, through the pop and fizz of intercepted airwaves, to voices from the enemy trenches.

The crackling words coming through the radio headphones made no sense at first. I picked up a transmission . . . *"Das Übel laüft . . ."*

I shook my head dismissively, thinking my mood still affected by my ghoulish dreams.

I kept on listening.

There it was again, clear this time. *"Das Übel laüft . . ."* Evil walks . . .

And then, *"Die Soldaten sind tot. . . ."* The men are

dead. . . . *"Geschlachtet wie Tier . . ."* Slaughtered like animals . . . *"Niemand bleibt. . . ."* No one left. . . .

Jenkins had predicted a quiet night. Could this news from the German trench be true?

I knew I must see for myself. I left the communications dugout and made my way toward the ladder. With every step my legs screamed with pain. My vision darkened at the edges as fever gripped me—making me shiver with heat, then cold.

Dawn mist poured into the trench, tinged yellow by the mustard gas. I grabbed hold of the ladder's rough wood and hauled myself upward.

Fog clung to the ground as I raised my head above the parapet. At first, I could see nothing. I heaved myself over the top and stood, swaying on the brink.

Before me lay the familiar stretch of ruptured landscape, eerily silent. Some small voice inside me attempted a warning. Above the trench, I was an easy target for the German guns. But the greater part of me was insensible to the threat of sniper fire. I made my way across no-man's-land toward the enemy trenches.

After a moment, the fog cleared. I gazed at my surroundings and my breath caught in my throat. I tried to scream, but no sound came.

My mind whirled. This could not be possible and yet—it was.

Through the clouds of mustard gas and the lingering light from shell fire and flare, I saw enemy soldiers—scores of them.

Their bodies hung from every post and tree. Their torsos and limbs were brutally mutilated. Their severed heads littered the twisted mounds of barbed wire, like grotesque berries on a bush.

As shells shook the ground, the bodies and heads trembled, as though life still pulsed through them.

No!

I grasped my head, pulled my hair in terror and confusion. These were the very images that haunted my dreams! How could they be here now, in the real world?

I fought to tear my sight away, but my eyes refused, drinking in every grisly detail.

Then *it* stepped forward.

Standing in the middle of this terrible slaughter was a hellish, hound-like beast with eyes that blazed red in the predawn light.

It locked its gaze upon me.

In its mouth, it carried a severed head. The head's clouded eyes stared blindly, its tongue lolling lifelessly from the mouth, its white-blond hair matted with blood.

The great beast stalked toward me. Closer. Closer still.

The earth seemed to tilt. I heard a roaring in my ears— and saw no more.

As I write these words, I am huddled in my dugout—back in bed.

How did I come to be here? How did I return from no-man's-land?

I wonder, did Jenkins really ask me to relieve Butler? Did I actually see what I have just related? Or have I been in my dugout the whole night?

My mind feels frayed at the edges. I am beginning to shake. I must stop now.

I cannot think anymore. . . .

Journal of
Mary Seward

30TH AUGUST 1916

Part of me now wishes I had not read Lieutenant Shaw's journal. How will I ever drive the images of terror and suffering from my mind?

The poor man! Surely the real horror of war is enough to bear without one's mind also playing tricks? The words in these pages show that his fever had gotten the best of him long before he was admitted here. Half of his present suffering comes not from wounds to his body, but to his psyche.

My course of action therefore must be to soothe his mind with the balm of kindness and compassion, the very thing absent from his experience at the front. I confess it will not be difficult.

As for Captain Harker, it is chilling to see what monsters war makes of men, but I must pity rather than condemn such monstrous acts, for I know our soldiers at the front fight for the noblest of reasons. I still shudder at the cruelty meted out to Private Smith, but nobody can deny the nobility in Captain Harker's carrying Lieutenant Shaw through the raging battlefield to safety.

I must try to get some rest now, or I shall be of no use to anyone in the morning. I approach sleep with trepidation, my mind still full of the horrors about which I have read. I only pray that common sense will guide me through the next few hours.

31ST AUGUST 1916

Today we lost three men to fever and injuries, and John Shaw was no better than yesterday.

Whenever I am near Lieutenant Shaw, his nightmares seem to ease. He looks upon me with the most childlike expression of awe. He holds my gaze at times. He mumbles that word—*angel.*

My heart twists in sympathy for the pain I know he is suffering. My instinct is to remain by his side as long as possible, to do as much as I can—without raising Sister's suspicion.

As I tend to Lieutenant Shaw, I speak to him softly of the beauty of the gardens outside the sanatorium walls and of our days as children, before the war.

I only hope that my words are reaching some part deep inside him where the real John Shaw—the one who wrote of his sister's kindness—still thrives.

I had hoped for some recovery before my visit to Carfax Hall so that the news I carried to his sister, Lily, would be easier to bear.

I had not seen Lily Shaw since the garden party, and I remembered her as a shy, fragile child. I felt determined to find some note of hope for her to cling to in all of this.

Still, I struggled to find the right words to ease the blow of her brother's condition.

At the end of my shift, I made my way through the grounds of the sanatorium to the high stone wall that surrounded our northern neighbor—Carfax Hall. I was glad I had my umbrella with me, for it was raining quite hard.

I pushed open the estate's heavy oak-and-iron gates and slowly began to make my way up the long drive.

What a fearful great house it is, so dark and imposing. It frightened me as a child, and I was surprised to find some of that old nervousness remained. My heart was pounding as I rang the bell at the huge, black front door.

The woman I knew to be John and Lily Shaw's housekeeper

and former nurse answered. I was surprised to find that she had changed very little since our last meeting five years ago.

She is a tall, imperious woman with a handsome but harsh face and graying black hair scraped back in a bun. An old memory of Miss Shaw as a child, new to the village, flashed into my mind; I could just see her nestling shyly into the stiff skirts of this stern-looking woman.

"May I help you?" she asked, her words swathed in a thick Eastern European accent.

"My name is Mary Seward," I replied. "I should like to speak with Miss Shaw."

"What is it in connection with, miss?" the housekeeper asked.

"It is a personal matter, and quite urgent," I replied.

The housekeeper frowned, then beckoned me in. She took my wet coat and umbrella and showed me into a parlor. "Please wait here," she said curtly.

To my astonishment, I heard her announcing my arrival to Miss Shaw out in the garden! To be outside in such a storm? Why would anyone would brave these elements unless it was a matter of necessity?

Moments later, Miss Shaw ran into the room, quite soaked through. Her face betrayed her surprise at my visit. "It's Miss Seward, isn't it?" she asked.

I nodded. "Hello, Miss Shaw," I began. "It has been quite some time since we last met. I've come from—"

I was interrupted by the housekeeper, who rushed in, carrying towels.

Ignoring me, she chided Miss Shaw. "You should have come in long ago, child. Imagine wandering around in the rain with a cold; you'll catch your death." She pulled off Miss Shaw's sopping wet coat and boots, then began to pat her dripping dark curls with a towel.

"But it was such a beautiful rainstorm, Antanasia," Miss Shaw replied, smiling. "And it *is* warm out."

"I think Miss Shaw would benefit from some hot tea," I told the housekeeper. She shot me an indignant glance. Clearly she was peeved by my attempt to secure some privacy.

"Yes! Tea for two, if you would be so kind, Antanasia," Miss Shaw added. "I hope Miss Seward will stay for a cup. It's so kind of her to call." She looked at me hopefully, clearly delighted to have company. My heart ached as I thought of what I had to tell her.

I nodded. "Thank you, Miss Shaw. It is my pleasure to join you."

Her eyes lit up with glee. I noticed that they were the same deep blue as her brother's, her lashes thick dark smudges against her creamy skin. She shivered in front of the fire, dark tendrils of hair clinging to the curves of her face and neck.

"Please, call me Lily," she instructed. "There is no need to stand on ceremony."

I blinked, taken aback by her instant familiarity. "Thank you," I said, recovering myself, "and you must call me Mary."

"Mary." Lily smiled enchantingly. "Yes, I remember now. Your father is Dr. Seward, from Purfleet Sanatorium, is he not?"

I nodded. "He is retired. His health declined just before the sanatorium was commandeered for the war effort. I work there myself now, as a VAD nurse. Which brings me to the reason for my—"

"Here we are," Antanasia interrupted. She swept into the room carrying a tea tray and a long cashmere shawl. While she wrapped Lily in the shawl and pulled her chair closer to the fire, I poured the tea. Without asking, I put sugar in Lily's cup, remembering Father's advice that sweetness prepares the body for shock. I passed the cup and saucer and prepared another for myself.

I remained silent while Antanasia stoked up the fire and fussed about the room. At last, giving me a rather pointed look, she took her leave.

"I am so pleased to have someone to share afternoon tea with," Lily said happily. "But tell me, to what do we owe the pleasure of your company?"

"Lily, I have come about your brother . . ." I began carefully.

She raised her eyebrows in surprise. "My brother? But John is in France. Fighting." Her voice cracked as she said the word.

"He's not there now," I said quietly.

Lily stared at me, eyes wide, her pale cheeks flushing in alarm.

I rushed to explain before she could grow too distressed. "He's safe, back here in Purfleet—at the sanatorium. A shoulder wound and trench fever have made him ill. . . ." I leaned forward to take Lily's cup before it slid from her shaking fingers.

"Did he tell you to come and fetch me? Shall I go to him?" Lily's voice was now high and reedy with worry.

I knelt beside her and took her hands in mine. How could I explain to her that her brother would not know her if she went? "John has not yet regained consciousness," I said softly. "At least, not properly."

"Properly?" Lily's smooth brow creased in confusion.

"His fever from the trenches is rather severe."

"Fever?" she echoed anxiously.

"Fever is quite common amongst soldiers in the trenches. It can be very debilitating—causing pain and delirium—but it's not fatal. He is in no immediate danger. . . ."

I tried over the next few moments to reassure her. But it became clear that she would not rest until she'd seen her brother for herself.

"Come," I said, getting to my feet. "I will take you to him."

Journal of
Lily Shaw

Oh, Mother, Father! Our John is injured! He is at the sanatorium here in Purfleet. I pray that you are looking down on him from heaven and sending your blessing for his recovery. I cannot lose him too! I'm told he's almost healed from his physical injury, but a virulent fever from the trenches has robbed him of all reason.

Mary Seward, a girl from the village who now works at the sanatorium, brought me to him. She has been most kind to me during this terrible hour.

I arrived at John's bedside and stared at the poor creature lying before me. The familiar features I love so well were stiff and startled, as if trapped beneath ice.

Tentatively, I touched his arm. He turned his head toward me but did not recognize me. At least, I hope it was not his beloved sister he saw, for he pulled away from my touch and scrambled into a hunched-up crouch on his bed, rocking rapidly—back and forth, back and forth.

Peering down at his fingers, he began feverishly crushing his fingertips and thumbs together, seeing something there that no one else could.

"You suck my blood," he muttered. "I kill you and claim it back."

Then he sucked his fingers greedily and sighed with what seemed like pleasure.

I stepped away, chilled and sickened. My darling John, whatever could have happened to him?

When the doctor came, he could give me little comfort. "Your brother is not a well man, Miss Shaw," he said gravely. "This is one of the most severe cases of trench fever I have encountered." Then, seeing my distress, his expression softened. "I feel confident he will recover, given time. And from what I've heard, your brother is lucky, considering . . ."

I stared at him, wondering what luck he could see in poor John's condition.

"When Lieutenant Shaw was injured, his commanding officer carried him back from the enemy lines," the doctor explained. "If the captain had left him, your brother would surely be dead."

For a fleeting moment I wondered if it were better that John had died. Then reason flooded me with regret; at least I have him near me once more, and he must recover.

Mother, Father, your son is a fine, strong man. He will not be lost to this madness for long.

Your spirits guide me at this hour, and I know what I must do. I must write to John's commanding officer—a Captain Harker, I believe John mentioned—and thank him for his courageous act. If he is good enough to reply, I may find out what happened to John in France to so break his spirit.

Please, continue to watch over us both, as you have all these years. We have great need of your presence now.

Your loving daughter,

Lily

CHAPTER 6

*Journal of
Mary Seward*

2ND SEPTEMBER 1916

I arrived on the ward early this morning to find another soldier in the bed John had occupied. Shock and grief tightened my chest. There was only one reason that I could fathom for this change: John had succumbed to his fever during the night.

I could not speak at first, but after a moment I gathered myself and turned to Sister. "What has happened to Lieutenant Shaw?" I asked her.

Sister looked up from her desk. "Doctor had him moved to the secure wing in the night. His ravings were disturbing the other patients, who have their own nightmares to contend with."

Relief flooded through me. It was as if my heart had resumed beating.

Then the weight of Sister's words reached me. I paled at the thought of John in the secure wing—that dark corner of the hospital, where the worst of Father's patients had been locked in cells for safety.

"The secure wing?" I asked. "But Lieutenant Shaw is fevered, not insane."

Sister shook her head. "I am sorry. It is for the lieutenant's own sake as well as that of the others. Doctor's orders."

I frowned. The grim aspect of the wing could only worsen John's condition, which had seen precious little progress since his arrival.

Yet I dared not voice my disagreement.

"May I go and see him?" I asked.

"Once you've emptied the bedpans," Sister replied firmly. She looked down at her files, and I knew she had finished with me.

I worked as quickly as I could and, before long, was knocking on the locked door of the secure wing. Sommers, the aged attendant, opened it. I told him whom I was there to see.

"Follow me, Miss Mary. He's in Renfield's room." Sommers lumbered down the corridor toward the room where John was imprisoned. Ever the storyteller—Sommers had regaled me in my youth with the most unsettling of tales from the ward. Though my mother disapproved, each one thrilled and surprised me.

Despite the fact that I was now grown, I knew he was eager for another chance. I felt grateful for his comforting presence in this dreary place and so indulged him.

"Renfield?" I asked. "Who is that?"

"Man of that name occupied the cell—many years ago now, afore you was even born," Sommers explained. "A strange case, he was. Killed hisself in the end. Broke his neck. Your father never used the cell again—right up to the day he retired. Me and the rest of the men used to wonder if Renfield's spirit was still there—haunting the thing for the rest of eternity."

I gazed up into his face. He gave me a wink and a smile.

We finally reached a small door at the end of the hall. I peered through the iron bars and found John sitting on a small iron bedstead, the only furniture within the padded cell.

He was sitting up now, I noted. Gaining strength. His body was healing. I could only hope the same was true of his mind.

I watched for as long as I dared. Clearly something was troubling him, for his gentle features held a look of confusion. He stared intently into nothingness, occasionally gesturing, as if he saw something there.

Suddenly he spoke. "It is most odd, Jenkins. The trench walls have become soft and clean. Can you see? I keep looking for the mud, but can find none."

Then his expression darkened. His eyes grew wild. "I can still smell the rats, though. Can you smell them, Jenkins? The rats . . . and the blood . . . and *death!*"

He grasped his head in his hands. Then lay back on his pillow. "I hear cries out in no-man's-land. But I cannot find a ladder. Help me get to them! Jenkins, help me!" he screamed.

I turned away, unable to bear seeing him like this.

Sommers placed a rough hand on my shoulder. "Been repeating those things since they brought him," he said gently. "Poor chap."

It seemed natural to give in to despair. Yet I knew I must not.

John was improving and if he was to improve further, he must be removed from this horrible place.

And so I have made a vow to do everything within my power to see Lieutenant Shaw well again. No matter what I must do to help him.

Report of Dr. McLeod,
Purfleet Sanatorium

Patient John Shaw, Lieutenant, no. 467842

Volunteer Mary Seward has shown a special interest in this patient, and since she is a calm and sensible girl, I have assigned her to his care. She will report back to me on the patient's behavior.

DM, 2 September 1916

Journal of Mary Seward

8TH SEPTEMBER 1916

I have been visiting John Shaw in the secure wing for nearly a week now. When I look into John's face, I know that he is in great need of me. I feel that I am the only one who can reach him.

In the time we have spent together, I have grown to understand his delirium. I have attempted to bring him back into reality gradually, so as not to overtax his mind. I feel strongly that we are making progress.

LATER

Sommers was in a rare, ill-tempered mood when I arrived at the door to the wing this morning. "A rat got in through the window of 'is cell," he told me sourly.

I wondered if he blamed me for the rat's intrusion. It was I who had left the barred window open, in the hope that the sweet scents of an English summer might help restore Lieutenant Shaw to his senses.

I heard a high-pitched squealing from his cell as Sommers led me down the corridor.

"Caught it with his bare hands," he muttered, barely disguising the disgust in his voice. "I tried to get him to drop it, but he won't let go."

I peered through the bars of the lieutenant's cell in disbelief. As Sommers had said, he was holding a large rodent by its tail.

Lieutenant Shaw shrieked with laughter as the rat struggled to free itself. "Jenkins! Hurry up with that bayonet!" he shouted. "This is a fine fat specimen."

I grasped the locket that hung around my neck, pity and revulsion vying in my breast. I took a deep breath and gathered my senses. "Unlock the door," I told Sommers. "And fetch a porter."

Sommers began to argue. "But Miss Mary, you can't. I—"

"Do it!" I commanded. "Quickly."

Sommers turned the key in the lock, then hurried away for help.

As I entered the cell, John caught sight of me. "Have you brought it, Jenkins?" he demanded. "I want to spear the damn thing. We'll roast it tonight."

"Lieutenant," I urged. "Let the rat go. Let it out of the window."

"What!" he exclaimed. "And waste a perfectly good meal? Are you mad? Hand me your bayonet!"

"I don't have one," I explained as calmly as I could. "And I am not Jenkins."

"Then fetch him!" John shrieked. He cursed until the porter arrived, Sister following close behind him.

"What's going on here?" Sister demanded. "Porter, restrain this patient and take that vile creature away!"

The porter stalked forward.

Lieutenant Shaw backed into a corner, his eyes fearful at the thought of someone stealing his catch.

"No! Don't upset him," I implored. "Please. I can reach him. I know I can."

Sister's tone grew impatient. "Miss Shaw, this is no time for games. Leave the lieutenant's cell this instant."

I ignored her command and turned my eyes to John. Holding his gaze as best I could, I called to him softly. "Give the creature to me," I said. "Jenkins will take it away and kill it for us."

"Can we roast it?" he asked, his eyes lighting up.

"Yes," I lied.

He looked distrustfully from me to the porter, who nodded. "I'll take it away and cook it up just how you like it, sir."

I felt perspiration gather on my brow. The filthy creature in John's grasp twisted and gnashed its sharp teeth.

Slowly, slowly John held out the struggling rat.

I gingerly lifted it from his fingers and handed it—still dangling it by the tail—to the porter. He carried it from the room, shaking his head.

I breathed a sigh of relief.

Sister regarded me for a moment with admiration in her eyes. Then she spoke, more gently this time. "I'm afraid we will still have to restrain him, Miss Seward. He is clearly beyond all sense."

Her words struck me like a blow. "But why? I can reach him. And he has hurt no one!"

"Mary, he is a danger to himself," she pointed out. "What if that rat had bitten him? The lieutenant doesn't need blood poisoning to add to his woes."

I nodded, fighting back tears. How could I disagree?

As Sommers held John down on the bed Sister strapped one of his wrists to its frame.

"No! No! No!" he yelled. "Do not leave me with Private Smith!"

I tried to soothe him—smiling despite my despair. "Hush now, Lieutenant. We will not leave you." I bent and, as tenderly as I could, fastened the other strap.

"What is happening?" John asked me, his voice softening, a look of confusion on his fine face. "Please, tell me what is going on?"

"It is just for a while," I whispered. "Just a short while . . ."

10TH SEPTEMBER 1916

I am relieved to see the soft leather bands only chafe John's skin a little. Distressing though it is to see him this way, it is almost more upsetting to see what it does to poor Lily.

When she arrived to visit him yesterday, I warned her as gently as I could. But as I pushed open the door and she saw for herself, she gasped and swayed on her feet. I ushered her from the room so that she might catch her breath.

Tears streamed down her cheeks and she turned her face away. "Oh, Mary, I can't bear to see him brought so low!"

"Please don't despair, Lily," I begged, grasping both her hands in mine. "This isn't really your brother—it's just his fever. We will have him back. I know it."

Lily looked at me, lifting her wet lashes to stare at me hopefully. "I believe you care for him, Mary. And so I trust your words."

I flushed with embarrassment at Lily's directness—and at my own transparency. I longed to explain my feelings but could not find the words.

Luckily, Lily required no explanation. "Tell me, Mary, when the fever passes . . . ?"

"He will be the brother you have always known and loved," I promised, hoping with all my heart it was true. "You must not give up. Lieutenant Shaw needs you to be strong."

Lily nodded. "Then I shall be." She slipped her hands from mine, wiped her eyes, and returned to the cell.

She shed hardly a tear as she sat at his bedside. She tried so hard to be brave and cheerful, but I saw her tears once more as she bade me goodbye.

How terrible it must be to have a loved one treat you as a stranger.

I must confess to feeling something of this myself. For Lily is right. I have come to care for John Shaw—yet I'm not sure he even knows I exist.

16 SEPTEMBER 1916

John remains locked in his own dark world. But today, as I left his cell, he commented, "I believe we've been visited by an angel, Jenkins. Did you see her golden hair? Her hands were so soft. . . . I wish she would stay. . . ."

His words made my heart swell. I know that every day we are together, he moves further from the horrors that pursue him.

LONDON CHRONICLE
18th September 1916

Woman Attacked on Quayside

A Miss Nancy Merrick of London was found unconscious on the docks yesterday evening, victim of a mysterious attack. Miss Merrick was found lying beside a warehouse by a young private who had recently disembarked from his troopship. Private Collins reported that he saw Miss Merrick's body in the moonlight and was startled by the sight of a great black hound running from her.

"I thought at first the fleeing dog must have attacked her," he said. "But I was mistaken. Aside from being weak and pale, the only injury Miss Merrick appeared to have on her person was a scratch on her neck. I only called a constable because I was worried about such a dog being loose in the area."

Miss Merrick said she remembered no such dog, only the man she'd been taking a stroll with on the quayside. She described him as being, "tall and proper handsome, with glossy black hair." Miss Merrick also told police, "He had the most piercing eyes. Sent me right light-headed when he bent close to me, they did. I think I must have fainted. Then that horrid hound came along. Thank heavens Private Collins noticed me when he did!"

Letter from
Captain Quincey Harker

THE ARMY AND NAVY CLUB
36–39 PALL MALL
LONDON
18TH SEPTEMBER 1916

Dear Miss Shaw,

How gracious of you to write. Your letter caught up with me here at my club in London, as I left the front shortly after your brother's own departure. I have business at the Foreign Office and shall be in England for some while.

I assure you I could have done no less than save your brother's life and know it was his dearest wish to return home to his beloved sister.

It is good to hear that John is getting the best of care at Purfleet Sanatorium. It sounds as though he is in good hands. You make Miss Seward sound like a guardian angel.

I plan to visit John shortly and do hope that I shall have the pleasure of meeting you as well.

Yours sincerely,
Captain Quincey Harker

Journal of Mary Seward

20TH SEPTEMBER 1916

John was particularly restless today, twisting himself into his sheets and struggling against his restraints. I didn't want to leave him and asked Sommers to take a message to Father on his way home. I scribbled a few lines, telling him that I would be working late. Father does worry so.

As the evening drew on, John seemed to be experiencing something of a crisis. I sat with him, bathing his flushed face with cool water, trying to calm him. I was glad that I had persuaded Lily to go home. She would have been beside herself if she'd seen him suffering like this.

But then John's breathing altered, deepened. I feared what new change in him this might signify. I felt his forehead and, to my surprise, found it cool. And as I withdrew my hand John opened his eyes.

He blinked, as if in bright light, even though his cell was shadowed. Then slowly he focused on my face. For the first time he seemed to actually see me. "Are you—are you really an angel?" he whispered, his voice hoarse and slurred.

Heart thudding, I shouted for the night porter. "Please, fetch Sister!" I told him.

"What is it, Seward?" Sister asked when she arrived at my side. Automatically she reached for John's wrist, still restrained in its leather strap. She looked at her watch to check his pulse.

"I think he knows where he is!" I told her excitedly.

"I have no idea where I am," John croaked.

I smiled. He had heard me. And his words were those of a rational man.

Sister raised her eyebrows. "You are at Purfleet Sanatorium," she informed him.

"Back in Blighty?" John breathed incredulously.

"Back in England, yes," Sister confirmed. She glanced at me. "I'll fetch Doctor."

As Sister strode away, I found John staring at me.

"I've had such bad dreams," he said, his voice still weak and cracked with thirst.

I lifted a glass of water to his lips, supporting his head with my hand.

He tried to move his arms and found them restrained. "Why?" he asked.

"You've had a fever . . ." I began cautiously, anxious not to let him know how wild and strange he'd been since his arrival. I pressed the water to his lips, insisting he take a sip.

He lay back on his pillow. "I feel quite myself now." He tugged again on the restraints.

"The doctor will be here soon," I assured him. "I'm sure he'll undo them. And then I must go and fetch someone else to you. Someone I know you'll want to see."

Joy brightened John's pallid features. "Lily?"

I nodded. "She's been here every day," I told him.

He furrowed his brow. "You have too," he ventured. "Your face. I remember—"

I felt a flush in my cheeks. "Shhh. You must save your strength," I interrupted him. "Lily will be here soon. You'll want to be at your best."

I hurried over to Carfax Hall as quickly as I could, though it was late and a chill wind sent wispy clouds scudding across the night sky.

I walked up the long drive toward the hall—and stopped short. A figure stood ahead of me in the moonlight, clad in white, walking through the grounds.

Her nightgown fluttered around her bare feet and she seemed to glide along the lawns. So eerie was her demeanor that a shiver crept up my spine. Was this some sort of apparition?

The figure walked on, drawing closer. I recognized the mass of dark hair and delicate frame. Lily! She seemed insensible to her surroundings.

I checked my instinct to call out to her, for I thought she must be sleepwalking. Father had taught me never to shock a sleepwalker into wakefulness, so instead I hurried after her, overtaking her and turning to block her steady procession.

Her eyes were open—dark, vacant pools in the moonlit pallor of her face. She did not see me as she pressed forward with the same unerring step.

The stress of her brother's illness must have driven her outside in the night, I thought. Poor Lily. So fragile. This is all simply too much for her.

"Lily . . ." I whispered her name. But she did not hear. Only when my fingers tightened around her arm did she seem to become aware of me. She looked at me with a haunted gaze, not really seeing.

"Lily," I repeated, with all the gentle fondness I could summon. "Come inside now; it is cold."

I led her in the direction of the house. But she paused and looked back in the direction she had been heading.

I followed her gaze. Nothing there but trees and a small, still lake, shimmering peacefully in the moonlight.

"We must go in, Lily," I urged, pulling on her arm.

She stared blankly at me. Then her eyes rolled back and she fell into a dead faint. I gasped and just managed to catch her before she crumpled onto the ground.

With the weight of Lily in my arms, I looked around desperately for help. To my great relief, I saw Antanasia running toward us across the lawns.

Between us, Antanasia and I carried Lily to the house. As we entered I looked back, still searching for a clue to Lily's delirious destination. Other than a solitary bat swooping over the lake, all was still.

I hurried inside to help Antanasia return Lily to the warmth of her bed.

"Mary?" Lily said groggily once returned to her bed. "What . . . what are you doing here?"

"I've come with good news, Lily," I told her gently. "It's John—his delirium appears to have broken. He is recovering, and he is anxious to see you!"

"Oh, Mary . . ." Lily breathed joyfully, "that is *wonderful* news!" She tried to sit up but was clearly exhausted, her sleepwalking episode testament to that.

I sat with her for a while until she eventually drifted off to sleep.

The moment we were certain that Lily was resting peacefully, Antanasia accompanied me to the front door and bade me a stiff good night.

I made my way back down the long drive, feeling exhausted after my long day. As I neared the wooded area by the gate, I noticed something lying on the grass. A sense of foreboding gripped my heart as I approached it.

It was a fallen deer, its pelt glistening with blood. I pressed my fingers to my lips when I found the fatal wound—a gaping tear in its throat.

The deer's legs twitched one—twice, then fell still. Whatever animal had killed this creature was likely nearby.

Trembling, I hurried on through the heavy estate gates, now desperate to get to the familiar comfort of home.

CHAPTER 7

Journal of
Mary Seward

21ST SEPTEMBER 1916

John was moved back to the general ward today. I was so
pleased there was an available bed on the south-facing side—
his window will look out onto the countryside.

After settling him into his bed, I drew back his curtain.
"After so long in that dark cell, this view should do you a
world of good," I told him.

He gazed wistfully out the window at the trees and flower
beds of England. It was his first view of home since leaving
for the front. His face betrayed the emotion that he struggled
not to show.

I fussed a bit with his sheets and his hand brushed mine.
I looked up and found myself locked in his gaze.

"I have no need of sunny views, Miss Seward," he said
shyly. "Not as long your visits brighten my day."

I smiled as lightly as I could at his compliment, but even now my heart flutters to imagine that he could think of me so, even in jest.

22ND SEPTEMBER 1916

Today John asked for his journal. My cheeks burned, for it was still on my desk in my bedroom. I made an excuse to go home and rushed to collect it. On my return I told Sister I'd found the journal in the box of reading books we keep for the more recovered patients, where it must have been put by mistake.

*Journal of
Lieutenant John Shaw*

22ND SEPTEMBER 1916

How long it seems since I last put pen to paper in this journal.

I awoke two days ago to find the angel in my dreams sitting next to me. She is, in fact, Mary Seward—a local girl from Purfleet. Miss Seward has been looking after me since my arrival here at the sanatorium.

Yesterday, I was moved from my solitary cell to a bright sunny ward. No sooner was I settled than my darling sister, Lily, arrived to see me.

She embraced me as though I had returned from the dead, tears of joy trickling down her cheeks. She looked so happy that I am surprised she did not burst! I thought she would never stop weeping.

"Everything is going to be all right now, Lily," I reassured her, but she would not let go her grip on my hand. I am glad she did not, for it was wonderful to feel her fond touch once again.

It is so strange to be away from the trenches. I cannot get used to the whiteness of the ward. When I awoke this morning, I thought I must be dead. The world was never this clean. At least not the world I've inhabited lately.

I feel so terribly tired, as if I have made a great journey— yet Miss Seward assures me I have been in bed for weeks.

Miss Seward . . . what shall I say about her? Though she is not the celestial creature I imagined, I hold fast to the notion that she is sent to me from above.

I remember little of the time when she cared for me. And yet I do remember her face, her tenderness. Though she will not admit as much, I am certain that she has been with me every day during my sickness.

Sommers, the guard in the secure area, hinted none too subtly at the state I have been in these past days. To think that Miss Seward has seen me in such a state! The things she must have endured for my well-being! It is all I can do to hide my mortification.

I only thank God for her kindness and her tenacity. For it is she who saw me through the darkness clouding my mind.

I look forward to her visits each day. I believe they are as frequent as her supervisor, the stern head nurse, allows. When we talk, I feel as if I have known Miss Seward all my life. Her quick wit never fails to lift my spirits.

Her beauty matches her agreeable personality. Her hair is as golden and shining as my dear departed mother's and her face holds a subtle prettiness. How wonderful to be back in a world where one can notice such things and take pleasure in them!

Today I believe that Miss Seward noticed me staring while she took my temperature, for she turned quite pink and put a hand to her hair self-consciously. I looked away then, but I could not help but smile.

My current circumstances ensure that Miss Seward and I speak every day. Once I am discharged, I hope she will agree to continue in my company. I long to show her how, in the very short time I have known her, she has grown quite dear to my heart.

The war is behind me now and I am determined to leave its horrors in the past. It is time to begin a new life. It is my hope that this life might involve Mary Seward.

Journal of Mary Seward

22ND SEPTEMBER 1916

After my shift, I walked home with a happy heart. John seems to take pleasure in my company, and it is such a joy to see the newfound peace in his eyes. I even dare believe there is warmth in them when he rests his clear blue gaze on me.

The sun was sinking quickly below the trees as I strolled into the village. I saw a courting couple ahead of me, strolling arm in arm, clearly wrapped up in each other. I smiled, comfortable in their unwitting companionship.

But soon they stopped and turned toward each other. The gentleman, a tall, dark man, his face in shadow, bent down and kissed the girl in a way I could not help but consider too passionate for a public place.

Doubtless they did not know I was behind them and supposed themselves to be alone. Still, the impropriety of it shocked me.

I turned down a different path, wishing to leave them in solitude. But I was not quick enough to avoid hearing the girl's gasps of passion as her beau pulled her tightly to him and lowered his mouth to her throat.

To my relief, the couple remained oblivious to me. But

even now my cheeks flush red at the memory of their indiscretion.

They grow redder still when the memory leads me to thoughts of John. I cannot help but wonder what it must be like to be kissed in such a manner. . . .

Journal of
Lieutenant John Shaw

23RD SEPTEMBER 1916

I fear I may have suffered some sort of relapse last night.

I had been drowsing and awoke feeling rather odd. The shadowy ward seemed to swim about me. As I gazed about, I caught sight of a figure standing in the doorway.

Panic gripped me—the figure was that of Captain Harker. There was no doubt in my mind. No mistake. Surely nobody else shared that imposing silhouette?

The figure moved down the ward toward my bed. I realized incredulously that though the light was behind it, the figure cast no shadow before it on the polished ward floor. I wanted to run, but I felt frozen in place—like a frightened deer.

My surroundings began to swim again. I do not

remember the figure reaching my bedside, but I awoke this morning with a horrible, uncertain feeling I have not had since the front.

I will not tell anyone about this nightmare, for now the doctor has taken away those hateful restraints, I would not want them back.

CHAPTER 8

Journal of
Mary Seward

23RD SEPTEMBER 1916

This evening, when I returned to the ward from fetching fresh linen, I found a stranger standing at John's bedside, watching intently while he slept.

"Who is that, Sister?" I asked immediately. The visitor was an officer, immaculately turned out and impressive in stature: tall and broad, with sleek black hair.

Sister raised an eyebrow. "You are very interested in Lieutenant Shaw's personal affairs, Miss Seward."

"I'm sorry, Sister," I apologized.

"It is the lieutenant's commanding officer," she told me, bending a little. "The very man who saved his life."

"Captain Harker," I murmured.

"How did you know that?" Sister looked surprised.

"Lieutenant Shaw, or perhaps his sister, Lily, mentioned him," I replied quickly.

Sister must never know I have read John's journal. And now, once again, I wished that I had not. For gazing at the captain, I could not forget his cruelty to Private Smith, his passion for battle, and the monstrous images John wrote about in his delirium.

"Captain Harker wants to know how Lieutenant Shaw is progressing," Sister went on. "Why don't you go and tell him?"

I nodded and walked slowly toward the man, struggling to quash my trepidation. John's newly recovered psyche could not withstand this brutal reminder from the past. Best to give Captain Harker the information he sought and send him on his way, I reasoned.

"Hello," I greeted the captain. "I'm Miss Seward. I understand you've come to inquire about Lieutenant Shaw's health."

"Good evening, Miss Seward. It is a pleasure to meet you at last. I am Quincey Harker, at your service."

The gentleness of Captain Harker's voice was unexpected and had the effect of throwing me off balance. I took his outstretched hand. "Captain Harker," I replied. "How kind of you to visit the lieutenant."

The handsome officer smiled down at me. "I could do

nothing else. I understand from Miss Shaw's letters that you have been taking very good care of the lieutenant."

Feeling uncomfortable under the intensity of Harker's stare, I turned toward John. He continued to sleep peacefully.

"The lieutenant has emerged from his fever and grows in strength each day," I told the captain. "But his mind has been badly scarred by his experiences in the trenches. The brutality of war affects some men that way."

"Perhaps," Captain Harker said, "but Shaw is strong. He will recover." He spoke with a flat certainty that vexed me.

"I am doing everything in my power to ensure that he does," I reported.

There was an awkward pause. After a moment, I gestured toward the door. "Thank you again for your visit, Captain Harker."

Harker frowned slightly. "I understand your eagerness to be rid of me, Miss Seward. I am sure you have much to do."

I bit my lip. Though I wanted Harker out of the hospital, I had not meant to be obviously rude. "I—I will let Lieutenant Shaw know you were here, of course," I tried to recover myself.

Harker nodded. He made for the door. I could feel my anxiety easing with each step he took.

"If you like, I will update you on his progress," I called after him. "Where may I write to you, sir?"

The captain turned. "That is most kind of you, but it will

not be necessary to write. I am staying at Carfax Hall. Miss Shaw has graciously invited me to be her guest."

My eyes widened. I had to suppress a gasp. How could Lily invite a brutal man such as Captain Harker into her home?

Then I remembered—she had not read her brother's journal. Only I had. To Lily, Harker was not a bloodthirsty warrior. He was the savior who pulled her wounded brother from the battlefield.

"Will you be here in Purfleet for long, Captain?" I asked, my voice wavering slightly.

Harker smiled broadly. His long teeth were blindingly white. "My business in England may take some time, Miss Seward. I shall be staying indefinitely."

Journal of
Lily Shaw

25TH SEPTEMBER 1916

Oh, Mother, how you would enjoy this! We are to have our first houseguest! It is John's commanding officer, Captain Quincey Harker. When he wrote to tell me he was planning to visit, of course I invited him to stay at Carfax Hall.

I met Captain Harker at the entrance to the sanatorium this morning. He was just leaving John's side.

When the captain greeted me, I confess, my breath was quite taken away. He is a most disarmingly tall and handsome man.

"You must be Miss Shaw," he said softly. "I am Captain Quincey Harker." He took my hand and bent his head to press his lips against my gloved fingers.

I had not expected the gesture, and at the touch of his lips I went quite light-headed. I admonished myself for being such a silly, sheltered girl. I quickly drew my hand in an effort to gather myself.

"John often mentioned you in his letters to me, Captain Harker," I replied. "I felt from his words that you were a great strength and inspiration to him."

I looked up into his aristocratic face and felt I might drown in his gaze. His eyes were deepest brown, fringed with long black lashes.

"Your brother is a fine soldier," the captain said. "Take comfort. When John has recovered, he will be all the stronger from his experiences."

"Do you really think so?" I asked, desperately wanting to believe the captain's words.

"I am certain of it," he assured me. And then he smiled.

How can I describe the quality of Captain Harker's smile? His finely shaped mouth parted to reveal the whitest, most perfect teeth I have ever seen. His beautiful eyes warmed to a golden color.

"I should leave you to have some time alone with your brother," he offered, stepping down from the entryway.

"Please stay," I said, suddenly bereft at the prospect of losing his strong presence in this melancholy place.

"I would, but I'm afraid I have arrangements to make," the captain apologized. "I am looking forward to joining you at Carfax Hall this evening. You are quite generous in extending your hospitality. Especially to a virtual stranger."

"Think nothing of it," I said immediately. "It is the least we can do to thank you for all you have done for John."

Captain Harker gave a small appreciative bow. "That is most kind of you, Lily. Some home comforts are a welcome thought after the trenches."

Captain Harker's use of my given name stirred a warmth within me that I have never felt before.

Oh, Mother! To have a guest—and one so charming and agreeable! It is sure to dispel the loneliness I have felt all these years in our home. I can barely wait for the captain to have his belongings brought to the hall!

LATER

Mother and Father,

Before I sleep this evening, I must bring you more news

of our Captain Harker. He is now settled here at the hall.

Not wanting him to think me improper, I immediately explained our family situation. Antanasia would have to act in the dual role of housekeeper and chaperone—at least until John was well enough to come home to us again.

Captain Harker quickly put my mind at ease. He expressed sympathy for the terrible way I lost you, my dear parents, and admiration for my resilience given our circumstance.

I offered him the blue room, for it gets the morning sun. However, he confided in me that he suffers from a mild form of porphyria—a condition brought on by the mustard gas used at the front that causes great sensitivity to sunlight.

I had the red room prepared for him instead, as it remains in shade for most of the day.

We shared a most pleasant dinner this evening. I asked Antanasia to serve us in the dining room and to use the best china. I am so accustomed to sharing supper with her in the kitchen it was delightful to dress up and dine by candlelight.

"That is a lovely gown you are wearing," the captain commented as I took my place at the table. "Is it from London?"

"Oh no," I answered quickly. "I'm afraid you will think me terribly provincial, but there is a lady in Purfleet who makes all of my dresses."

"Provincial? Not in the least. She is clearly a woman of taste," Captain Harker noted. "That pale blue silk looks well against such pale skin. It sets off your delicate features."

I was lost for words and found myself blushing.

What stories Quincey (for that's what he now insists I call him) told me about the war and about his life before it! My dinner went quite cold as I listened, thrilled.

As he bent to sip from his wineglass, a raven wing of black hair fell across his noble brow. I longed to push it off his face, run my fingers through it. Such a thought, entering my mind unbidden, shocked me.

Antanasia hovered around the table the whole time. I suspect she is as taken as I am with our new houseguest and anxious to perform well in her role as chaperone.

Oh, Mother, Father, if only you could meet this astonishing man. It is uncanny—already, I feel as if we are old and dear friends.

Antanasia has suggested we hire a housemaid since we have company, and I told her to do so at once—I would hate for the captain to find us too rustic.

It quite amazes me. Since Quincey's arrival I feel more certain than ever that everything in our little corner of the world will be all right again.

Journal of Lieutenant John Shaw

What tricks the stresses of war have played on my mind.

I have proof now. I am not mad, merely the victim of an uncommon set of circumstances.

I know this because Lily came to visit this evening—with Captain Harker at her side.

Miss Seward was sitting with me, as she does every evening. She was in the middle of relating a story when her face paled. I looked up and saw the approach of my imposing former commander. I must admit the sight of him caused my heart to race. Involuntarily I grasped Miss Seward's hand.

"Hello, old chap!" Harker greeted me. "You're looking fine. I knew you'd be back to your old self before long." His words were filled with such cheery warmth that I had to shake my head. Was this affable man really the bloodthirsty fiend I'd seen on the battlefield?

Harker spoke to me animatedly and at some length about several topics, including the state of the war, his favorable impression of Purfleet, and his new role at the Foreign Office in London.

I was surprised to learn that he and Miss Seward had already made each other's acquaintance. Further, I was astonished by Mary's obvious discomfort in Harker's presence. For after speaking with him for just a few moments, it was clear that he is no more a monster than I!

After some time, Sister called Mary to make her rounds of the other patients. She excused herself reluctantly.

Lily beamed happily at me, cheered by my good spirits.

"John, Captain Harker is going to be in England for quite some time," she announced. "He is keen to keep an eye on your recovery. So I have invited him to stay at the hall. I hope you don't mind."

I frowned slightly at the news. My irrational fears about Harker were all but erased by his normal, friendly demeanor. But regardless, he was still a man of the world—and Lily a young, unmarried woman.

"Oh, John. Please do not tell me that this troubles you," Lily cried when she noticed my expression.

"I am sorry," I protested quietly, "but propriety dictates—"

"We have a chaperone," Lily interrupted, anticipating my argument. "Antanasia is with us always, and when you are well enough, you will join us too! Quincey has already brought such life into Carfax Hall. And I am no longer lonely in our great home. Oh, please, John, I could not bear your disapproval."

At that moment, I pitied my sister. Her life at the hall

was certainly difficult. Could I really begrudge her this companionship?

"Lily has been most hospitable," Harker told me. "It's been a pleasure getting to know her. She's a wonderful girl. I wish I had such a caring and devoted sister."

His words eased a bit of my worry. It was a very proper sentiment.

Lily blushed at the compliment. She hasn't changed a bit. She always blushed at the drop of a hat.

I glanced from one to the other. Lily gazed at me expectantly. "Captain, we are glad to welcome you to our home," I said.

Lily wrapped me in a great hug. We spoke a bit longer, then Lily and Captain Harker took their leave.

After they had gone, Mary came over to my bed. "How did you find the captain?" she asked.

"He seems well. It's kind of him to come," I answered.

"Yes. It did seem kind of him." She looked at me most curiously and then she smiled as if dismissing some thought or other.

"Captain Harker is charming," she commented. "I think your sister is quite taken with him."

I shrugged. "It is nothing more than a schoolgirl's crush, I am certain. But you are very astute to notice it."

Color warmed her cheeks. "Mother always joked that my sharp wits will stand between me and marriage."

"Why? Intelligence would be a fine quality in a wife," I replied.

Then self-consciousness gripped me. How horribly forward I must have sounded! Inwardly I could not deny my admiration for Miss Seward, but to say as much so blatantly . . .

"I'm sorry. I—I didn't mean . . ." I stammered.

"I know," she replied quickly, smiling to banish our embarrassment. "But Lieutenant, do have a care for Lily. Captain Harker is . . ." She paused, then began anew. "I simply mean, a dashing officer can turn the head of even the most sensible girl."

"I know. But Captain Harker is an honorable man," I assured her. "I am quite sure that he will conduct himself with perfect propriety."

Miss Seward seemed about to say something more. But then Sister called her, and she hurried off to see to another of her patients.

*Journal of
Mary Seward*

26TH SEPTEMBER 1916

"You've been looking uncommonly happy these last few days, my dear," Father said. He glanced at me over his paper at me as I poured our evening tea.

"Uncommonly, Father? Am I usually gloomy?"

He laughed and folded his paper. "Of course not, my dear, but you've been quite preoccupied in recent weeks. I was becoming concerned that working at the sanatorium was proving too much for you."

"Not at all," I replied firmly, handing him a teacup. It rattled in his saucer as he took it with a feeble hand.

Father smiled. His eyes shone teasingly. "Of course. There is nothing you couldn't manage, Mary. I pity the man who marries you, for you will be a formidable woman."

"Father, I don't know whether to be flattered or insulted. You make me sound like I conceal the heart of a harridan."

"You have a brave heart, Mary Elizabeth, which will always guide you toward rightness. Never be ashamed of your strength."

"Oh, Father! All this grand talk!" I chided him. Yet his fond words warmed my heart.

I took a sip of tea, wondering where to begin—or if I should begin at all. Lieutenant Shaw and I had grown closer than my heart had hoped for lately. It was my wish that our relationship would continue after his discharge.

If it did, it was proper that Father should know. But was I too sure of myself, bringing it up now?

No, I decided. John's words and actions indicated that his feelings mirrored my own. I would let Father in on the news.

"There has been a patient at the sanatorium, a young lieutenant . . ." I began hesitantly.

Father regarded me with curiosity.

"He was delirious for some weeks," I went on. "Wounded and fevered, and terribly affected by some of the things he saw in the trenches. But he seems to have recovered his senses at last."

"And it is he who has brought a new flush to your cheeks?"

Though Father was ailing, he had lost none of his shrewdness.

"Something drew me to him as soon as he arrived," I explained. "And now he is himself, he shows such sweetness and charm . . ."

"Handsome, is he?" Father suppressed a smile, but I could see his eyes twinkling with amusement.

"I suppose some would say he is," I replied. "It is Lily Shaw's brother, John, from Carfax Hall."

Father's eyebrows shot up. "Ah! So that is why you and Lily Shaw have recently had so much to do with each other." He took a sip from his cup, then settled back into his chair. "John Shaw . . . can't say I've ever spoken to the lad. Bundled off to boarding school as soon he and his sister arrived at the hall by that stern-faced housekeeper of theirs. And then plunged straight into the war, poor chap . . ." He shook his head in sympathy.

I went over to the dresser drawer to fetch Father his pills.

"Well, I hope he appreciates what a blessing he's found in you, my dear," he said as I handed them to him.

I laughed and kissed the top of his dear head. As usual, my father and I hoped for the same things.

Journal of Lily Shaw

27TH SEPTEMBER 1916

Antanasia has wasted no time in obtaining a housemaid—a young girl from the other side of Purfleet by the name of Dora Hughes.

Dora seems a little rough and ready, and I confess, I'm surprised at Antanasia's choice, she being so fastidious herself. Still, Dora adds a certain cheeriness to the place with her singing and loud laughter. And her flirting with the delivery boys seems to bring our grocery orders to the door in double-quick time! I cannot let her know that I have seen her make advances. As mistress of the house, I should be seen to disapprove. But in reality part of me envies her freedom of spirit!

4TH OCTOBER 1916

I shall invite Mary to dine here at the hall. I want her to get to know Quincey better. He is such a fine man.

If I am honest, my own feelings for Quincey have become far stronger than admiration. What a comfort and pleasure it is to have someone with whom I can share my evening walk around the estate. He stays up long after I have retired, seeming to prefer the night to daytime. At first, this struck me as odd. Then I remembered his condition.

I thought Antanasia would disapprove of his strange hours, but she sends Dora to bed and stays up herself to see to his needs, without a word of complaint. And she leaves us alone together to talk, when I'd have thought she'd be the strictest of chaperones.

Who would have thought it? He has clearly melted her heart too!

7TH OCTOBER 1916

Dear Mother and Father,

Something happened tonight. Something wonderful!

After dinner, Quincey and I took our coffee in the parlor as usual. We were sitting tête-à-tête on the small divan, an evening rain drumming against the windows outside. I pressed my fingertips against the cold glass, admiring the storm.

Perhaps it was the wine, which I may have had a drop more of than usual—but for some reason I could not stop thinking of you and the good times we had in the past.

Oh, my dear parents! As Quincey and I grow closer, I find

myself wishing more and more fervently that you could know him. I am certain that you would love him as much as I have grown to. And after tonight there is even more reason to wish that you could speak to the captain.

But I am getting ahead of myself.

"Such beautiful weather," Quincey said, following my gaze out the window. He gave me a wry smile. "Sometimes it seems as if the sun will never appear in England."

I shrugged. "Most people think the rain unpleasant. But I enjoy it. I find beauty in its dark and tempest."

"Really?" he asked, raising an eyebrow.

"Of course," I prattled on foolishly. "The sun is blinding—and gives objects a harsh glare. But in a storm, one can see without discomfort. The rain softens the edges of everything."

"You are a most unusual girl," Quincey remarked, taking a sip of his deep red port.

I sat upright, putting a hand to my breast. "Oh, Quincey! Do you think me odd?"

"No," he reassured me. He took my hand and replaced it on my lap, allowing his palm to rest on mine for a moment.

The strong, rough feeling of it sent a warm wave through me. I struggled to keep my composure.

"You are not odd," Quincey continued. "Your ability to find appeal in what others carelessly disdain is admirable. Please, continue." His eyes urged me on. He was interested in knowing more of me. And this night, it was as if we were the only two in the windswept world. It was not long before I found myself telling Quincey about John's and my child- hood, about your deaths—and the dark years that followed.

"Perhaps that is another reason I so love the storm," I ventured. "Mother and Father left us on a rainy evening— and never returned. When it rains, I am reminded of the last time we were all together."

"Poor sweet child," Quincey murmured, taking my hand again. "It must be difficult for a girl so young, so fragile to be without those she loves most."

I tried to ignore the warm current his touch sent through me.

"But I am not without them. Not really."

"How so?" he asked.

I blushed again. "I speak to them," I confided in him. "No one else knows of it. I write letters telling them everything that is happening with me and with John. I know it is fool- ish, speaking to the dead."

"Oh, Lily. It is not foolish," he said, touching my shoulder. "It is more real and true than the understanding of reason- able people."

I bent my head back to look up at him. His fingers traced the line of my throat.

It felt so easy to share the sadness that lingers in my heart with him. I wondered how I ever lived without his strength and presence in my life.

Then he took my face between his smooth hands and lowered his lips to mine. I stiffened at first, surprised by his action. But then, the closeness of his massive frame overwhelmed me. His lips tasted headily of the wine we had sipped at dinner. I found the scent of his skin intoxicating— like that of the woods after rain. It awoke something within me, made all my senses spin.

I had dreamt many times of my first kiss, imagining it would be with a sweet boy. Never could I have imagined it would be with a captivating man like Captain Quincey Harker.

I wanted to linger in that kiss for eternity, to hang on to the fiery pleasure it awoke in my body, which drowned out all fear and sorrow from my heart.

But slowly, he drew away, letting his hands again trace lightly along my throat. He shuddered. Then taking hold of my trembling fingers, he whispered, "You surely are the sweetest soul. . . ."

I looked into his eyes, confused by what I saw there— desire—but also a trace of melancholy. Was there pity mixed in with his regard for me? I could not bear that. I shook my head to clear it and, whispering a hasty good night, withdrew up to my room.

Sleep is impossible now. I can still feel the trail of Quincey's fingertips on my heated flesh. I marvel at these new sensations. The night seems filled with magic.

The storm has cleared, and I could sit and watch the moon's silvery light caress the distant hills all night.

Lovingly,

Lily

LATER

I have just seen something from my window that has quite altered my mood—a great black hound prowling across the grounds, pacing restlessly back and forth. The sight of it quite chills me. Where has it come from? Why is it here?

I am now even more thankful for darling Quincey's presence in the house.

I have drawn my curtains so that I cannot see it and shall ask Antanasia to mention it to the gamekeeper tomorrow. It is time I went to bed.

CHAPTER 9

*Journal of
Mary Seward*

14TH OCTOBER 1916

This evening I went to dinner at Carfax Hall with Lily and Captain Harker. Lily had invited me a week earlier, and I was glad of the invitation.

It has been more than two weeks since Harker took up residence at the hall and I am worried that a man such as he shares a home with sweet Lily.

There have been several occasions, at the hospital, when I have witnessed interactions between the captain and Lily that give me pause. There have been lingering glances and even physical contact between them that seems too intimate.

I have told Lieutenant Shaw what I have observed and though he has tried to quell my concern, I cannot rest properly until I am certain that Harker is the honorable man he appears to be.

At the hour, I knocked at the front entrance of the hall. A young woman I hadn't seen before opened the door.

"What is it, then?" she asked.

"Good evening, I am Mary Seward. I'm here to join Miss Shaw for dinner," I replied, taken aback by her rough manner.

Just then, Antanasia loomed up behind the girl. "Dora— get back to the kitchen," she snapped. She pulled back the front door to let me in.

"Blasted girl!" she muttered when Dora had returned to her post. She took my cloak and hung it up.

A loud clang echoed down the hallway—the sound of a large cooking pot dropped from some height. Antanasia muttered something under her breath and hurried off toward the source of the noise.

I blinked. It seemed I would be left to my own devices. Though I had no idea where my hosts might be.

I gazed down the hallway and noticed a light shining from beneath a closed door. The muffled sound of gramophone music and laughter emanated from within.

With no Antanasia to announce me, I decided to make myself known. I let myself into the room.

I was greeted with a sight that rooted me to the spot. Lily was in the arms of Captain Harker. She was tracing his mouth with her fingertips, rapt fascination on her face. I watched as he grabbed her small white hand in his own and kissed her palm, then lowered his head to place his lips over hers.

My gasp broke them apart.

"Mary!" she cried, slipping from Harker's embrace, her face flushed. "You're here! Come in!"

Not surprisingly, she sounded flustered. But her eyes shone with an exhilaration and joy I could never imagine seeing in the normally pale, haunted Lily. She hurried over and grasped my hands, pulling me eagerly across the room. "I'm so pleased you came! Now you and Quincey can get to know each other. I'm sure you shall become great friends!"

I was lost for words. Instead of embarrassment, I saw nothing but pride in Lily's eyes.

"Quincey?" I asked, finally regaining myself. "I had not realized that you and the captain were so informal with each other." I stared at Lily, my expression full of meaning.

"We have grown so close in these past weeks that formality began to seem . . . foolish." Captain Harker's eyes were hard, but his tone was warmly civil. "A pleasure to meet you again, Miss Seward."

I bristled at Captain Harker's rude dismissal of my concern. But as Lily smiled at one, then the other of us, I determined that I should make the best of things, while keeping eyes and ears fully open.

Dinner was an uncomfortable affair—although there is no denying the captain is a man of great charm and wit. He steered the conversation like a master helmsman, while Lily sailed merrily through the evening as happy as a child.

I tried my best to join in and not betray my dismay at the manner in which their relationship has obviously been allowed to develop. It was beyond unseemly, and more, I felt sure that Lily was in danger of falling under Harker's sway.

I was affronted by the manner he affected, conducting himself as though he were the master of the house, when that title clearly belonged to John.

I noticed, too, the overly familiar way Dora, the new housemaid, lingered at Harker's side when she cleared away his dishes. Lily seemed quite oblivious to this—to anything but Harker himself.

Perhaps Harker was busying himself with the maid? If so, Lily might be safe. But I could not be sure, and I could not leave it to chance.

The captain left Lily and me alone after dinner, excusing himself to do some Foreign Office paperwork in his room.

Lily and I returned to the parlor. Once there, she grasped me by both hands and led me to sit with her on one of the sofas. "I am so happy, Mary!" she exclaimed. "As you saw . . ." She blushed a little. "Quincey and I have become . . . very close. . . ."

I smiled, but failed to mask my concern completely.

"Why do you look so worried?" Lily asked, noticing my expression. Then her eyes widened with sudden fear. "Is it John?" she gasped. "Has he relapsed? Tell me!"

"No, no," I reassured her. "John was sleeping peacefully when I left the sanatorium this evening. I am just a little tired, that is all."

She looked on at me searchingly, as though she did not believe my excuse.

I swallowed hard and decided to speak my mind. After all, Lily had always surprised me with her candor. And she had led such an uncommonly sheltered life, she might value some sisterly advice. "I am worried for you, Lily," I began haltingly. "You are such an innocent. And Captain Harker is clearly not . . ."

A frown clouded her lovely face. "Surely Quincey has seen much. But I am not sure of what you mean."

"Lily, it is unwise to be alone with a man . . ."—I was lost for words delicate enough to describe what I had witnessed— "in the way you were when I arrived here this evening."

"Mary, Quincey has been nothing but wonderful to me from the moment he arrived." She lowered her voice conspiratorially. "Though I must admit, there is something between us. I do believe that he loves me!" Lily smiled broadly.

"Even if he does, you must realize what such . . . such passion can lead to! What trouble even the most levelheaded person can find herself in," I insisted.

"Quincey would never take advantage of me!" Lily prickled in defense of her sweetheart.

"Has he spoken to you of marriage?" I asked, as calmly as I could.

"No," Lily admitted. She turned and sat on the edge of a satin-covered couch, picking at the fringe of an embroidered pillow. "But I am sure that he loves me. I trust him, Mary. I wish that you could too."

Just then, the door opened and Captain Harker entered. Had he heard us speaking?

His face betrayed nothing but polite charm. "May I join you ladies for a nightcap?" he asked. "My work took much less time than I had anticipated."

I took this as my cue to depart. "I must be getting home to settle Father for the night," I said, and made my goodbyes.

I fear so that Lily mistakes Captain Harker's passion for love. I pray that she does not give in to her desires. Her sweet heart will broken—or even worse circumstances may befall her.

Journal of
Lily Shaw

14TH OCTOBER 1916

Dear Mother and Father,

I saw the black hound prowling outside again as I drew my curtains. I am glad I offered Mary my carriage home, for

I would not like to think of her walking through the estate while such a beast roams free.

I fear my dear Mary and darling Quincey will not easily become friends after all. Though they were perfectly polite to each other at dinner, I sensed a guardedness between them that I have never before seen in either. If only they could be friends, for they have both grown so dear to me in the short space I have known them and they both care so much for John.

Mary did not linger long after dinner. She said she must return to see her father before he retired to his bed. I hope that this was true and that it was not our company that drove her away.

"And what did you and Miss Seward discuss while I was gone?" Quincey asked teasingly when we were alone again.

"She is concerned for my reputation!" I smiled back as I told him, trying to make light of her advice.

"Does she believe I would let you come to harm?" Quincey asked, turning to face the window.

"Of course not!" I laughed. I moved behind him and circled his frame with my arms. "How could anyone think that you would hurt me?"

He turned and held me in his embrace. He stroked my hair with a hand so gentle I did not realize he had removed my comb until I felt my hair tumble around my bare neck.

"Dark and soft as a summer's night." His voice was like

the rumble of distant thunder. His beautiful face looked magnificent in the firelight—his eyes lit by the reflecting embers in the hearth. His gaze seemed to enter my very soul and stake its claim—as if this had always been my destiny. I ached to be kissed and touched by him, as he had done before Mary interrupted us. I stroked his cheek. It felt smooth and cool under my fingertips.

He touched his lips to mine, then gently moved his mouth along my jaw and down to my throat.

I felt so breathless and excited I thought I might faint. Mary's caution sounded in my mind, like a distant church bell drowned by the roar of a storm. But I could not resist the power of these wonderful new feelings and pressed my body closer. I could feel my heart beating strong and fast.

"Please," I whispered.

Then he gently pushed me from him. "Lily, we cannot. Not yet," he said. His voice had a ragged edge.

His sudden rejection stung me, but as my passion subsided I realized he was only echoing Mary's sensible advice.

"Our time will come," he said as he left me at my bedroom door.

The thought keeps me warm as I write in the chill of the night. I should reassure Mary that Quincey has shown himself to be a man of honor. But how can I be fearful of the passion Quincey has aroused in me? I yearn to embrace it—for it seems to promise joy powerful enough to banish fear forever.

Something odd occurred this morning. Dora did not strike me as the fainting type, yet she swooned clean away while serving breakfast. And when she came to, she was so pale I feared she was truly ill. I insisted on calling the doctor, though Antanasia seemed to feel it unnecessary.

The doctor could not explain Dora's bloodless pallor. He said she may be anemic, yet she seemed so robust—even yesterday. He recommends she rest for a day or so and eat red meat and eggs.

I hope she has not been kissing too many butcher's boys and landed herself in trouble.

*Journal of
Mary Seward*

"So how is your new friend Lily?" Father asked at breakfast. "You seemed a little distracted after your dinner with her at the hall."

"I'm afraid I did not warm much to her houseguest," I confessed.

"She has a guest?"

"John's CO—Captain Harker."

The name seemed to awaken a light in Father's eyes. "Harker?"

"He came to see Lieutenant Shaw, and Lily took him in."

"Harker . . ." Father repeated. "I once knew a man by the name of Harker—Jonathan Harker. A fine man . . ."

Father turned his gaze away as he drifted off into his memories. I knew it would be kinder to leave him there than to disturb him with my anxieties about Lily, so I sipped the rest of my tea in silence.

Journal of
Lily Shaw

15TH OCTOBER 1916

Dora has disappeared. Her bed lies unslept in, her wardrobe cleaned out, its doors and drawers left opened as though she left quickly. I thought she was happy here. But perhaps I was right when I suspected her fainting might have betrayed more than poor diet. I fear the poor girl has got herself into trouble.

What a pity she did not have someone like Mary to guide and caution her as I do.

Journal of
Lieutenant John Shaw

I slept without dreams last night. It was like being freed from hell.

Opening my eyes this morning, I felt a vigor that had not stirred within me for weeks. The sky outside gleamed a deep, rich blue in the morning light. A more beautiful day could not be had.

Mary Seward appeared at her usual hour to fuss with my bedsheets and help lay out my breakfast. As usual my heart filled with delight at the sight of her.

Miss Seward is a most uncommon girl. I am lucky to have her in my company, but my time at the sanatorium soon comes to a close. I will return to Carfax Hall, and my friendship with her will end. I want so much for it to continue—to turn into something more. I have tried many times to express my feelings, but at each attempt, I find myself tongue-tied.

How can I tell Mary my feelings and not offend her? Worse, what if my feelings are not returned? I am so ignorant in matters of the heart, but I must take courage and hope I can make her understand.

I have done it, and I will explain all here.

"You're looking well!" Mary approached me with her usual cheerful smile at the end of her evening rounds.

"I feel better and better each day," I told her, smiling back. "And it is due to you that my improvement has been so rapid."

"Nonsense," Mary argued playfully. "How can changing sheets and taking temperatures be thanked for your recovery?"

"You misunderstand," I corrected her.

"Really? How so?" she asked.

I frowned, searching again for the proper words.

"Lieutenant Shaw, what is the matter?" she asked when she noticed my expression. "Are you in pain?"

I shook my head, then gestured toward the chair next to my bed. She lowered herself gently into the seat.

"Miss Seward," I began, "you have seen me brought so low. Even today I am ashamed that you witnessed my horrible state."

She began to protest, but I interrupted.

"I am anxious to improve," I continued, "because I want so much to show you the man I can be. A man I hope you will consider worthy of your continued company. I wish to ask you—may we continue to see each other after I am discharged from your care?"

She stared at me a moment, expressionless. I held my breath. This was not the response I had hoped for. Was she repelled by my suggestion?

My fear was banished in a moment, for her eyes warmed, and she smiled. "Lieutenant, your bravery and strength have proven you more than worthy. I should love to keep your company after you are discharged."

I took her hand. Her small, soft fingers squeezed mine firmly. "My, you are very bold today," she teased.

"I slept well," I told her, smiling back. "No nightmares."

"What nightmares are these?" Captain Harker's voice came from behind us.

Mary and I both turned with a start. Neither of us had heard him approach. The surprise of him seeming to materialize at the end of my bed set my heart hammering. Mary let go of my hand and stood up.

"My nightmares of—of the trenches, sir," I stammered.

"Ah . . ." he replied sympathetically. "That is to be expected. But you must put our time in France out of your mind if you are to focus on your recovery."

There was a heavy pause. Mary looked away from Captain Harker, a troubled expression creasing her brow. I felt surprised. Did she have no greeting for the captain?

Captain Harker broke the silence. "Please, John. You must call me Quincey," he announced. "It seems odd for you to call me 'sir' while your sister calls me by my first name."

My mouth opened slightly in surprise. Had Lily and Harker grown so intimate in so short a time? I was about to ask that very question when Mary took a thermometer from her pocket and popped it beneath my tongue.

"Lily is such a sweet soul . . ." she commented, still not looking at Quincey. "So trusting . . ." She flashed me a glance I felt was laced with meaning. It had the effect of sharpening my concern.

Captain Harker—Quincey—anticipated my worries. "I'm sure you have noticed, John, that your sister and I have very quickly become dear friends. I hope you do not find our familiarity distasteful. It is Lily who insists upon it. I believe she is glad to finally be close with someone."

I allowed myself to relax. Once again, Quincey assured me that he harbored only the most appropriate feelings for my sister.

Mary snatched the thermometer from my mouth, shook it sharply, and looked straight at Quincey. "Shall you be returning to the front soon, Captain Harker?" she queried.

I was surprised and confused by her sharp tone. What could she find so distressing about our conversation?

"For the time being, I remain on special duty in England," Quincey told her politely.

"And you intend to remain at the hall with Lily?" Mary's question sounded blunt to the point of rudeness.

"Of course he should remain at the hall," I interjected,

keen to smooth over the bristling tension between them. I stared at Mary's hard expression, struggling to understand her actions. Perhaps she was disconcerted by Quincey's interruption of our intimate moment. Or perhaps—

"Miss Seward!" Sister's voice rang out across the ward. "I think you have spent enough time with the lieutenant this morning. There are other patients who need your attention."

"Yes, Sister." Mary bowed her head, pocketed her thermometer, and walked away, forgetting to record my temperature on my chart. It was most unlike her.

PURFLEET CHRONICLE
16TH OCTOBER 1916

BODY RECOVERED FROM RIVER

The body of one Dora Hughes was dragged from the river last night just outside the Carfax estate. Miss Hughes had been working as a maid at Carfax Hall. There were no evident injuries to the body apart from a scratch at the neck, deemed insignificant by the coroner. It is assumed she drowned after having imbibed too much alcohol. Miss Agnes Hughes, sister of the deceased, told the police that the two of them had spent the previous evening at the nearby Dog and Duck public house. "It was her one evening off a week; why shouldn't she enjoy herself?" the distraught Miss Hughes said. "That vinegar-faced housekeeper at the hall worked poor Dora ragged. Pale as a ghost she was.

"We left the Dog and Duck at closing time and Dora was going to walk back to the hall along the river like she always did. That was the last I seen of me poor departed sister," Miss Hughes sobbed.

On further investigation, Dora Hughes's name has been brought into question. The housekeeper at Carfax Hall has let it be known that jewelery found on Miss Hughes's body belonged to her employer, Miss Lily Shaw.

Journal of
Lily Shaw

16TH OCTOBER 1916

Dear Mother and Father,

I am filled with sorrow at the news of Dora Hughes's death. The poor girl is dead. Drowned.

Antanasia showed no pity at the news. "We can find another maid," she said coldly. "One who is more honest."

"More honest?" I looked at her in surprise.

Antanasia informed me of Dora's thievery. I rushed upstairs to my jewelery box and saw that one of my ruby earrings was missing. So it was true. I had come to think of Dora as a member of our household, and she had been stealing from us all along!

That evening, when I told Quincey of the matter, he bristled with rage. "That girl deserves a worse end—for taking what is not hers and for daring to do so underneath my nose."

I was surprised by his anger at first, but Quincey's harsh sentiment springs from his own guilt. I am certain that he feels partly to blame for the loss of my earring. As we have shared intimacies, he has grown quite protective of me.

I care not about jewelery, but I pity Dora. That poor girl. Something awful must have driven her to steal from us. Her crime was not deserving of such an end. Fate has meted out a harsh justice indeed.

19TH OCTOBER 1916

As I sit with John, I see Mary staring anxiously as she goes about her work on the ward. I know what she is thinking. But Quincey behaves like a perfect gentleman and I like a proper lady. I see desire burning in his eyes, and I feel it in my heart. I would not be so dishonest as to deny it. But my sweet Quincey restrains his ardor, and so do I. I only pray that he also dreams of marriage. Then we may at last be respectably united and give full rein to our passion.

When John is fully recovered, I know in my heart that Quincey will see to it. Then he and I will be united for all eternity.

CHAPTER 10

Report of Dr. McLeod,
Purfleet Sanatorium

Patient John Shaw, Lieutenant, no. 467842

The patient has now been fully lucid for nearly a month. In my opinion he is now recovered enough both physically and mentally to complete his recuperation in his family home. Therefore I am discharging him.

DM, 20th October 1916

Journal of
Mary Seward

Today John was released from the sanatorium to complete his convalescence at home. Lily came to collect him in their carriage.

"I shall miss talking with you every day," I said as he climbed, a little shakily, into it. I forced myself to give him a cheerful smile, for though Lieutenant Shaw and I spoke of continuing our relationship, I had no idea how frequently he wished to see me.

"On the contrary," he replied. "I will order our carriage to fetch you and take you home again each evening. Our conversations must not be interrupted."

I smiled again—and this time it came naturally. "I would be delighted to visit you."

John covered my hands with his own. "Dear Mary . . ." he murmured. "You must come as often as you can. You have been my strength these past few weeks."

I was quite taken aback by the fondness that shone in his eyes. I leaned forward and kissed him gently on his cheek. I knew it must seem forward, yet my heart compelled me to such affection. "I will come tomorrow evening . . . John," I promised.

He took my hand and kissed it. My heart fluttered like a bird caught in a net. "Until tomorrow," he said. The driver cracked his whip, and John and Lily were off to their home.

As I watched the carriage recede, I smiled at the notion that I might, someday, be a part of their very household. Because of this, I must tell John that I have read his journal. There should be no secrets between us now. I pray it will not turn him away from me.

Journal of
Lieutenant John Shaw

Being home is a mixed blessing; I find myself in an ill temper.

Our newcomer, Quincey, seems utterly at home here. He moves around the place as if he has known it all his life. It is as if I am the houseguest and he the host. An easy familiarity has grown between him and Lily and even Antanasia, which, I must confess, makes me feel a little like a latecomer to a party.

Further, I have noticed certain intimacies between Lily and Harker that hint at their desire for a deeper relationship. Though I have no doubt that Harker has kept his word to me and treated Lily with nothing more than brotherly affection, I am troubled by this development. Perhaps I will seek Mary's counsel about this when she visits the hall tonight.

Mary . . . perhaps my ill temper is as much to do with the fact that I am missing her, having grown used to her sweet presence close by me for most of the day.

LATER

Mary brightened the hall with her visit this evening. She came straight into the parlor, where I was resting on the sofa.

As she took off her coat and gloves and whisked the hat from her head, I felt I was watching a flower blossoming, filling the room with its freshness.

"Did Lily not greet you when you arrived?" I asked, wondering where my sister was.

"No, Antanasia told me she was taking a walk in the grounds," she replied. She settled herself across from me—on the white Queen Anne chair that had been Mother's favorite. "Tell me. How are you feeling?"

"It is strange to be home." I sighed, feeling no need to disguise my true feelings.

"I'm not surprised." Mary smiled encouragingly. "A lot has happened since you were last here."

"Quincey, however, seems very comfortable," I commented. "He strides around as though it is he who owns this place."

"The captain would be comfortable wherever he was." Mary sniffed. "He has that air about him."

I smiled. "Would you admire me more if I had that same confidence, Mary?"

She turned her wide, frank gaze on me. "Oh, John, of course not," she replied. "And I would call him arrogant rather than confident." She busied herself adjusting my pillows, then sat down beside me on the sofa. She took both my hands in hers. Her touch had the effect of a tonic. I felt life and vitality surge through me.

Then I noticed Mary's expression. There was anxiety in

her pretty face. Something was troubling her. I longed to help banish whatever worry plagued her.

"Dear Mary, tell me what is wrong," I urged her.

She took a deep breath. "John," she began, "there is something I must confess. When you were first brought into the sanatorium, I felt so drawn to you. Seeing you lost distressed me more than I can say. I longed to help you, yet there seemed nothing I could do. So I sought to discover what had paralyzed you with such fear."

She looked down at her fingers.

"Continue, Mary. You need not be afraid."

She lifted her gaze and faced me with an uncompromising directness. "John, I took your journal and read it."

I guessed from her expression that she expected me to be angry or indignant, but I felt only a surge of embarrassment. "You read that nonsense!" I exclaimed, putting a hand to my forehead to cover my discomfort. "What can you think of me?"

Mary gazed once more at her hands and then began hesitantly, "War causes people to do monstrous things. . . . And fever can make people imagine scenes even more wild and terrible . . ."

"Then you understand," I said, relieved.

She nodded. "You are not angry with me?" she asked tentatively.

"No, my love!" I exclaimed. "You did it only to help me— how could I be angry with you?"

We both realized at the same moment that I had uninten-
tionally revealed how deeply I felt for her.

"It is true, Mary," I confessed. "My hours without you are
empty. I should like to have you always by my side."

She blushed a charming pink, and I knew she felt similarly.
She smiled, then regained a more serious expression. "John, knowing the things that Captain Harker has done on the battlefield, I
am concerned about his residence in this house. He is a brutal
man. And I am afraid I have witnessed moments that indicate
there is quite a bit more than friendship between him and Lily."

"Yes. I have seen these things myself," I confided to her.

"You have?" she asked incredulously. "And you are not
concerned?"

"I am," I admitted. "But what am I to do? Had Lily been
in love with the Harker I described in the trenches, I would
forbid her from ever seeing him again. But I cannot trust my
own descriptions. The Harker I know now is considerate and
charming. I must believe his intentions are honorable."

"Still, John. When I saw them—" she began to argue.

I patted her hand softly. "Do not worry. Now that I am
home, I intend to keep a close eye on the situation. If
Harker's intentions are ill, I will find him out."

She touched my cheek with the palm of her hand. "I have
no doubt that you will." Then she leaned over and kissed me
on the cheek. "I must go," she said. "Father is not expecting
me to be late tonight."

"Must you leave already?" I protested. "Let me call for the carriage as I promised. We wouldn't want the wolves to catch you, Miss Riding Hood."

"Wolves, sir?" she replied, her voice light. "I did not know you kept them."

"Lily tells me she has seen a strange, rather fearsome-looking hound at large in the grounds at night," I confessed. "Antanasia's mentioned it to the gamekeeper. I won't have you wandering back alone in the dark until the beast is caught."

Mary shuddered, then told me of her distress at coming across a savaged deer when making her way home from the hall on a previous visit.

"Oh, Mary," I said. "When I think that you may have been in danger . . ."

Mary smiled. "I'm sure it will be caught in no time," she said.

I helped Mary into the carriage and waved her off. In the distance, I noticed Lily and Quincey strolling together in the twilight. As I watched, Lily took his hand and gazed at him admiringly.

I must confess, the sight caused me trepidation, but I shook my head, dismissing my fear. The Quincey Harker I had imagined was a creature of fiction, created by an addled mind. I had to believe that. To suppose anything else would be unbearable.

Journal of Lily Shaw

23RD OCTOBER 1916

Dear Mother and Father,

I fear the worst has happened. I fear I may have lost Quincey forever!

Since John's return to the hall, my beloved has stemmed the expression of our passion. He tells me that we must exercise restraint—out of respect, as well as concern for John's health.

Naturally, I want to do everything I can for my brother, but my lack of contact with Quincy seems to have heightened my desire for him. Now, even the slightest brush of Quincey's hand causes an aching within me that is not easily dispelled.

So when Quincey arrived home from the Foreign Office this evening out of sorts, I fretted. He didn't even come to say hello. Instead, he told Antanasia to send his apologies and went straight to his room.

I could not bear the lack of my beloved—and my want of him caused me to hunger even more for his touch. So as soon as John retired to bed, I crept to Quincey's room.

The hour was late. My way was lit only by a dim lamp burning in the hall.

I knocked on his door. When he did not answer, I grew worried. I turned the handle and let myself in.

"Quincey?" I whispered. The room was dark, but I saw his supper tray on the table near the hearth, untouched.

Bewildered by his absence, I moved over to the window and looked out, wondering if he'd taken a walk by himself.

A whispering of movement behind me made me spin round. Quincey stepped out of the shadows.

"Lily." His voice rumbled, raspy and seductive. The look of hunger on his face thrilled me.

He came toward me slowly. My whole body seemed to pulse with every footfall. I waited for him, my skin tingling in anticipation of his touch.

When at last he grasped me, I felt breathless at his strength. The lamplight shone down on his beautiful face and his eyes seemed to burn with a passion stronger than I have ever seen. The sight of his mouth fueled my desire, and I could not stop myself. I arched my body toward him. I felt a shudder flow through him as I kissed his lips, his neck. My desire to give myself to him was nearly overwhelming.

"This is maddening," he growled. "I must have you." He bent toward me, parting his lips until I could see his white teeth gleaming with a strange, sharp perfection.

"Yes," I gasped, feeling his mouth on my neck, his teeth scraping slowly against the tender skin. "Yes, my darling. I love you. I love you with all my heart."

He froze then and let go of me so suddenly I fell back against the velvet drapes. He turned, sweeping up his great-coat.

"Quincey, what is it?" My heart hammered with fear. Was it my expression of love that had driven him from me?

"I must leave tonight," he said harshly. "I have business in London."

The thought of his leaving pierced my soul, but I tried to hide my distress. "How long will you be gone?" I asked.

"Only a day or two."

"Please, don't leave," I said quietly. "I shall miss you,"

"I *cannot* stay here tonight, Lily." The anger in his tone cut to my heart like a knife. He pushed a lock of black hair back off his forehead and moved to the door.

As he let himself out of the room, I could hardly find breath, my heart twisted so with pain. I tried to remember he would be gone only a short time, but still, my eyes burned with hot tears.

I turned to the window and, pressing my face against the cool glass, let them flow unchecked. As I stared out into the wide indigo sky, a great bat swooped over the lawns. Through tear-clouded eyes, I watched the rhythmic thrust of its huge outstretched wings as it glided out into the great world beyond our gates.

CHAPTER 11

Journal of
Lieutenant John Shaw

I have spent the most wonderful week with Mary Seward!
Her presence in my life makes me happier than I ever
thought possible. We have spent days strolling in our gardens
here at Carfax Hall and evenings taking tea by the fire.

Though we have stayed within the bounds of propriety,
the deep affection I feel for Mary is undeniable. Her happy
laughter sounds like bells to me, and when the sun strikes
her golden hair, she does indeed look like the angel I imagined all those weeks ago.

Yesterday afternoon in the garden, I crept up behind
her to give her a playful fright. I grabbed her around the
waist, and she yelped with surprise. When I whirled her
around to face me, we found ourselves standing just inches
from each other—lips so close it would have been easy to

kiss. I expected Mary to turn away, but she stood fast. Though the color built in her cheeks, her clear blue eyes gazed expectantly into mine. How I wanted that kiss! But I also knew that I wanted Mary to regret nothing about our courtship. I turned my face slightly and pressed my cheek to hers.

"In time," I whispered in her ear.

She sighed softly and closed her eyes. I felt her long lashes brush the side of my face. "John Shaw, you are the gentlest man. I wish for all the time in the world with you."

My heart soared, hearing her words. With a woman like Mary at my side, my life could be truly complete.

I only wish Lily weren't so out of sorts. Since the captain's departure her manner has been morose. I have tried to comfort her, to explain that an important man such as the captain is needed in the world beyond our gates. But she will not be consoled.

So I am in a curious predicament. For Lily's sake, I wish for Quincey's speedy return. Yet as it concerns my dear Mary, I wish the captain to stay away for good. There is no doubt that she is far more at ease and far more herself when Quincey is not about.

It is their personalities. Like oil and water, they do not mix well. I hope that someday the two of them can see their way to an amiable truce, for it is my fervent wish that soon Mary will become a part of our family.

It seems that though I am not fit to return to the front, I can still be of use to the war effort, which pleases me greatly. Quincey returned to the hall this evening to inform me that my translation skills will be required at the Foreign Office over the next few days. He has even made arrangements for me to stay in town at his club, rather than tire myself by traveling back and forth.

My only disappointment in all of this is that I won't see my dear sweet girl, Mary, while I am away. I shall sorely miss her. Indeed, we have been so close these past days that I scarcely know how I will survive without her.

Quincey's return has cheered Lily as expected. However, I have instructed Antanasia to keep a watchful eye over the two lovebirds while I am gone.

She has always been so strict with us. I have no doubt that I leave Lily in good hands.

Letter from Miss Mary Seward to Lieutenant John Shaw

PURFLEET SANATORIUM

PURFLEET

1ST NOVEMBER 1916

Dearest John,

My plan is to slip this note into your bag, unnoticed. Are you surprised at seeing it? I hope that it will bring you comfort on your journey to London.

The days I face ahead without you will be long and dreary. But I will busy myself with my work at the hospital and look forward to the day when I can again behold your dear face and warm myself in the glow of your gentle love.

Though I have never confessed the depth of my feelings before, I want to tell them to you now, John. You must think me a coward, doing this in writing, but I did not want you to leave Purfleet without knowing the truth.

I love you, my darling.

It occurs to me that I may have loved you since our first meeting five years ago. Do you remember it? You were fourteen and a dashing boy. Your charm made quite an impression on me. So I think it must be Fate that brought us together again—that saw you through the battlefield and into my care.

I will think of you until we are together again.

Yours always,

Mary

Letter from Lieutenant John Shaw to Miss Mary Seward

THE ARMY AND NAVY CLUB

36–39 PALL MALL

LONDON

2ND NOVEMBER 1916

My darling Mary,

I am missing you more than I could ever have thought possible. You have become the safe haven my soul seeks and I cannot imagine life without you.

Darling Mary, I love you! And your letter tells me that you feel the same for me. I never wish to be without you again, and so I must do this now—even though I cannot kneel before you and ask you in person. I must do this while I have the courage and without delay.

I, too, feel that our lives are intertwined. We are meant to be together.

Mary, nothing would make me happier than if you would do me the great honor of becoming my wife. Please marry me and make me the luckiest man on earth.

There—now it is said. I count the hours until I have your response, and if I should see welcome in your eyes when I return, I will approach your good father for your hand in marriage.

My eternal love,

John

Journal of
Lieutenant John Shaw

5TH NOVEMBER 1916

My handwriting is not as steady as I would wish, for I am aboard the train back to Purfleet. How I am looking forward to seeing Mary again and receiving her answer.

My time with the gentlemen of the Foreign Office was puzzling. I wonder they asked me to come at all for there was hardly anything for me to do there. Perhaps Quincey will shed some light on this when I see him at the hall.

I have been counting the hours until I see Mary again. I can hardly wait.

Journal of
Mary Seward

John arrived back from London this evening. "Oh, my darling!" I exclaimed, embracing him, delighted he had come to me so soon. "The answer is yes! Yes! Come in," I entreated, pulling him over the threshold and into the hall. "Father is keen to meet you."

And then I saw his anxious expression, the bewilderment flickering in his eyes. My hand dropped away from his. "Have you not come here to ask Father for my hand?" I asked uncertainly.

"Oh, dear Mary . . . I wish that were my reason for being here . . ." John replied. "But something dreadful has happened."

As he spoke, I noticed how quickly he was breathing. "My love, what is it?" I asked, alarmed now. "Come into the parlor. Sit for a moment and regain your breath."

But he just stood there, shaking his head. "It's Lily . . ." he said at last. He held out a letter.

As I took it from him, a horrible coldness crept into my heart.

Letter from Miss Lily Shaw to Lieutenant John Shaw

CARFAX HALL

3RD NOVEMBER 1916

My dearest John,

I hope you will forgive me, but we could not wait for your return. Quincey received word today that he must travel to Romania immediately. He does not know when he will be free to return to England, and we cannot bear to be parted from each other. Dear brother, Quincey has asked for my hand in marriage!

For propriety's sake, Antanasia is with us, and we shall, with her blessing as my guardian, be wed in Transylvania, in the castle where Quincey grew up.

I must leave now. The carriage waits to take us to Whitby, whence, Quincey tells me, we shall sail to the Bulgarian port of Varna on the Black Sea and then travel overland to Transylvania.

I beg you, John—do not feel badly when you find this note. Instead, rejoice! I am to be united with the man I love! We shall all be together and happy again when this war is over. Your Lily has nothing to fear in Quincey's tender care.

With all my love,

Lily

Journal of
Mary Seward

5TH NOVEMBER (CONTINUED)

"Well, are you going to bring the young man in, Mary?"

The sound of Father's voice calling from the parlor flustered me. These were not the joyous circumstances I had envisioned for his first meeting with John.

I returned the note to my love, squeezing his hand as I did so. I could see the great effort it required for him to gather his stormy emotions as he stepped into the parlor to take my father's hand.

"Dr. Seward, do forgive me," he began. "I've had unpleasant news, and it distracts me. It will, I fear, spoil my hope of impressing you in our first meeting."

Father smiled kindly at John. "That Mary deems you worthy as a husband impresses me enough, sir. Let us not bother with formalities now; there is clearly something troubling the pair of you. I would like, if I may, to help."

"Thank you, sir," John replied. "I would value your advice."

Father gestured to the sofa. "Sit and tell me what causes two young people to look so worried."

As John and I seated ourselves, I looked at Father with some surprise. His voice was stronger than I had heard for a long while. Perhaps having his advice sought had restored some of his former vigor. I felt a prick of regret that I'd tried so hard to shelter him from the horrors I'd seen these last months.

John ran his fingers nervously through his hair, then addressed Father. "I have just arrived at my home—Carfax Hall—to find my sister, Lily, gone. It pains me to say it, but she has eloped with our houseguest, Captain Harker."

Father frowned deeply. "Why did she feel the need to elope rather than stay and marry in Purfleet?"

"That, sir, I do not know," John replied. He handed Father Lily's note.

I was surprised to see Father become rather shaken as he read it. He turned to John. "I did not realize that the Captain Harker Mary mentioned was a Captain *Quincey* Harker." He handed the note back to John and straightened in his chair. "Tell me, John. Do you know something of his origins?"

"A bit, sir," John informed him.

"Was he born in England, then taken to live in Romania?"

John nodded, wide-eyed. "How did you know, Dr. Seward?"

Father sighed. "It is as I feared. He and the Quincey Harker I once knew are one and the same." He turned to me. "As a small child Quincey Harker visited this very house with his parents, Jonathan and Mina. We were good friends then. But Jonathan died shortly after Quincey's first birthday. Soon afterward Mina took Quincey to live in Romania with Count Tepes, her future husband."

I blinked. "Why did I not know of this?" I asked, confused.

"It happened long before you were born, my dear," Father explained. "And when Mina left, your mother and I never heard from her again. We made our disapproval of her relationship with Tepes clear. We suspected something untoward going on between them while poor Jonathan was still alive."

Father turned back to John. "I'm sorry to hear that Quincey has inherited his mother's haste. My wife and I felt that she acted improperly, too—marrying Tepes so soon after poor Jonathan's death." He shook his head sorrowfully. "I understand that Quincey was your CO?"

"Yes," John confirmed. "When I arrived at the front, the men regarded him as something of a mysterious hero, known for his night raids. Unless he was leading into battle, he was hardly ever seen during the day."

Father stared at him. "Tell me about these . . . night raids. . . ."

John swallowed. "I still struggle to separate the true horrors I witnessed from the fevered imaginings that haunted me afterward, sir."

But Father would not take no for an answer. "This is vitally important!" he insisted, striking the arm of his chair with his fist. "You *must* describe them to me."

John slowly described the gore-filled nighttime atrocities I'd read of in his journal, and a chill seemed to enter the room. By the time he had heard all John had to say, Father had become quite gray.

"Father, we did not wish to trouble you so!" I cried, alarmed for him.

He shook his head. "Believe me, it is most important that you did, for I believe that I may be the only one left who can help you." He breathed a long rattling sigh. "My dear daughter, I fear an old enemy has returned. An enemy my friends and I had hoped our children would never know."

He turned to John. "My boy," he said, "I do not believe your testimony of Quincey Harker's demonic activities is that of a fevered mind. For I have encountered such behavior before. From what you have told me, I believe Quincey Harker must be descended from the same evil, parasitic presence I helped remove from the world thirty-five years ago. One Count Dracula . . ."

"Dracula . . . I have heard that name before," John whispered. "In the Romanian folklore of my childhood—but surely those monstrous tales cannot be true . . ."

Monstrous tales? A deep chill shook me. What could John mean? "Believe me, my boy, they are," Father assured him gravely. "And though Dracula himself was destroyed a full six years before Quincey was born, it is now clear that his evil bloodline continues—and it must be through *Tepes*." He spat out the word. "Poor Jonathan . . . none of us knew that the bouncing baby boy he adored was not truly his own— but the spawn of the devil himself."

John's eyes were filled with stark despair. "But sir, what does this mean for my sister?" My heart twisted as I saw the pain and worry in his face.

"It means that your sister's very soul is in danger. Quincey Harker is undoubtedly a bloodsucking demon. A vampire. And he has taken Lily to Castle Dracula to make her his own—as Tepes did with Mina. Lily's only hope is for you to follow—armed with the knowledge I can provide. I shall furnish you with essential reading for your journey. But you must go immediately—leave tonight. Or Lily may be lost forever."

CHAPTER 12

Journal of
Lily Shaw

4TH NOVEMBER 1916

Dear Mother and Father,

We arrived in Whitby in time for dinner at the Hope and Anchor—a quaint harborside inn where we are booked for the night. Quincey has chartered a vessel, and we are set to leave on the early morning tide, weather permitting.

A storm rages as I write here in the room I share with Antanasia. She dozes in her chair, but I can hear Quincey pacing restlessly next door. He hates to be ruled by the elements, I suspect!

I, too, am restless. My body trembles with a mixture of fear, excitement, and anticipation. We left Carfax Hall so quickly I did not even have time to rejoice with Quincey at the prospect of our future wedding. There has been scarcely a moment alone with him. How I long to feel his arms

153

around me—to tell him how I look forward to our union.

But I must leave him to tend to our affairs, for we pass through dangerous territory on our journey and we must arrive safely. I have no doubt that in Quincey's care, no harm shall come to us.

Your loving daughter,

Lily

LATER

What changes these last hours have brought to me. I am reeling from the memory of them, but I shall try to record them here.

It was around midnight. I thought Quincey had turned in for the evening. But then I heard his door open and close—and his footfalls passing our door. Heart beating fast, I rushed over and opened it. When I gazed down the hall, he was already halfway down the shadowy staircase.

"Quincey!" I whispered after him. "Where are you going?" But he did not hear me.

Confused, I turned back into my room to get my coat. Antanasia slept on peacefully. I threw my coat around my shoulders and headed after Quincey down the stairs.

Outside, the storm raged. Quincey leaned into the wind and made his way toward the harbor. I wondered, what could drive my love from his room in the middle of the night?

I had to know. I had to follow. I walked out into the darkness.

My heart hammered against my rib cage as I moved stealthily behind him. There was nary a soul on the cobbled streets of town—and no wonder. The rain drove hard, stinging me as it soaked through my hair, my coat, my nightgown.

Quincey paced the streets, then turned at the water's edge. He ascended a path to the windblown sea cliff that towered beside the harbor. I glanced up. It was a terrible height. Near the cliff's edge was a church surrounded by a large graveyard.

I feared the wildness of the wind at such an exposed height, but Quincey strode along, staring straight ahead.

His determination set a new fire within me. I had to discover what my beloved sought with such resolve.

Quincey was moving at such a pace that I was breathless by the time I reached the long flight of stairs to the cliff top. He began to climb, two steps at a time, unbowed by the lashing rain. My legs trembled as I stumbled behind him.

Halfway to the top, a strong gust swept the hem of my coat into a nearby bramble. Try as I might to free the fabric, it would not come loose! The thorns were like talons, holding me back.

Fearful that I might lose Quincey, I tore the coat from my frame and continued to climb.

As I reached the top of the stairs, I discovered him

striding the path to the churchyard. He swung open the gate and moved between the gravestones until he arrived at the cliff's very edge.

Clouds tussled on the dark horizon in front of him. The light of the moon brought shape to their swirling mass. The gusting wind made the grass around the graves seem to flow like water; I felt its chill pierce my thin gown and reach into my bones.

Quincey seemed elated by the tempest that whipped around him, sending his coattails flapping like a cloak behind him. I gazed with awed adoration at his powerful frame, the brightening moon illuminating his noble features. He seemed a creature equal to the storm. He stared out to the wild sea, challenging the turbulent sky. His eyes bored into the horizon, as if he were trying to see beyond it.

Clearly a troubled mind had brought him to this place. But what could disturb him so? Whatever it was, I wanted to console him.

"Quincey," I called. But he could not hear me over the howling wind. I stepped toward him, carefully making my way to the cliff's edge. "Quincey," I called again.

I was nearly at his side when I stumbled on a gnarled tree root. I lost my balance and, screaming, pitched toward the edge.

The world tilted and I beheld the rocky beach below. I began to tumble—

Then the strong arms of my beloved caught hold of my
waist. He leaned forward and scooped me up in his arms as
though I weighed no more than a child.

My body shivered. I clung to him as the wind tore at me,
fearing it might rip me from him. He laid me down on a
smooth stone slab—a grave, I realized. I breathed deeply,
struggling to slow my pounding heart.

Quincey paced before me, then knelt and took my face
roughly in his hands. "What are you doing here?" he
demanded, forcing me to look into his eyes.

"Please, do not be angry with me." I yelled to be heard
above the storm. "I only saw that you were troubled. I
wanted to comfort you."

"It is dangerous for you to be here," he growled, shaking
me violently. "You have no idea."

"I don't care," I argued, staring directly into his fiery
gaze. "You are the master of my heart. Quincey, I want you.
And I want to be with you—forever!"

His eyes softened. He seemed almost surprised by my
words.

Then, for the first time, he truly looked at me. His eyes
roamed over my body, now exposed by the thin wet fabric
of my gown. He lifted his hands and pushed the dripping
hair from my face. Then his hands wandered over me,
tracing the curves of my breast, my waist. He lingered over
me, savoring me.

I knew that I should be ashamed, but my body would not—could not—respond as if this was wrong. I leaned my head back, reveling in the feeling.

"You should not have come here," he said, kissing my ear, the line of my jaw.

"I am glad I did," I replied. And I spoke the truth—for there, safe in his arms and far from the quiet, calm world I have known, I felt truly alive. "Please. I am yours. Take me."

Quincey shuddered. He leaned forward and kissed my neck. I felt a delicious pain as his teeth pricked my skin. Waves of pleasure broke over me. The world swam before my eyes and in a moment, all faded away.

*Journal of
Mary Seward*

6TH NOVEMBER 1916

I write from the train. We are due to arrive in Whitby around six p.m. I must admit that I had trouble leaving Father in such a state. But ever selfless, he insisted that my place was with John.

"My time in this world is near its end," he said. "John

and Lily—they are your future. They need you now, more than I. . . ."

We stopped off in London so that John could draw money from his bank. He asked for it in gold, as that will be welcomed anywhere.

As the train pulled out of Kings Cross station, we opened the parcels that Father provided for us. We found a sheaf of papers and notebooks along with a leather bag. Beside the bag's catch was a name, clearly engraved: *Van Helsing.*

We opened the leather bag first. Its contents seem to shed little light on the matter.

Amongst the mundane but useful items—an oil lamp, candles, and various tools—we also found a bundle of wooden stakes, each about three feet long.

I drew one out and handed it to John. He ran his fingers along its length—felt its sharpened point. "What can it be for?" he wondered.

Deeper inside the bag, I discovered some dried blossoms so old they turned to dust at my touch. I lifted the powder to my nose and smelled the musty scent. "Garlic," I reported.

Reaching into the bag again, I drew out a small cotton bundle. I unfolded it and found it contained a silver crucifix and the crushed remains of a few wafer-like biscuits. "Holy wafers . . ." I guessed.

John shook his head. "This is ludicrous. There must be something in there that makes more sense." He reached inside the bag himself. "Ah. Now this I can understand," he declared, lifting out an old revolver.

I was shaken, having not yet dared to think of what we might need to do to recover Lily.

John, sensing my fear, laid a hand on mine. "Do not worry. The war has made me accustomed to killing," he said quietly. "And I swear I shall protect you from all harm. Let's start reading the notes now. Your father assured us they would explain all."

And so I write while John begins to leaf through the pile of papers Father gave us. I hold Van Helsing's crucifix in my other hand and take some strange comfort in its presence.

I only hope that we will not be too late to save Lily from this monster.

LATER

We arrived in Whitby to find the place in the thrall of a terrible storm. The wind and rain lashed the station and John struggled to open the door against the gale that howled along the platform. I am glad we brought so little luggage. John was able to carry both our bags while I hurried through the ticket office and secured a carriage to take us to the docks.

Our small coach rocked in the fierce wind as we clattered

over the rough road to the quayside. The driver stopped by the harbor wall and climbed down from his seat to help us from our carriage. "We've not seen squalls like the ones we've had these past days for many a year," he told us. "Fishermen who went out afore this one blew up dare not come back in, and those who stayed in dare not go out. There'll be a few empty tables in the town tonight, I reckon."

John grasped the driver's arm. "So no boats have left in recent days?" he asked, his voice raised over the wind. His face was taut with renewed hope.

My heart leapt too—I hardly dared hope that Quincey and Lily had not yet been able to set sail.

"A ship went out in the lull during yesterday's early morning tide," the driver responded. "It was such fleeting calm, she was lucky to catch it. Slipped out of the harbor while she could, like a cat through a closing door." He grinned.

"Where was the ship bound?" John asked urgently.

The driver shook his head. "I couldn't tell you that. But old Jacob, the harbormaster, is sure to know." He gave a throaty chuckle. "You'll more than likely find him in the Hope and Anchor." He pointed toward a harborside inn.

Jacob told us that the ship had been bound for Varna. Our flicker of found hope was snuffed out.

I found us rooms here at the inn while John has gone in search of a vessel that he might charter to follow Harker and Lily.

John has struck a deal with a Dutch captain and we board the *Katwyk* tomorrow at dawn to catch the early tide—so long as the storm has eased. The wind outside is beginning to weaken, and I pray that it means God is with us.

We sit before the fire in my room, still warmed by our supper. I suppose we are lucky to have found accommodations so comfortable, but we have little thought for our surroundings. Instead we pore over the notes and journals in Father's collection.

Included amongst Father's reading matter are pages from his own diary, in which he made notes on one of his asylum patients, one R. M. Renfield. It was Renfield's cell in which poor John was confined! The coincidence chills me to the bone. I dare not mention the connection to John; he does not know whose cell he occupied. But the more I read of my father's notes, the more unnerved I become.

Referring to Renfield's predilection for eating bugs, spiders, and the very lowest of creatures, he wrote:

I shall have to invent a new classification for him and call him a zoophagous (life-eating) maniac.

As I read this, I remembered John wanting to kill and eat the rat he caught. I wondered if Renfield's haunting presence might have affected him in some supernatural way. . . .

Just a week ago, I would have considered such a possibility ridiculous. Now I know that there truly are monsters in the world. Any of the horrors that haunt us as children may resurrect themselves to threaten us now.

"Look at this," John said, handing me a book from the pile. "Professor Van Helsing was an old mentor of your father's—a philosopher and a metaphysician—and an expert in obscure diseases. His help was sought when Dracula preyed upon one Lucy Westenra. Dracula desired Lucy. He came to her repeatedly and slowly drained her blood. . . ."

I read the pages that John had given me.

She was ghastly, chalky pale. The red seemed to have gone even from her lips and gums, and the bones of her face stood out prominently. . . . Van Helsing's face grew set as marble, and his eyebrows converged till they almost touched over his nose. Lucy lay motionless and did not seem to have strength to speak. Van Helsing beckoned to me, and we went gently out of the room. . . . "My God!" he said. "This is dreadful. There is not time to be lost. She will die for sheer want of blood. . . ."

I took hold of John's hand.

"The notes say your father and Van Helsing found Lucy like

that time after time," he continued quietly. "Do you think he has done this to Lily? Do you think he has drawn her blood?" His voice was calm, but his eyes betrayed the depth of his fear.

I embraced him, my heart bursting with pity. As I clung to him, hopelessness threatened to overtake me. Then I realized— we had to remain calm. We had to apply our minds to the facts at hand.

Though I wanted nothing more than to forget these horrible documents, to distance myself from them forever, I could not. I read on.

After digesting the tragic tale of Lucy Westenra, I turned to John. "Dracula drained Lucy's blood over many nights," I observed. "And after each bite, Lucy grew weaker and weaker. But Lily has *never* shown this weakness. And we have not seen the telltale marks on her neck. Harker must not have bitten her while he stayed at the hall."

Then the image of Dora Hughes flickered through my mind.

"While you were ill, Lily told me of a maid she had hired who fainted dead away. The longer she worked at Carfax Hall, the paler and paler she grew." My stomach tightened as I deduced the truth of the situation. "Harker must have been feeding from her instead of Lily."

"So she *was* safe. But what about *now?*" John asked. "Is Harker draining Lily's blood right now?"

I considered the possibility, then shook my head. "I do not think Quincey would touch her while they travel. The resulting lethargy would make her a burdensome traveling companion."

"Yes." John sighed with relief. "Of course, you're right." He rubbed his tired eyes, worsening the dark circles around them. He hung his head in his hands.

"Perhaps you should rest, my love," I suggested. "We will need our strength for the voyage . . . and whatever lies ahead."

"You are right again," he said, standing up slowly. He took my hand and pressed it to his lips. "You must retire too, darling. I shall need you to give me courage for the long road before us."

I nodded my agreement. John took his leave and went to his room across the hall.

LATER

I undressed and tried to sleep, but I could not find slumber. Father's papers called out to me. I needed to learn all I could.

I returned to the chair by the fire and continued reading the notes on Lucy Westenra. I was shocked to learn that they did not end with her death. Through Dracula's repeated draining of her blood, Lucy became a demon just like Dracula himself.

Despite Father's belief that Lucy was gone and buried, Lucy roamed the night in her white gown. She called to children in her sweet voice and when they left the safety of their bedrooms and came to her, she drank of their blood.

I felt utterly repulsed. How a good and pure woman had transformed into such an evil creature was beyond my imagination. I would not allow Lily to meet such a fate.

Then another image came to me. Lily sleepwalking, trancelike, her white nightgown flowing, the very evening before Harker made his presence known in Purfleet.

Harker could not have intended to harm Lily then; he'd had endless other opportunities in the weeks that followed. I decided he must have lured Lily from her bed that night simply to get a look at his prey, toying with his powers as a cat does with a mouse.

Why would Harker restrain himself? Is he preserving Lily for some darker purpose . . . something we all have yet to imagine?

*Journal of
Lily Shaw*

6TH NOVEMBER 1916

We are aboard the *Alexandru*. The cabin I share with Antanasia is painted gray, lined with rivets and stained with the grime of a hundred sea voyages. It is most gloomy, but I care not a jot. I feel like a princess traveling on a liner— because my darling Quincey is with me. He is truly a fine and honorable man, and I am privileged to be his betrothed.

The day after our encounter in the storm, Quincey came
to me. I felt quite tired and drained after such a wild night
and so relaxed in my bed. Antanasia was in the sitting room,
packing for our voyage, when Quincy entered.

He regarded me silently.

In that moment, I worried. With the perspective of a new
day, what he would think of me? Would he think me cheap
for giving in to my desire?

He walked to my bed and stood formally beside me.
"Lily," he began. "I come to see how you fare."

I reached for his hand and he moved a pace away, ensuring
that I could not get hold of him. I felt tears pricking the corners of my eyes. After a night of passion, was my lover now
shunning me? "Quincey." I gulped out the words. "I am so
sorry. In my mind, I am already your bride and yours forever."

He knelt beside me then. "Poor, sweet child. You are still so
innocent." He gently smoothed back my hair with his strong
hand. "It is true, we are bound to each other, but you are not
yet my bride. I promise you now I will do my best to respect
your honor until we are truly married—at my father's house—
for all eternity."

He left me then and all my fears were dispelled.

Since that time he has been most tender and caring to me.
Proof that his heart is true. When I long for Quincey's touch,
I will remember our night of passion by touching the
memento of it that I hide from Antanasia.

It is a small love bite—no bigger than two pinpricks on my neck.

We set sail not long after, and I shall count the seconds until I am Quincey Harker's bride!

LATER

Antanasia has pinned up her embroidered shawl to cover the dull wall beside my bunk. "That should feel more homely." She smiled.

For a moment, I wondered at how permissive she has been—and how easily she had accepted my decision to elope with Quincey. When we were children, she was always so stern.

Perhaps she has a soul sensitive enough to appreciate the love Quincey and I hold for each other. As someone who cares for me, she must value it as I do—as a precious gift it would be foolish to throw away.

There was a tap on the cabin door. "Come in," I called.

My heart soared as Quincey entered. I was as excited as if we had not seen each other in days, though it had only been an hour since we'd dined with the captain.

I had understood precious little of the captain's conversation over dinner. He and Quincey had spoken entirely in Romanian, and I had not held a conversation in the language since I was a small child. However, I'd sensed a tension in the old sailor. And now it would appear that it was because of Antanasia and me!

"I am sorry, ladies, but you must keep to your cabin," Quincey informed us.

"Really?" I asked Quincey, surprised. "Why? Have we offended the captain in some way?"

Quincey shook his head. "No, Lily," he said. "It is nothing that you have done. But you see, sailors believe it is bad luck to have women on board."

"Bad luck?" I echoed, mystified.

"It is an old-fashioned superstition, but one they seem attached to," Quincey explained. "The captain says that seeing you has unnerved his crew, so you must stay out of sight from now on." He glanced around the room. "I shall go and see what I can find to make the cabin more comfortable for you. Do not trouble yourself with anything on deck. I will deal with the crew."

Captain's Log
The Alexandru

9TH NOVEMBER 1916

We are only a few days at sea, yet two of my men have fallen ill. They are pale and move about the decks as if there is no life in them. I have ordered them to forgo their measures of rum until they recover.

Damn! This is nothing but bad luck, brought upon us by these women in our ship. At least the Englishman has paid a hefty fee for their passage. I only hope our passage will be a swift one. I am anxious to be rid of these passengers once and for all.

CHAPTER 13

Journal of Mary Seward

7th November 1916

The *Katwyk* carries us away from England's familiar shores. Our cabins are basic, but dry and warm enough. The sailors look at me warily. Women on board are supposed to be unlucky, but Captain Volkersen told me he will not pander to such superstitious nonsense, so I ignore their hostile glances.

Captain Volkersen has invited us to sup at his table. He is a friendly man, but we dare not share with him the truth of our mission. We shall save such talk for when we are alone and sit together reading Father's notes.

Later

The cheerful talk at the supper table with Captain Volkersen eased my heart—perhaps too much, for when John and I returned to our cabin to read more of Jonathan Harker's journal, we were not prepared for the horrors we were to read of Count Dracula. . . .

> The bag which the count had thrown upon the floor moved as though there were some living thing within it. He nodded. One of the women jumped forward and opened it. . . . There was a gasp and a low wail, as of a half-smothered child. The women closed round, whilst I was aghast with horror. But as I looked, they disappeared, and with them the dreadful bag. . . .

These horrible creatures preyed upon infants! They would care not a bit about Lily's gentle nature—her innocence.

How could Father have lived with these horrors etched in his heart and never betrayed it? If he helped vanquish such evils as this, then I love and admire him more than ever.

I passed the page to John, and as he read it, I saw him pale. "I thought I had witnessed every cruelty imaginable when I fought in the trenches," he whispered, "but to think there are even worse deeds in the world chills my very soul."

He must have been thinking of his dear Lily, though we dare not speak her name for fear of awakening imaginings too horrible to bear. The poor girl surely has no idea of the haven to depravity she travels toward.

I know I shall not sleep tonight.

Journal of
Lily Shaw

9TH NOVEMBER 1916

I write now at a little table Quincey has managed to procure for me. I have no idea how he has found such things, but my cabin has been transformed into a cozy hideaway, draped with rich cloth and with rugs upon the floor and lanterns hanging at every side. To me, it is like the bedchamber of a queen and all the dreary dampness has been banished. Even the porthole is covered so that I would not know I am on board a ship if it were not for the steady rocking of the floor beneath my chair.

My only small disappointment is that I cannot find the hand mirror that I packed. I have not seen my reflection in days. I fear I look a fright! But the mirror seems to have disappeared—and neither Antanasia nor Quincey has one either. I asked Quincey if we might borrow one. But he told me there are none to be found on board.

"Sailors rarely worry about their appearance," he joked.

In these past days we have slipped into a habit of sleeping by day and wakening at night, the three of us cocooned in this strange all-at-sea world, so far from the cares of the real world. Quincey and I talk, while Antanasia sits quietly sewing in the corner.

It is as if Quincey has replaced the sun in my universe and it is around him that I spin and from him that I take my warmth.

My one link with the outside world is a smallish grate above the door, through which I can hear the creaking and groaning of the ship's deck, the crash of the waves, and sailors' voices. They sound like a rough lot, and I am glad not to have to bother myself with them.

Captain's Log
The Alexandru

11TH NOVEMBER 1916

My two ill sailors have perished and now two more appear wan and lifeless. I am beginning to fear there is something unwholesome about our passengers.

I shall instruct the crew to be wary, to hang garlic, and to protect themselves in whatever ways necessary. We must pray the tides are with us. For the faster we make port, the sooner we are all out of danger.

Journal of
Lily Shaw

It was stupid of me to go up on deck after Quincey's warning, but I could not sleep and longed for some fresh, cool air. Antanasia was still slumbering.

I supposed it must be nearing dusk. Even if I was too late to catch the sun, I might see the stars. I would not invite trouble by venturing far.

I climbed the iron steps to the empty deck and emerged into the half-light. At the rail I leaned forward and stared out at the horizon, watching the stars beginning to appear in the vast dark sky above the sea's inky surface.

I thought the footsteps behind me must be Quincey's and prepared to beg his forgiveness with a kiss, smiling to myself as I anticipated the feel of his strong warm arms around me.

But then I caught the acrid tang of garlic—something I'd never smelled on Quincey.

I turned quickly and came face-to-face with one of the crew. His lined face was reddened with weather and rum, and his lustful expression made me stiffen in fear. I gripped the rail, feeling it smooth against my back, and started to slide away from him.

But the sailor followed, pushing against me until I was hard against the rail, leaning out over the ocean. I could sense the waves below me, speeding beside the hull. I longed to scream, but he lifted a rough finger to my lips.

"Hush, pretty one . . ." His thickened voice breathed in my ear. My rusty Romanian was no match for the rest of his words, but the menace in his tone terrified me. I wondered the hammering of my heart did not awaken the whole boat.

He let his finger move from my lips and reach for the edge of my bodice. I gasped, feeling the jagged coarseness of his nail against my flesh, and saw the sailor smile as my breast heaved beneath his hand.

I closed my eyes in terror and heard my gown rip as he roughly tore the bodice apart. The world seemed to swim inside my head and my knees began to buckle beneath me.

Then a wild shriek sounded out. The shock of it startled me into wakefulness and I opened my eyes to see Antanasia throw herself at the sailor, hitting and spitting like a wildcat, her face creased with fury.

The sailor cursed and staggered backward. Antanasia rushed at him again, hate blazing in her eyes. She hit him over and over with the vigor of one possessed! The sailor dropped to his knees, covering his head and still cursing her.

And then I heard more footsteps. I felt strong arms around my waist, sweeping me up with a gentleness I recognized at once. Quincey's sweet voice sounded in my ear. "Lily, Lily! Are you all right?"

I clung to him, cold with shock, trembling in terror as he carried me back to the safety of my cabin.

The next thing I knew, I was back on my bed, Quincey sitting at my side, feeding me Antanasia's reviving sweet tea. He stared at me so intensely I feared he was angry I had disobeyed him. I looked at him from beneath my lashes, humble and penitent. "I'm sorry," I breathed. "I only wanted the air."

But there was no reproach in his eyes, only concern. He put down the tea and leaned close to me and softly kissed my hair. "There is no need for an innocent like you ever to be sorry," he murmured.

*Journal of
Mary Seward*

9TH NOVEMBER 1916

I made more chilling discoveries today as I progressed with Father's diary. John and I sat reading by the light of a lamp swaying from the cabin ceiling, its yellow glow illuminating the pages.

"Look at this, my love," John said. He gave me the page he had been reading. "It records how they destroyed Lucy Westenra after she had become vampire. . . ."

I braced myself for new horrors and then began to scan the words. They were Father's:

> She seemed like a nightmare of Lucy as she lay there, the pointed teeth, the bloodstained, voluptuous mouth, which made one shudder to see . . . seeming like a devilish mockery of Lucy's sweet purity. Van Helsing, with his usual methodicalness, began taking the various contents from his bag and placing them ready for use. "Take this stake in your left hand, ready to place the point over the heart, and the hammer in your right. . . . Strike in God's name, so that all may be well with the dead that we love and that the undead pass away." Then he struck with all his might. The thing in the coffin writhed, and a hideous, bloodcurdling screech came from the opened red lips. The body shook and quivered and twisted in wild contortions. The sharp white teeth champed together till the lips were cut, and the mouth was smeared with a crimson foam . . . whilst the blood from the pierced

heart welled and spurted up around it. . . . Finally it lay still. The terrible task was over.

I threw the paper onto the bunk, aghast at what lay ahead of us. So that was what the wooden stakes in Van Helsing's bag were for.

With trembling hands I opened the bag and drew out one of the stakes. I ran my fingers, damp with fear, along its smooth shaft to the sharpened tip. With this cruel weapon we must destroy Harker.

Journal of
Jily Shaw

12TH NOVEMBER 1916

Both Antanasia and I drifted to sleep but were awoken before dawn by raised voices up on deck, filtering down to us through the grate in our door.

I heard feet running on the deck and more shouting but could make no sense of it. I pulled the bedding up around me and sat huddled, fearful of what further aggression might be occurring.

"What do you think is going on?" I asked Antanasia, who

had decided to brew tea on the stove in the corner of our cabin.

She shrugged. "Who knows what trouble those sailors have got themselves into?" she said disdainfully.

The door opened just then, and Quincey stepped into the room. "How are you, my love?" he asked, coming at once to my side and taking my hand.

I kissed him on the cheek. "Much better, thank you." I smiled to reassure him he had no reason to worry. The nightmare of a few hours ago was beginning to fade, and remembering Quincey's strong arms carrying me away from it only strengthened my feeling of safety in his care. "But what of the commotion up on deck?" I asked him.

"One of the sailors drank too much and had an accident," Quincey explained gravely.

"What happened?" I asked.

Quincey shook his head. "He must have taken a fall on deck. When they discovered him, it was determined that he had snapped his neck."

"Oh, the poor soul!" I gasped.

"Poor fool, more like, for wandering around a ship too drunk to walk straight," Antanasia put in. "Captains are always too liberal with the rum ration."

But my heart tightened with grief for the dead man. I felt my eyes fill with tears.

Quincey took a handkerchief from his pocket and

dabbed my cheeks. "Do not waste your pity on him, Lily," he said quietly. "It was the brute who attempted to molest you."

His words afflicted my heart even further. For I found that a part of me was glad! I took Quincey's handkerchief and began to sob.

"There, there . . ." he said, stroking my tearstained cheek. "What a time you've had. We reach Varna in just days. Do not worry, poor sweet creature. Your ordeal will be over soon."

*Journal of
Mary Seward*

13TH NOVEMBER 1916

I could only pace my cabin this morning, unable to read anymore, anxious to be away from this ship and on our way, frustrated by the slow pace of the voyage. John read on, however, his concentration not wavering as he neared the end of the documents.

"Look," he said. "The final page." He held it up for me to see. The paper, though still yellowed, did not seem quite so old and worn as the others. "Jonathan Harker added this note seven years after Dracula was destroyed."

Seven years ago we all went through the flames. And the happiness of some of us since then is, we think, well worth the pain we endured. . . . Our boy's birthday is the same day as that on which Quincey Morris died. . . . His mother holds, I know, the secret belief that some of our brave friend's spirit has passed into him. . . . We call him Quincey. . . .

I looked at John. We'd read of the brave American, Quincey P. Morris of Texas, who'd died heroically in the defeat of Dracula. But it wasn't Quincey Morris's spirit that had passed to the child. . . . I shuddered and read on.

In the summer of this year we made a journey to Transylvania and went over the old ground, which was, and is, to us so full of vivid and terrible memories. It was almost impossible to believe that the things that we had seen with our own eyes and heard with our own ears were living truths. Every trace of all that had been was blotted out. The castle stood as before, reared high above a waste of desolation. . . .

"Poor Jonathan." I sighed. "Tepes might well have been in residence then. But why would they return to a place of such dreadful memories?"

"Because Tepes *was* there," John said slowly. "He already held sway over Mina Harker. Perhaps he wanted to see his son."

I lowered my eyes to read the rest of the note. Its ending was chilling:

> Van Helsing summed it all up as he said, with our boy on his knee, "This boy will someday know what a brave and gallant woman his mother is. Already he knows her sweetness and loving care. Later on he will understand how some men so loved her that they did dare much for her sake."

I thought sadly of how mistaken they were about Mina. She had already been lost to them—like the boy Quincey.

I pray Lily will not follow in Mina's footsteps.

Now that we have finished reading all of Father's notes, we understand the articles contained in Van Helsing's bag. We must find replacements for the perished garlic—though from where, at this time of year, I do not know. Holy wafers should be easier to procure. We can only hope that together, all these will provide protection enough to save us from the horrors that await us.

Captain's Log
The Alexandru

14TH NOVEMBER

We have passed into the Black Sea and shall make Varna tomorrow. I am thankful the weather has been with us all the way for I long to be rid of my cursed cargo.

Journal of
Mary Seward

17TH NOVEMBER 1916

After a long and arduous voyage, Captain Volkersen has stayed true to his word and has delivered us in Varna. Lord knows how we shall ever return home, but there is not time to worry on such things as that now.

We stood at the top of the gangplank, which clattered with the sound of the crew passing up and down it.

"I have been ashore already and asked about *The Alexandru*," Captain Volkersen told us. "It docked two days ago and brought with it no cargo, only passengers. It seems your sister's crossing was not an uneventful one," he added darkly. "The captain of *The Alexandru* has been cursing the voyage since he docked."

"What do you mean?" John asked urgently.

"Three sailors were lost," Captain Volkersen explained. "You are a brave pair to travel in these dangerous times and deserve the blessing of heaven."

John and I thanked him and made our way down the gangplank onto the busy quayside.

A chill wind was blowing and oily puddles lay on the dock from the recent rain. Bulgarian soldiers milled among the crowd and I felt exposed, keen to find shelter in the city. We walked as calmly as we could, weighed down by our bags, toward the buildings that lined the water's edge.

Varna is old, its buildings ornate and brightly painted, its streets narrow and busy—which is a blessing, for it is easy to travel through them unnoticed.

We stopped to buy a crucifix for Lily from a small shop filled with religious paraphernalia. I had my own—Father had always been strangely insistent that I wear one, and now I knew why. John would carry the silver cross we had found in Van Helsing's bag.

It was too late in the day to find a means of traveling to the Danube, where we would cross into Romania, so we found an inn to stay for the night.

The innkeeper was a tall man, gaunt and stooped; he

eyed us suspiciously as John tried first in German, and then in Romanian, to request rooms.

The man stared at us blankly. So John unfastened his purse and took out a gold coin. Suddenly, the man seemed to understand our request. He picked up our luggage and led us up a creaky staircase.

As he handed over the keys, a woman bundled in thick skirts and a grubby apron shuffled past. The innkeeper muttered something to her.

I recognized German as she began to address John. I waited, my palms prickling with anxious curiosity, as the two conversed. I saw the woman glance repeatedly at John's purse until finally he opened it and took out two more gold coins.

"What were you talking about?" I asked after the woman had left.

"Mrs. Cinzov has agreed to arrange a way out of Varna for us," he told me.

"Already!" I gasped.

"Gold is a great incentive." John smiled wearily. "Especially in wartime. The sight of it encouraged our hosts to place every assistance at the disposal of a German-speaking visitor to their town. I told Mrs. Cinzov the story just as we planned, that you were my sister and we had to get you out of Bulgaria before my leave was over."

"And she believed you!"

"I don't think she cared about anything more than my money," John answered. "But no matter. She told me that her husband has a brother who will be traveling to the river Danube tomorrow, where we can cross into Romania. He's a tanner, with a cartload of hides to deliver. We may travel with him for a price. I have paid half now and will give the rest to the brother when we arrive safely at the Danube."

"Can we trust them?" I asked worriedly.

"I doubt it, but what other choice do we have?"

"But what if they try to rob us or worse?"

"I have Van Helsing's revolver in my coat. I will use it if necessary," John told me resolutely.

He is right—what choice do we have?

Journal of
Lily Shaw

18TH NOVEMBER 1916

I have not written these past few days since we left the ship, for the journey across Bulgaria has been tiring. We have hurried from train to coach then train again.

"Where are we headed for now?" I asked Quincey as we

settled into our private train compartment. The blinds had been pulled down against the sunshine outside, for which I was grateful. I had grown unused to its bright light during our voyage, becoming quite the nocturnal creature since our ship's passage.

"We are going to the river Danube," he told me with a smile, "where we shall cross into Romania."

I tensed as I saw gray-uniformed soldiers stamping along the corridor outside our compartment. Their hats were topped with spikes. I recognized them from posters back in England, warning against the wicked Hun.

"Are they not German soldiers?" I asked, pointing through the compartment's smoky window.

Quincey nodded. "They will give us no trouble," he said calmly. "If we are questioned, I have documents to convince them to send us on our way."

I must have dozed for a while after that, resting my head on Quincey's shoulder, for the next thing I knew, Quincey's gentle hand was touching my cheek. I blinked into wakefulness. Lights burned inside the compartment and the sky beyond the window had blackened into night.

"Lily," he said, "we are nearing the station and must alight. A carriage will be waiting for us there."

I yawned and stretched as Antanasia got down our bags and gathered the luggage tickets. Quincey leaned out into the corridor and called, in German, for assistance.

The carriage took us to a ferry on the banks of the Danube. I stood at the stern, wondering at the great width of the river and how silently it flowed, disappearing into the velvet darkness of the night.

We are in Romania now, comfortable in a carriage Quincey says will carry us all the way to his home. The journey will take a few more days, but he promises it will pass quickly and that the inns along the way will give us comfort and warmth at night.

It feels so strange—and yet familiar, being back in the country where I was born. I had learned to accept the sights and sounds of England as the only ones possible and had forgotten that houses or people, landscape and animal could be any other way than the way I'd become used to at Carfax Hall. But now I remember how the strangeness of England disturbed me when first I moved there as a child of seven.

A myriad of memories are being awoken by all I hear and smell here in Romania—the Slavic accents and ancient buildings, the rough countryside and strong odors of food and animals, these are of the world I shared with Mother and Father. How I wish they were here to share it again. But I know that cannot be and so am doubly thankful for darling Quincey.

Journal of
Mary Seward

20TH NOVEMBER 1916

We have crossed the Danube. The tanner introduced us to a fisherman with a boat who agreed to ferry us across to Romania once night had fallen.

"What luck!" John whispered as we settled ourselves into the rough fishing smack.

"It is not luck but kindness that has brought us this far," I answered. "Be grateful. We have found humanity in a strange land."

"It is greed that drives these people. They help us only for the gold."

The disillusionment in John's voice surprised me. "They risk their lives," I pointed out. "Would they do that simply for money?"

John did not reply, only stared at the waves that stretched ahead of us. I felt his despair.

"My dearest, you have been through so many horrors," I murmured gently. I took his cold hand and kissed his fingers. "It has shaken your faith, but in time, you will forget."

He looked at me hopefully and pulled me close to him. "Do you think it is possible?"

"Of course, my darling."

"And what of the horrors we still have to face?"

"We will conquer them together." I looked at him intently, imploring him to accept my words.

"Yes," he said, stroking my cheek, "we will do it together. And when this is darkness is over, I shall return you to England, where we will be married in the sunshine."

He gazed down and in that moment I knew he was going to kiss me. I tilted my head back as he pressed his soft lips to mine. The sweetness of our embrace made me ache for home and everything I knew.

Yes, to stave off these nightmares, I would have to believe that soon John and I would have in our day in the sunshine.

Chapter 14

Journal of
Lily Shaw

21ST NOVEMBER 1916

Quincey tells me we are now only a day's journey away from his home. We have stopped at an inn for the night at the foot of the mountain where the castle is situated. He has gone downstairs to collect a letter that was waiting here for him.

"Who could have sent it?" I asked Antanasia.

She looked up from unpacking our bags and was about to say something when Quincey returned, the letter in his hand.

I stared at it inquisitively.

He smiled and silenced me with a kiss. "It is from the castle. But no questions, eh? You will know all once we arrive."

His words filled me with excitement. But though I am now quite unused to resting at night, Quincey says I must, so that I will remain fresh for our arrival at the castle tomorrow evening.

Shortly after midnight I awoke suddenly, unnerved by the sound of screaming. I sat up in bed—and found no noise disturbed the room except the peaceful ticking of the clock.

I looked at Antanasia. She snored on. I wondered if the screaming had been a dream.

Reluctant to disturb her, I decided to seek comfort from Quincey. I pulled on my dressing gown to go next door. I knocked lightly. When I received no answer, I turned the handle and let myself in.

The room was empty. Though disappointed, I did not think too much of it, knowing Quincey rarely slept during the hours of darkness.

My eye was drawn to the letter on the mantel. I longed to know its contents—knowing it would likely provide a clue as to what might await me at the castle.

And though my conscience told me not to, a wilful curiosity impelled me to lift the creamy envelope and take out the letter.

Letter from Mina,
Countess Tepes

CASTLE DRACULA
20TH NOVEMBER 1916

Dearest Quincey,

It is so long since you left us, my son. But soon you will back where you belong, at the heart of your family—and with you, such a prize! I need not tell you how eagerly we await your arrival. . . . At last, your bride is ripe for the union we have planned these long years.

The preparations for your wedding are all in hand. What a glorious St. Andrew's Eve it shall be! And not a moment too soon—for we sorely need your strength to carry us through this time of darkness to a new age where once more the House of Dracul shall be triumphant.

Your loyal mother,
Mina, Countess Tepes

22ND NOVEMBER (CONTINUED)

St. Andrew's Eve? But that was just days away, on the 29th of November! Pleasure and confusion seemed to war in my breast. My wedding to Quincey was close at hand. Soon we would be united for all eternity! Yet I wondered, why did my love not tell me of his intent to marry on this day?

There was more that perplexed me about the letter. Quincey's mother spoke eagerly of my arrival—her tone showed the very same warmth and affection I love so much in her wonderful son. But what did she mean by "the union we have planned these long years"? Who were the others "who eagerly await" our arrival? What was the House of Dracul? And what kind of triumph was the countess talking about?

Sighing with frustration, I wished that Quincey were less reluctant to talk of his family. I refolded the letter and put it into its place back on the mantel.

LATER

It is almost time to embark on the very last leg of our journey. Quincey wants us to be on our way before dawn.

Antanasia has gone to buy provisions from the inn's cook.

I have written to John to tell him that the wedding will take place on the 29th of November and that I am safe and well and very happy. I have no idea when the next mail coach will pass through this remote village to collect the letter. But even though John will not receive my reassuring words for some time, it was a comfort nonetheless to imagine his face as he reads them.

*Journal of
Mary Seward*

22ND NOVEMBER 1916

We race across Romania toward the castle, taking whatever transport we can find. I cling ever more tightly to Van Helsing's bag as we near our goal, but it is gold that is our most important tool in this foreign land. It buys us passage and eases our way through nations disjointed by war.

We traveled last night huddled on the flat back of a wagon, open to the lashing rain.

This morning, as our "carriage" rumbled over the rutted roads, I looked out at the passing countryside. Out in the fields women, the elderly, and children worked the land. I

supposed it must be the same here as it is back in England—
the war drew all the young strong men away to fight.

The landscape is imposing, its wildness crowding the villages and roads. As we travel farther into Romania's heart, it grows ever more rugged and mountainous.

LATER

We found shelter at an inn tonight. Though the food was poor, it warmed us and we have dry beds for the night. But the knowledge that we come ever nearer to Castle Dracula fills me with trepidation. I am only thankful I have my dear John and that we face the hellish peril side by side.

*Journal of
Lily Shaw*

22ND NOVEMBER (CONTINUED)

It is difficult to write as we travel in the coach along rough dirt tracks. We are in a splendid black caleche, which I believe has been sent from the castle. Antanasia is dozing in the corner and Quincey seems lost in thought.

I left my letter for John with the innkeeper. Even though

the hour was ungodly early—not yet dawn—I was touched that the innkeeper had roused himself to see us away.

I know that my adored Quincey cuts an impressive figure, but I have noticed that the locals all regard him with an awe and reverence that surprises even me. I am beginning to wonder at his family. They must be even grander than I'd guessed. I must admit, the possibility makes me even more nervous.

As we began to take our leave, a fearful shriek sounded outside and a man burst through the doorway, shouting to the innkeeper. I struggled to grasp what he was saying, but he was quite incoherent.

He had clearly not seen our party waiting in the shadow of the doorway, for when Quincey stepped forward—I assume to ask the poor fellow what was the matter—he jumped in surprise and backed away. His jabbering mouth fell silent, hanging slackly as he stared up into Quincey's face. He crossed his chest with a trembling hand and slunk out of the door, running down the muddy street. My initial alarm dissolved into pity, for it seemed that he must not be of sound mind.

"Did you catch what was troubling that poor strange fellow?" I asked Quincey.

Quincey shook his head. "Probably drunk," he muttered. He lifted his hand, and his black cloak enveloped me as he placed his arm around my shoulders. "Come, Lily," he said gently. "Let's not keep the driver waiting any longer."

We went out to the carriage. The black velvet sky was

beginning to warm with the onset of dawn. I heard the door of the inn being closed firmly behind us and its bolts being fastened.

Quincey helped Antanasia and I into the vehicle, then climbed in himself and secured the door. He pulled down the shades and signaled to the driver to set off.

Though the blinds are down for Quincey's comfort, I can, by leaning my head close to the window frame, see a sliver of scenery through the gap between the blind and the glass. As we progress up the winding mountain road, the shadows cast by the thick forest surrounding us never seem to disappear, no matter where the sun appears in the sky. Large black birds circle and swoop, high above the treetops.

The carriage sways along and makes me drowsy. Though I had hoped to enjoy the countryside in the light of day, I think I shall stop now and sleep.

23RD NOVEMBER 1916

I am now at Quincey's home—the castle. Though midnight has passed, I cannot find peace in sleep—so I shall write, by lamplight, of the horrible events that befell us as the carriage made its approach to this place.

As the sun began to sink behind the treetops, the road grew steeper. Quincey pulled up the blinds, and for the first time, I was exposed to the full force of our fiercely majestic surroundings. Transylvania was truly beautiful.

As I watched the scenery go by, a chill penetrated my shawl. I began to experience the strangest sensation that we were being watched.

I caught glimpses of movement through the trees—a sleek pelt moving here, another there. Suddenly, an unearthly howl rang out.

Alarmed, I looked to Quincey.

"We are perfectly safe," he assured me. "The wolves have been protectors of this place—and my family—for many centuries. They are to be welcomed rather than feared."

I nodded and despite my trepidation gave him a smile. I was determined to meet my future with a boldness that he could be proud of.

A strange creaking noise began to sound from beneath us.

"What is that?" Antanasia asked curiously.

"These old roads are hard on the carriage," Quincey replied calmly. "Nothing to fear." He pointed out of the window. "Look, Lily . . ."

I glanced out the window to the top of the peak we were climbing. Perched on the corner of a vast rock far above us was the castle—three towers blackly outlined against the bloodred sunset.

The fourth tower appeared to have collapsed some time

ago. It tumbled down the almost sheer drop that surrounded the structure on most of its sides.

"How old is the castle?" I asked.

"At least five hundred years," Quincey replied. "The Tepes family have occupied Castle Dracula for many generations."

The creaking of the carriage became louder as the incline grew steeper and stonier. All at once I heard a crack like a tree snapping in a gale. A second later, it was as if the world tumbled over! The carriage spilled and crashed onto the ground with a sound of splitting wood. Outside, the horses whinnied in protest.

"Lily, are you all right?" Quincey grasped me, pulling me up from where I had fallen to the floor of the caleche.

I waited to see if pain afflicted any part of me and was relieved to find that none did. "I'm fine," I assured him.

Antanasia dusted off my skirt, then straightened her hat, which had been displaced with the pitch of the carriage.

"It feels as though we have lost a wheel," Quincey announced, reaching past me to unlatch the door and let it swing open. He leapt out and lifted me down and then Antanasia.

Quincey was right. The great wheel at the back had cracked in two and lay crushed beneath the carriage. "We have a spare one," he told us, and signaled to the driver, who had already climbed down from his seat.

It was the first I had seen of the driver. I could not make out his face, shadowed as it was beneath a wide-brimmed black hat and a tall upturned collar. The effect of the outfit was strange. I should probably be quite unsettled by it if Quincey had not been with me.

More howls came from the trees. And now I could see pinpricks of light—eyes gleaming amongst the thickets.

Though Quincey said we had nothing to fear from the wolves, they frightened me. Now that we were exposed— outside the safety of the cab—my fear of them doubled.

Antanasia took my arm. "Don't worry, child. We shall be on our way in no time." She led me to a boulder a few yards from the carriage. "Let's sit and wait here."

I sat beside her and watched the driver unfasten the spare wheel from the underside of the caleche. Quincey stripped the broken wheel from its axle as the driver rolled the new one to his side. Then, with strength so massive it stopped the breath in my throat, Quincey took hold of the axle and raised it from the ground so that the caleche balanced on three wheels.

How he supported the weight of the coach, I could not say. I watched in awe as the driver rolled the spare into place and hammered it onto the point of the axle that rested in Quincey's hands. Each blow made the carriage shudder and Quincey with it, but he just gazed down, concentrating on his task.

So absorbed was I by this that the sudden piercing scream next to me turned my blood to ice.

I turned to reach for Antanasia—and recoiled in horror.
She was being pulled violently backward by a huge wolf,
who gripped her neck with its pure white fangs.

I wanted to shout out for help, but my voice died in my
throat. A loud crack met my ears, and Antanasia's head
twisted in a brutally unnatural angle. I stared into the bloodied face of my beloved guardian, her unbelieving eyes fixed
in death, as she was hauled into the bushes.

Another scream rang out around the trees and echoed
against the dark and empty sky. I felt Quincey at my side,
pulling me to him, and realized that the screams were my
own. "No!" I sobbed, not wanting to believe in the unthink-
able horror I had just witnessed.

A loud rustling sounded through the undergrowth. More
wolves were slinking toward the site where the murderous
beast had taken Antanasia. The noise of them feeding on
flesh, gnawing on bone, made me nauseous and light-headed.
Only Quincey's arms kept me from falling. "We must hurry
back to the carriage," he told me. He enclosed me in the
darkness of his cloak, shielding me from the sound of
Antanasia's bloody dismemberment.

I barely registered my surroundings as we continued on our
journey. Then the noise of the wheels changed, sounding out
on cobbles instead of dirt. We passed through huge wooden
gates into a courtyard. We had arrived at the castle.

"Introductions will wait," Quincey told me. I buried my face into his chest, desperate for his comfort as he carried me immediately to my rooms. He placed me gently on the bed and took off my boots. Then he placed a coverlet over me and sat with me until I fell into an exhausted slumber.

I awoke, an hour or so later, to discovered a silver tray of food on the small table beside my bed. I have no appetite, however. I can only grieve for the loss of my guardian and pray for slumber to ease my suffering.

LATER

My mind will allow me to sleep no more and so I have gazed about my rooms. They have a severe, nightmarish aspect to them that chills me to the core.

The ancient stone walls of my chamber arch into vaults far above my head. Shadows collect there, thick like cobwebs. There is a huge stone fireplace, which gapes at me like a giant mouth. Though a fire rages in the grate, I feel no warmth.

My mind tortures me with terrible imaginings of ghouls and ghosts and all the demons that filled the stories of my childhood. I imagine footsteps at my door but upon investigation see only shadows in the unlit hallway.

It must be the shock of losing dear Antanasia that makes me see things through this sinister lens.

Oh, where is my darling Quincey? Why has he left me alone in this strange place? I pray the dawn comes soon!

Journal of
Mary Seward

25TH NOVEMBER 1916

We have arrived in the village at the foot of the mountain. At its crown is our imposing destination.

I notice with a sense of foreboding there are far fewer sheep and cows in the lush meadows around the village than we have seen earlier in our journey—yet many more shepherds—who guard them with ferocious-looking crooks topped with crucifixes. Clearly it is not wolves or bears that prey upon God's creatures here, and the thought makes me want to turn and flee this place.

John noticed my trepidation at the sight of these shepherds and took my hand in his. "Steady," he coached me. "I am with you." I gazed up at him, and the set of his strong jaw gave me courage.

We have found rooms at an inn and will spend the night gathering all our wits for the battle to come.

The innkeeper's eyes widened when John signed the

register. Grasping John's hand, he gabbled something urgently and disappeared into a back room.

"He has a letter for me, "John told me excitedly. "He says a young lady left it with him a few days ago to give to the next mail coach. It must be from Lily!"

The man returned and pressed the letter into John's hand, talking once more in a most agitated manner.

"He says his heart bled to think of that poor innocent girl traveling to the castle with that fiend!" John translated for me. The innkeeper's words had brought a glow of perspiration to John's brow. He ripped open the letter.

Letter from Miss Lily Shaw to Lieutenant John Shaw

22ND NOVEMBER 1916

Dear John,

I am writing to let you know I am safe and well and that we will arrive at Quincey's home tomorrow. Our journey has been so smooth it is hard to believe a war rages. Quincey has ensured we have traveled in peace and safety.

Countess Tepes, Quincey's mother, is eagerly awaiting our arrival and is very pleased about our betrothal. Oh,

John, not having had a mother of my own for so long makes me hope that she will treat me, and indeed love me, as a daughter.

The wedding ceremony is planned for St. Andrew's Eve—the 29th of November. Quincey and I both so wish that things could have been different and that you could be there with us.

I hope you have not been fretting too much about me. As you see, I could not be in safer hands, my dearest brother.

I pray you are wishing us joy.

All my love,

Lily

Journal of Mary Seward

25TH NOVEMBER (CONTINUED)

John read the letter first, then passed it to me.

I scanned the words. "St. Andrew's Eve!" I exclaimed. The fateful wedding date struck further terror into my heart. We had read of this date in a sheaf of Van Helsing's notes. St. Andrew's Eve was the time when vampires, and indeed all dark forces, were at their strongest—and it was just five days away!

"We must take Lily from the castle and make our escape before then," John stated. I knew he was right. If we could not liberate Lily before then, we would not stand a chance.

John began talking in a quick and serious tone with the innkeeper, who answered him earnestly. "The villagers here will assist us however they can," John translated.

Then the innkeeper shook his head and murmured something to me.

"But he is begging that you do not go," John added gravely. "He says that he cannot bear to see another innocent lost to the darkness." John paused, then placed his hands on my shoulders. "Mary, this man may be right. The evil we face is great, and I could not bear to see harm come to you. Perhaps you should reconsider."

My heart warmed at John's protective instinct, but I had already made up my mind. "Darling, I cannot allow you to face this threat on your own," I told him. "I must go with you." I turned to the innkeeper. "Unless this concerned gentleman would like to volunteer to go in my place?"

I stared the innkeeper straight in the eye. Though John did not translate my challenge, I think the man must have understood, for he lowered his eyes in shame. He signaled for us to wait there before hurrying away. To our great surprise and relief, he returned with a canvas bag filled with dried garlic. He pressed it into my arms while gabbling an explanation to John.

"Like Van Helsing, the villagers know of the protective nature of garlic," John confirmed. "They grow it and store it here to protect their families."

I gestured my thanks to the man. "Ask him where we may find holy wafers," I urged John.

He did so.

"We can obtain some from the village priest before we leave tomorrow morning," John told me.

And so we are almost prepared for battle: we have Van Helsing's tools, our garlic—and holy wafers tomorrow, God willing.

Now all we need is to secure transport for our journey to the castle.

LATER

No one will take us to Castle Dracula—not for any amount of money. But thankfully, John has been able to purchase two horses on which we shall ride ourselves. He will go and collect them while I visit the priest tomorrow morning.

I will be glad to see him. I will ask for a special blessing, for John and I will both need it.

CHAPTER 15

*Journal of
Lily Shaw*

Having lain awake for most of last night, tortured by my grief and my fearful imaginings, I was calmed a little by the arrival of daylight, which brightened the room considerably.

Pushing my blanket away, I rose from the bed and went over to look out of the large casement windows. I squinted. I had been so long without the sunlight that the brightness of it caused me some discomfort.

The window on the northern wall looked down onto the castle's cobbled courtyard, which seemed deserted. I moved over to explore the view from the western window—and drew back in shock. There was nothing below the window but a sheer drop onto the great rocky precipice that lay below me.

I went and sat back on the bed, feeling quite light-headed.

Realizing I was exhausted, I decided to try and sleep. I pulled a nightgown from one of the two bags that had traveled with me, changed into it, and got back into bed, glad of the heavy covers, for surprisingly, the sunlight brought precious little warmth to the room.

I awoke as the sun was dipping back behind the mountains. Night and its shadows were returning. I rose, shivering, to light the lamps.

The fire was dying in the hearth. I took a log from the pile beside it and leaned into the yawning fireplace to place it on the flames. As the dry wood caught and flared, I saw scuttling shadows around the fireplace. Great spiders crawled from the crackling flame, their long arched legs hurrying away from the heat.

I backed away, a shuddering panic gripped my body, and I hugged myself to stop from shaking, repulsed by the sight.

Footsteps sounded outside my door again, louder and more purposeful now. My heart, already hammering, tightened further and a flash of terror gripped me as the door creaked open.

With what wild eyes must I have greeted Quincey—for it was he who entered. I rushed to him, wrapping myself round him, desperate to feel his strength and reassurance, tears of relief coursing down my cheeks. "You have been gone so long," I choked. "I didn't know where you'd gone—when you'd come back to me."

"I have not been gone so long," he told me, stroking my hair. "I have had business to attend to all day, and you needed to rest, I think."

"I heard someone outside my door," I sobbed.

"You are in my care," murmured Quincey. "And while you remain so, nothing here will dare harm you. I shall give you the key to your door if it will make you feel more secure."

Trepidation chilled my veins at his words. Why did he not hasten to persuade me there was nothing in this gloomy place to fear?

"What is it, Lily?" Quincey asked, sensing my distress.

"It is just—Quincey, I know this is your home, but it is so dark here," I told him. "There are shadows everywhere. It seems as if they will swallow me up."

Quincey smiled. "You have been out of Romania too long, dear one. Everything here seems wild and dramatic compared to the civilization and formality of England."

"I suppose you are right—and I am sorry for my skittishness. I want to love your home—and everything else that you hold dear," I told him. "I want to see what you see."

Quincey stiffened slightly and retreated a pace. "Do not worry. You will come to appreciate this place as I do . . . soon enough."

He gave me the strangest look then, and I felt conscious

of the disheveled mess I must be. "Oh, Quincey. Here I talk about my silly fears when I myself must look a fright." I ran my hands through my hair, trying to smooth it.

Quincey's face brightened. "You look like a princess. Which reminds me—my mother is eager to meet you. She is on her way here."

"B-but I am not even dressed!" I stuttered, flustered at this sudden news. I had expected a little notice to prepare for this important event.

Quincey shook his head. "It's no matter. Mother knows of your loss. She will be glad that you have rested through the day."

"Still, I wished to impress her . . ." I responded.

Quincey smiled down at me. "Fine clothes are only a distraction in one as beautiful and pure as you. Mother will love you as you are, just as I do."

I could not help but smile, touched by his sweet words. I hugged him to me and pressed my lips to his.

A soft knock on the door broke our embrace.

Quincey crossed the room. He opened the door and led in a striking-looking woman. "Mother—this is my fiancée, Lily Shaw," he announced.

I was immediately taken by the youthful appearance of Quincey's mother—and her incredible beauty!

The countess's hair showed no sign of gray, but hung in rich glossy curls around her slender neck. Her eyes shone a surprising shade of blue and her full, beautifully shaped lips seemed to invite all to taste them.

She had a charisma that was nearly palpable. Yet so regal was her air, I felt the urge to curtsy before her.

"Countess," I whispered shyly. "It is a great honor to meet you."

The countess gave me a gracious nod. Her sapphire eyes glittered as she looked me over. I felt nervous at her close scrutiny but remained still, glancing under my lashes at Quincey to see if he was pleased with the impression I was making.

At length, his mother turned to him and, in smooth velvety tones, said just one word: "Magnificent."

I smiled, greatly relieved to have won her approval. "You are most kind, Countess Tepes," I said.

"I am nothing of the sort," she responded sportingly. She held out an elegant hand. "You must call me Mina."

I met her hand with one of my own, trying not to let it tremble.

She trailed the tips of her fingers slowly over my palm. Their coldness made me shiver. Finally she loosened her grasp and turned to Quincey. "Such warmth," she observed.

He nodded, responding with a tight smile.

"Have you eaten since you arrived, my dear?" Mina asked me.

I shook my head. "I noticed the food. You have been most kind in sending it, but I have not been hungry," I answered truthfully.

Mina clucked her tongue sympathetically. "Of course. Quincey told me what a frightful journey you had coming here. But you must eat now. We can't have you growing weak from lack of nourishment."

Touched at her concern, I nodded.

She strode elegantly over to the doorway, then turned back to look at me again. "I am sorry that the count does not feel able to greet you as well. He has made himself something of a recluse these past years. . . ." She glanced at Quincey. "He shall, of course, make an exception for his son's wedding, and you shall meet him then."

"Of course. I look forward to it," I told her.

Mina smiled broadly. Her teeth were as straight and glinting as her son's. "In the meantime, I will have supper brought to you both here. Dear Lily, I hope you will enjoy our company. Do make yourself at home." She left us then, the door creaking shut behind her.

"Do you suppose she really liked me?" I asked Quincey when dinner was through. I gulped from the silver goblet of port he had handed me.

I had drunk three glasses thus far, glad for its power to deaden my heartache over Antanasia—and my sense of foreboding in this strange, disconcerting place.

"How could she not like you?" Quincey answered. "You possess all the beauty, innocence, and purity of heart she would desire in my bride." A frown played upon his lips. He took a sip from his own glass.

"Quincey, my love, what is it that *you* desire?" I asked. I grinned at him, feeling fluid and relaxed. My eyes drooped a bit as I set my glass down on the table.

Quincey chuckled. "I think, my dear, that you are tired. I will leave you to rest." He began to stand.

"No, no." I stopped him before he could rise. I reached across the table and stroked his cheek. Then I slid over to his chair and placed myself in his lap.

He smiled again, shaking his head. "Dear, sweet Lily." He kissed me a tender good night on the forehead.

The touch of his lips was enough to leave me breathless. I gasped at the feel of them.

After a moment's hesitation, he gently moved his mouth along my brow, then down across my cheek, to meet my own lips.

For the first time since that rain-swept night, I felt our passion flicker, but he snuffed the flame before it could kindle and grow.

"Please. Stay," I whispered to him. "I am lonely here."

"I cannot," he told me, summoning his resolve. "It is not time yet to fulfil our destiny."

He moved me toward my bed, then took his leave.

I write sleepily now at the candle-wax-and-ink-spattered desk by my window. I will leave a lamp lit tonight for, though

though I would not offend Quincey or his mother by saying so, my room has a dismal air.

Though Quincey would not stay, I take solace in his words. He is my destiny, and in just five days' time our destiny will be realized!

CHAPTER 16

Journal of
Mary Seward

I have just come from the church.

I went early—the sun had barely risen above the mountain. It was a small, inconspicuous building, its stone walls
weathered and darkened by age. Its parapets were orna-
mented by grotesque gargoyles; the sight of those hideous
faces made me hurry through the weathered door into the
sanctuary of the chapel.

Beneath the plain ceiling, rows of pews crowded the nave,
their wood worn smooth—as if well used over the centuries.
The air was perfumed with incense and dust motes moved
silently through the stillness.

A priest knelt at the altar, bowed in prayer. There was an
air of weariness in the stoop of his back. Hearing the creak of
the door, he stood and came to greet me. His tired, wrinkled

face reminded me of Father, and my heart twisted as I thought of him, all alone back in England.

I did not know how I would explain what I sought, for I knew no Romanian. But it seems the priest was expecting me. Word of our arrival had spread through the village during the night. He took my hand and drew me toward the altar.

He gestured me to kneel. I felt such peace there, the morning light filtering through stained glass windows and checkering the stone pillars around me. The priest turned and took a pewter chalice from the altar. Intoning words I recognized as Latin, he pressed it to my lips. I smelled the spicy tang of wine and took a sip. The priest then offered a holy wafer to my lips. I put out my tongue and accepted it, feeling it dissolve in my mouth and mingle with the wine. I felt courage rise in my heart.

The priest pressed his hand upon my head. I closed my eyes and tried to hold the comforting sensation, knowing I would have need of it in the days to come.

The priest then led me into the vestry, where he put more holy wafers into a silken cloth, then folded it and pressed it into my palm. He also gave me three small glass bottles, making the sign of the cross as he did so. I guessed they must contain holy water—another tool Van Helsing used to fight the parasitic vampire.

I took it all from him gratefully, wishing I had the language to express my thanks. I did the only thing I could think of and kissed the priest on his weathered cheek. He smiled and patted my hand.

As I write, John sharpens the stakes we uncovered in Van Helsing's bag. I shudder to think of their ultimate purpose, but I must be strong. We have but four days to make our journey and return Lily to the safety of home. May God help us.

Journal of
Lily Shaw

25TH NOVEMBER 1916

Quincey did not come to me till long after sundown. "I have brought your key," he said, placing it on the table beside the door. I rushed into his embrace, not caring about the key while he was with me.

He pressed me to him. "I'm afraid you must be very bored."

I could not say that boredom was what afflicted me, for most of the time that Quincey was away, loneliness and trepidation had occupied my heart. Try as I might, I could not find comfort here at the castle.

"Why did you not come to me sooner?" I asked, unable to keep the reproach from my voice.

"My poor Lily." Quincey lifted my chin gently. "I hate neglecting you like this. But I have been away from home for so long, business has quite piled up. At least we shall have this evening together. . . ."

I looked up at him hopefully.

"Mother has planned a supper for us," he announced. "We are to go down to the Great Hall directly. She is already waiting."

A mixture of emotions troubled me. Any bride would welcome a formal supper with her future mother-in-law. Yet there was something about Mina that put me ill at ease. I felt acutely uncomfortable around her. Yet I could not explain why.

"Shall we join her?" Quincey asked, offering me his arm.

I summoned a winning smile—for his sake. "That will be lovely," I told him. I looked down at my dress with a hesitant glance. "Should I change?" The pale blue dress I wore had been packed for traveling. Until my trunk arrived, I had nothing formal to wear.

Quincey smiled and gently stroked my neck. "You need no adornment, my sweet," he said.

He took me down a spiral staircase that led onto the opulent entrance hall. It was ablaze with oil lamps burning with open flames. A pair of stone staircases curved up to meet in a galleried landing on the floor above.

As we crossed the white marble entry, I stared at the magnificent black-and-red dragon mosaic in its center. It was beautiful, and for a moment my heart wrenched looking at it; it was not unlike a pattern in the charm that Antanasia always wore around her neck.

We climbed the stairs to the landing. The castle seemed more alive at this end. Innumerable voices and the sound of laughter echoed beyond the closed doors we passed.

"Have you friends staying with you?" I asked him curiously.

He nodded. "The family always welcomes its friends. We reward allegiance with hospitality."

"Shall any of them be joining us for dinner?" I inquired.

Quincey paused before he answered, as though deliberating his words. "You will meet them at the wedding," he told me. "Tonight is to be a family occasion."

We passed through the first open door I had seen, which led to a sumptuously furnished drawing room. Just beyond that was the Great Hall.

Quincey led me into the huge, high-ceilinged chamber. The tapestries hanging from its walls were spectacular, though dulled by the dust and cobwebs that seemed to have taken hold throughout the castle. I peered up into the vast darkness above my head and wondered how high the ceiling stretched beyond the shadows.

Mina was already sitting at one end of the immense dining table. She looked dazzling in a violet satin gown that accentuated the creamy slope of her shoulders. "Welcome, my dears, do sit down," she said.

The table was laden with so many dishes; I wondered

that so much had been set out for so small a party. A roasted suckling pig lay at the table's center, its crisp skin glistening in the light from the candelabras that adorned the table.

The movement of a pale, thin figure caught my eye, but before I could regard it carefully, it disappeared into the shadows at the far end of the hall.

I supposed the stooped person to be a servant—the first I have actually seen at the castle.

Quincey silently took his place at the head of the table, his eyes drawn to the window, where the lamplight gleamed on the diamond-leaded panes.

"Do you always dine so late?" I asked tentatively, settling myself on one of the velvet chairs.

Mina inclined her elegant head. "It has been a custom of my husband's family for generations. I hope it is not an inconvenience."

I twisted my hands in my lap. I hadn't meant to be rude. "No, no. Of course not," I assured her.

"Then please eat, my dear," Mina murmured.

During the course of the meal, my future mother-in-law ate next to nothing, preferring instead her crystal glass of deep red wine. But she took great pleasure in watching me partake of the feast and urged me to indulge in whatever I desired.

Her manner was cordial, and yet, I could not shake my uneasiness about her. If I didn't know better, I would say that Mina regarded me in a detached and bemused manner—as a cat observes a canary in a cage.

"Which part of England do you come from?" I asked in an effort to make conversation.

"We lived in Essex, my first husband and I," Mina told me. "But I hardly think of those days anymore. I never really began to live until I came here."

"Have you not been back since?" I asked, surprised at how easily she had given up one life for another.

"Why would I go back?" she asked, astonished.

"Well, I cannot imagine what it would be like . . . never to return to England."

I dared not say how I really felt. I was horrified at the prospect of *anyone* living at this castle—day in and day out—for the rest of her life. Once Quincey's business was settled, I planned to return to Carfax Hall as soon as possible.

I peered at Quincey, hoping he would share my sentiment, but he did not meet my glance.

Giving no sign she heard or understood my gentle plea, Mina changed the subject. "How long, I wonder, till our other family member arrives?" she said, giving Quincey a long look.

"I have been informed that he is on his way. He should make the castle in two days' time," he muttered.

"I do hope so," Mina drawled. "For I would hate him to miss our celebrations." She raised her glass as if in toast and I wondered who this new guest must be.

"Are many coming?" I asked.

"Well, of course, my dear," Mina answered. "The marriage of my son is quite an event."

Quincey glanced down at his plate and I thought I saw a frown crease his brow. I studied him for a moment. The presence of his mother had a decidedly negative effect on his mood.

Mina went on, "That is why we have chosen St. Andrew's Eve, a special date, for the ceremony."

"Saint Andrew's Eve," I echoed, remembering Mina's letter. "Why is it so special?"

"It is like Christmas to the Tepes family," Mina answered enthusiastically. "A time to celebrate and rejoice. It has been the tradition for centuries." She gave a sudden smile and leaned forward in her chair. "Now, my dear, I am sure that in the rush, you did not have any time to acquire a wedding gown."

"N-no," I answered. "I had not even thought of it. Quincey and I packed so hurriedly for our journey."

"Well, do not worry. I have a gown that would suit you well. It is the one I wore for my marriage to Tepes. We look to be a similar build."

"Why—why, thank you," I breathed, touched by this generous gesture. "I would be honored to wear it."

Mina smiled. "Excellent. I shall have it brought out from storage and prepared for you." She turned to her son. "Lily shall make a most appealing bride, don't you think,

Quincey? And in my gown, she will be simply *delicious*."

I was happy at Mina's enthusiasm, but Quincey's brooding silence troubled me. I looked at him, praying he might show some interest, but he stared on at his plate till his mother chided him for his unchivalrous attitude.

"Quincey, I know men rarely appreciate the planning of a wedding," she said, "but your bride has no family to guide her through this momentous occasion. We must help her and show her kindness in the time that she has left—"

Quincey shot his mother a fiery stare.

"As an unmarried woman, I mean," Mina clarified her sentiment.

I tried to summon Quincey's gaze once more, but still he looked away from me.

My heart trembled. Suddenly, everything seemed wrong. Did Quincey no longer wish to marry me?

Tears pricked the corners of my eyes. My vision began to blur. I would have run from the table, but at that moment, I felt Quincey's hand grasp mine.

"Oh, Lily. I am sorry . . ." he whispered. He raised his eyes and I saw in them a dark remorse.

I wonder—what has changed since our voyage? I am sure that Quincey loves me, and yet the closer our wedding day draws, the more uncertain he becomes. What makes he, who has carried me along like a whirlwind, now hesitate?

I do not know how long I slept, but it was before dawn when something disturbed me into wakefulness. A shadow darkened my pillow and I became aware that someone was in the room. I sat up in alarm and drew my bedclothes to my breast.

It was Mina, her milk-white face looming over me, eyes gleaming with red reflected from the hearth. She moved closer and smiled. I felt a jolt of confusion. Two of her strong white teeth now appeared slightly pointed.

"My dear one . . ." Her voice came as a sigh. She reached her hand to my cheek and caressed it slowly. "Such sweetness is hard to resist."

Mina's words and her seductive tone kept me rooted in place. "Wh-what are you doing?" I asked. My voice came out a whisper.

"You have been so agitated since your arrival." Her voice seemed to echo about the room and through my head. "Relax, my pet. Relax . . ."

Her fingers moved to the collar of my nightgown, exposing the hollow of my neck. My breath quickened. Mina leaned forward—

A sudden clatter on one of the windows startled her. She spun in the direction of the noise. When she again faced me, I saw that her expression held no menace—only her usual smooth composure.

The lights in the room appeared brighter than a moment before.

I shook my head. Had I been dreaming?

"Dear Lily, I know that you were upset by Quincey's manner at dinner. I merely came to see how you were sleeping," she explained.

"Th-thank you," I stammered, not knowing what to make of her explanation. "I am fine."

After Mina had swept from my room, I leapt out of bed and locked the door behind her. Then I ran to the window, anxious to discover what had clattered against it. I pressed my face against the cold glass.

The shape of a large bat rose up in front of my window and soared away toward the valley. I stared at the great arc of its wings in awe.

In that moment, I wished that I, too, could fly away— could leave Romania with Quincey at my side. For whether the perils around me are real or of my own imagining, I am certain that I do not belong in this fearful place.

CHAPTER 17

*Journal of
Mary Seward*

Leaving everything but essential belongings at the inn, we set off as the sun was still rising in the sky. Our steeds were sorry creatures, culled from the few left in the village after the army had taken what they wanted.

We made slower progress than we had hoped.

We had ridden most of the day when at last, the castle loomed into view. It sat on its great rock, like a black-hearted giant, crouched in waiting—ready to pounce. My heart tightened as I imagined poor Lily imprisoned in that dreadful place.

Soon the path began to steepen and the horses became slower still. By their flattened ears and anxious whinnies I knew they sensed the danger we were driving them toward, yet they plodded on with noble courage. Then John's old nag stumbled on the rocky path and we decided, fearful we might lame the sorry creatures, to let the horses loose and go on by foot.

We dismounted and John untied the bags in which we had stored our equipment. Then he slapped the horses and sent them running back down the hill. They needed little more encouragement, for they galloped back toward the village with more haste than we imagined they possessed.

Together, we pushed on, hoping to reach the castle well before nightfall. Without the horses, however, the distance seemed impossible to cover.

John gazed toward the horizon. "The sun is setting. We're not going to make it," he surmised.

I agreed. "Perhaps it is best to camp here. No one at the castle knows that we are coming; we should be safe."

John pulled me to him in a tight hug. "Nonetheless, we will take the necessary precautions."

Using our bags for pillows, we lay down on a bed of soft pine needles a little way from the path. We ringed ourselves with holy wafers, and John fastened his crucifix around his neck. I touched the one I always wore, confirming its presence.

Father's notes assure us that even if a vampire should discover us here, they could not breach the ring of holy wafers.

Despite this, I shivered. We were in the land of the enemy, and we were at his mercy.

I heard the crack of a twig in the woods nearby and

bolted upright. I shot a glance over at John and saw that he too was disturbed by the noise.

We sat that way in the forest, ears pricked, for a long while. Finally, John whispered, "Nothing to fear. Just the sounds of the trees."

"Perhaps we should not sleep tonight," I suggested.

"But we must," John told me. "We will need our strength. Here, lie by me. I will keep watch while you slumber."

I moved my bag and snuggled next to John. He placed his arm protectively around me and I did indeed feel safe once more. My heart swelled. In a world where such evil was possible, how blessed I was to have John Shaw by my side!

I record all this now by soft glow of Van Helsing's lamp. John surveys the woods around us. I shall turn in, however, as my love is right. I must rest myself for tomorrow.

Journal of
Lily Shaw

27TH NOVEMBER 1916

In the early hours before dawn, my thoughts turned to Antanasia's trunk, sitting in the entrance hall next to mine.

Quincey had come moments ago to inform me that the two cases had been delivered. He disappeared again just as quickly.

The yearning to wrap myself in the comfort of my guardian's belongings became overwhelming. I took a candle and crept from my room.

I hurried down the spiral staircase and into the entrance hall. The lamps along the grand staircase were lit, and the rooms beyond the landing were filled with voices and laughter again.

Near the massive front door were the two trunks. Crossing the marble floor, I knelt before the great leather one Antanasia brought with her to England after Mother and Father's death.

I unlatched it with trembling fingers and lifted the heavy lid. I delved eagerly into the clothes and boxes stored inside Antanasia's trunk.

In one of the boxes, hidden under the starched skirts that I clung to as a child, I found a bundle of letters tied together with a red cord.

Drawing the first from the top of the pile, I recognized its stamp as Romanian. There was a strange familiarity to the handwriting, a rounded evenness I distantly remembered. Perhaps I'd seen the letters at Carfax Hall in passing; maybe they were from the sister that Antanasia had once mentioned.

Tentatively, I opened the yellowing envelope and unfolded the letter from inside.

Dear Antanasia,

Thank you for sending me news of John and Lily. Your account of Lily's 8th birthday brought me a bittersweet joy. I'm glad she liked my gift, though it breaks my heart she could not know it was from me.

Every day and night I berate myself for my moment of weakness—and will never forgive myself for what happened to my dear husband.

I pray you will foster in my children the strength and courage they shall need to face their future. But you must promise to love them as though they are your own, for they need a mother's affection.

I will write again soon. Until then, kiss Lily for me tonight when you put her to bed, and when John comes home for the holidays, feed him well and deny him nothing. I know how strict these English boarding schools can be.

> Kind regards,
> Rosemary Shaw

CONTINUED

I grasped the side of the trunk to steady myself. Our mother! This letter was from her! She had been alive when John and I believed her dead.

But how could it be?

Then another thought: Antanasia knew of this and never told us.

I fumbled through the bundle, looking for the last letter, desperate to know how recently it had been written.

I read the date on the postmark: 17th August 1916. Just months ago . . .

Was she alive still?

Questions raged in my mind. My heart seemed ready to burst with anger and frustration. John and I had been deprived of our mother unnecessarily. But why?

Did she give us up?

Where was she now?

With trembling fingers I hurriedly pulled the other letters out of their envelopes. I scanned each—but there was no address on any of them.

I staggered to my feet and across the marble floor to the staircase, my mind reeling from shock and disbelief.

I had to find Quincey. He would help me make sense of this.

I reached the top of the stairs, then rushed from the landing to the shadow-filled corridor. Its walls flickered red as my movements caused the lamp flames to sway. I moved along, rattling each of the door handles, hoping to find one that would give. I called my beloved's name. Surely he must be here in the castle somewhere.

At last, a handle twisted beneath my grip and the door swung open. I fell into the room—and saw a couple locked in a passionate embrace. Mortified, I was about to withdraw when the man turned at my disturbance. I froze in horror.

How can I describe what I saw?

The man glared at me with eyes that shone like rubies. His complexion was ghoulishly white and his lips gory from the blood that dripped from them. The girl in his arms hung limply, as if drugged or mesmerized. Blood streamed like tears from two punctures in her neck. I watched as it pooled into a red stain that blossomed over her breasts.

The man hissed, his eyes blazing redder, clutching his victim tightly to him.

"No!" I shouted in fear. I stumbled from the room and ran, not seeing where I fled. I tore down endless corridors. Scream after scream issued from my throat. I turned a corner—and came to a dead end. I could run no farther.

There were monsters here. True monsters! They had killed that girl—and they would kill me!

My mind whirled. I was going to die in this awful place!

I fainted then from sheer terror, and as the world faded to black, I heard my beloved's voice. "Lily, Lily, I am so sorry. . . ."

Journal of
Mary Seward

An eerie howl wrenched me from my uneasy sleep.

I sat upright. It came again.

Wolves.

John pulled me close. "Don't fret. If necessary, I'll use this." He pulled open his jacket to reveal Van Helsing's pistol in his belt.

The sound of footfalls padding through the undergrowth sounded around us. The howling became a chorus that spread and rose until the mountains around us echoed with the ominous sound.

I shivered as words from Jonathan Harker's journal came back to me:

> There seemed a strange stillness over everything, but as I listened, I heard, as if from down below in the valley, the howling of many wolves. The count's eyes gleamed, and he said, "Listen to them—the children of the night. What music they make!"

I tried to block out the mournful lupine cries, my eyes anxiously scanning the shadows through the trees.

Suddenly John sprang to his feet. He grabbed me with him and pulled his pistol from its holster with his other hand.

There, in the middle of the road, loomed a huge gray wolf. It lifted its head and howled into the sky. At its call, more gray creatures streamed in from the trees and gathered around their leader.

Another bloodcurdling snarl came from behind us. I turned and with a jolt of horror saw that the pack had surrounded us! Their mouths were open so that we could see their long fangs and their eyes fixed on us with terrifying intent.

They began to creep slowly forward—like an army bent on massacre.

The howling from the forest fell silent. Now all I could hear was the low growl throbbing from the throats of our attackers.

John took out his pistol and fired it at the nearest wolf. The bullet plunged deep into its skull. The wolf sank heavily to the floor, its crimson blood pumping into the dirt. But its companions streamed closer, undaunted.

John fired again, felling another, and then turned to fire upon the wolves behind us. Though he hit his mark, the wolves kept coming. By the look in their hungry eyes I could see their bloodlust had only been strengthened.

Fury boiled up in me. I would *not* have life or Lily's salvation torn from me so easily! I drew a stake from Van

Helsing's bag and raised it in defiance. If they came at me, I would die fighting. And Harker, the fiend who commanded these wolves, would see them bloodied and scarred.

The first wolf leapt at John, the great impact pushing him backward. I tensed every muscle, expecting him to fall. But he simply staggered, taking the weight of the wolf with relative ease.

"No!" he snarled. He shoved the wolf before it could sink in its fangs. "Get away!" he shouted. His tone was utterly fearless and he eyed the pack with such ferocity, I hardly recognized him.

At his command the wolves ceased their growling and began to back away.

I ran to him, trembling, as the pack turned and slunk back into the forest.

"I—I don't know what happened," he said, his strong chest heaving against me.

At last, we released each other. The forest had become ominously still—save for the bats that wheeled around us overhead. Looking up at them, I wondered if Harker already knew that we followed him.

If so, it is even more important that we wait here—until the safety of sunlight and morning. I only hope that Lily can hold on until then.

CHAPTER 18

*Journal of
Mary Seward*

In the reassuring light of dawn, we began to walk again. The castle loomed ever larger overhead.

As we rounded a bend, John grabbed me and pulled my head to his chest. "Do not look," he warned.

But I would not listen—and turned my face to see.

On the path, beside a broken carriage wheel, lay the head of Antanasia, neck ragged and bloody, eyes wide and staring in disbelief, as though her death had come more as a surprise than a sorrow.

My heart froze at the sight. Antanasia was already dead. Would we find Lily next?

I took John's arm as we walked past the hideous scene. "I am so sorry," I told him. "Antanasia cared for you for so long. You must be devastated."

John shook his head. "It is her fault that we are here now," he spat angrily. "She should never have let Lily leave the hall."

I stared at him a moment, surprised at the hatred in his voice.

We carried on in silence, walking quickly for most of the day. We knew that we must reach the castle as soon as possible. There were just two days until St. Andrew's Eve—when the vampire's strength would be at its height.

Finally, we approached the side of the great structure. I looked up and noticed a rosy glow beginning to color the afternoon sky. "It is not long till sunset," I said anxiously. "We must hurry!"

As we quickly skirted the perimeter of the castle keep, I noticed, with shock, that the huge entrance gates were slightly ajar. "Look!" I whispered.

John scanned for any signs of life. "They must think the wolves deterrent enough to keep out intruders," he observed. "Let's begin. There is no time to waste."

"Wait," I whispered. Rummaging in Van Helsing's bag, I drew out two bottles of holy water. I slid one into John's pocket and the other bottle into mine. John nodded in silent thanks.

I followed him as he hurried through the gates and crossed a cobbled courtyard to the great, studded front door of the castle building. No lights flickered in the windows. My

heart pounded as John turned the massive handle and
pushed the door open.

We crept into the vast stone entrance hall, where an elaborate twin staircase curved upward to the first-floor landing.
The massive stone walls were adorned with paintings and
weaponry that paid testament to the inhabitants' warrior
heritage.

The late afternoon light hardly made any impact through
the small defensive windows around the entrance. No
sounds emanated from within. The place seemed desolate—
vacant.

"Come, my love," John whispered. "We must hurry." He
pulled me forward to the grand staircase. I lifted my skirts
and took the stairs two at a time, desperate to find the place
where Lily was held captive—or Quincey Harker slept.

John pointed to a corridor to the left. We hurried into it
and crept along, trying the door handles on either side. All
were locked.

Then, halfway along, we came across a door that was
wide open. We stepped inside—and a dreadful sight met our
eyes.

A young woman lay facedown on a rich Persian rug. Her
dark, glossy curls were splayed around her head, creating a
halo of ringlets.

Her hair, her blue dress, they looked just like . . .

"Lily," I whispered.

"No!" John shook his head in disbelief. "It can't be!"

I took in her slender build and my heart wrenched. I noticed the girl's arm, lying by her side. Her skin was deathly white.

I wanted to grieve—to comfort John in that moment— but there was still something to be done. If Quincey had drained Lily of her blood, I needed to be sure he hadn't also ruined her soul.

According to Father's notes on Lucy Westenra, a vampire could turn his victim into one of his kind after a series of bites. The bite marks on Lucy's neck belied the state that would befall her, for they appeared quite severe and large before her burial.

I could not allow Lily's delicate soul to inhabit the wicked realm of the undead. If she *was* changed, we would have sooner need of Van Helsing's stakes than we expected.

I crept over to the body and rolled it over. It turned easily—its unseeing eyes fixed now on the ceiling. Its neck was broken.

I gazed at the poor soul that lay there—and breathed a sigh of relief.

Behind me, John slumped against the wall.

Her face—it was that of a stranger. Lily might still be safe somewhere in the castle!

I pitied this girl whose remains lay in this wretched place, yet my heart filled with hope. Perhaps we were not too late.

John pulled me away and we carried on. Open doorways
on either side revealed room after room, but all unoccupied.

There was no Lily—and no sign of a coffin anywhere.

Eventually, we found ourselves at the other end of the
wide landing overlooking the entrance hall.

We stole down the other side of the twin staircase and hid
once more in the shadows beneath it. "Where now?" I asked
urgently, glancing at the fast-reddening sky through the narrow window.

"There." John pointed. I followed his gaze to an ornate
stone doorway. I nodded. This must be the door to the vampire's crypt.

We hurried to it and saw that it opened onto a staircase
descending into blackness. The walls that enclosed it bore
elaborate designs in their ancient stone. I ran my hands over
the inscriptions, and my palms prickled.

We had found what we were looking for.

John peered past my shoulder and I knew he thought the
same, for he slid the revolver back into his pocket. If vampires slept there, the gun would be of no use to us.

I fumbled in Van Helsing's bag, drew out the oil lamp,
and, with trembling fingers, lit it.

"The descent into hell?" muttered John darkly. He
grasped my arm and took the lamp from me. "Stay behind
me, my darling. I shall go first."

I prayed the sun still hovered above the horizon as we

hurried down the smooth stone steps. At the bottom, a sickly sweet odor permeated the cold air. All was deathly still.

I squinted in the dim light of our small lamp. John and I stood in a long, narrow hall. The corridor of dank stone was punctuated with heavy wooden doors—each embellished with gruesome dragon head handles. Lamps, yet to be lit, hung between each door.

I touched the cold metal of the handle nearest and was prepared to turn it when John tugged my arm. He pointed to a door at the end of the corridor, wider and more elaborate than the others.

"Harker," he whispered.

Gathering all my courage, I followed John toward it. I heard a scraping from one of the other rooms as we passed, and a terrifying thought occurred to me—how many more vampires inhabited this place? When they woke at sunset, would we be able to defeat them all?

When we reached the door, John handed me the lamp. He turned the great wrought iron handle. It opened easily, swinging lightly on its hinges.

The rank air in the chamber beyond caught in my throat and made me gag. It was hard to imagine that any living creature had entered there before.

I held up the lamp. The stone walls were lined with rich tapestries, embellished with gold thread that shimmered in the lamplight. On a great plinth in the center lay two boxes, long and narrow.

"*Two* coffins . . ." I gasped. "If one is Harker's, then the other must be for . . ." I could not finish, for the thought that Lily already lay in the other made me sick to my stomach.

John said nothing. He took from the bag a stake and hammer and approached the plinth.

I forced my frozen limbs to follow, though every fiber of my body fought against it.

With silent purpose, John leaned over the nearest coffin. He lifted its heavy lid and rested it against the nearby wall.

"Hold the lamp closer," he instructed, leaning over to see in the darkness.

With a shaking hand I held the lamp above the coffin, illuminating what lay within. I felt John grow rigid against me and heard a clatter as the stake and hammer dropped from his hand.

"My God . . ." The words left his lips in a horrified gasp.

I stared into the coffin and saw a woman—young looking yet without the bloom of youth. Her face must have once been beautiful, but now it spoke of misery. Her pale lips barely covered her pointed teeth.

I glanced to John, whose eyes were fixed on this creature. His face was rigid and expressed a look of horror I had not seen since the sanatorium.

"John," I called. But he did not answer. He was frozen with terror.

I knew now was not the time for pause. Were this creature to wake, we would have to fight for our very souls.

Our horrible task must be completed—or our rescue would be over before it began. I thrust the lamp into John's petrified hands, then bent and picked up the hammer and stake. I raised them above the vampire's heart.

"No . . ." John gasped. He gripped my hands. "Mary . . . you cannot strike her. She is my mother!"

CHAPTER 19

Journal of
Mary Seward

John's appalling words made me freeze. His mother? But how could that be?

The eyes of the creature snapped open. She stared up at me in shock. Then she looked at John.

Her expression quickly changed to one of wild amazement. She covered her face, as though shamed by her unmasking. She let out a scream filled with despair.

As she did so, the lid of the coffin beside her began to move.

John was insensible to it. I knew I had to move quickly to save us both.

Dropping the stake and hammer back into the bag, I pulled John's arm. We hurried from the room and made our way down the narrow hall. As we reached the stairs, I heard the other doors along the hallway beginning to open. The vampires were emerging!

John began to regain his composure, and by the time we reached the top of the staircase, he was matching my pace with ease.

As we passed the lamps in the entrance hall, they blazed to life with a loud whoosh. At last we reached the studded front door. I pulled the handle—

"Good evening."

We spun around, hearts in our mouths.

Quincey Harker stood on the great landing, gazing down at us with a look that chilled me in its confidence.

"I have been waiting for you," he said, descending the stairs with purposeful steps. "You were spotted on the mountain last night."

The sight of him, now that I had full knowledge of the monster he was, chilled me to the bone. His eyes burned into me.

"I knew that John would come after Lily," he said, "but I confess I do not know why *you* deemed it appropriate to undertake such a journey, Miss Seward."

As he reached the bottom of the staircase, I fought to recover my self-possession. "Lily is my friend and John my fiancé," I countered. "It is right that I should help them."

"Fiancé?" he echoed, a fleeting frown betraying his displeasure at the development.

I felt a small satisfaction in unsettling this fiend—but Harker's discomposure did not last. "What a definite sense of right and wrong you have, Miss Seward," he went on coolly. "I almost envy your simplicity of outlook."

I turned then, searching for another way out. Behind us, streaming from the crypt's doorway, were the waking vampires!

"Splendid. You have arrived in time to meet my friends. Don't worry, they won't bite . . . yet." Quincey's voice dripped with malice.

I gazed at these creatures—cursed souls with evil in their eyes. There were six of them in all—men and women of all shape and size.

Unlike Quincey, their appearance was animalistic . . . feral. They gazed at us hungrily, licking their lips. I grasped John's hand and fingered the cross around my neck. As long as I had the protection of this holy ornament, the vampires would not dare attack me.

John's hand squeezed my own. I saw fury building within him.

"I see from your new trinkets that you have deduced my true nature," Quincey taunted.

"I've always had this," I answered defiantly. "I never had need to show it."

"You monster," John growled. "Where is Lily?"

"She is in her room." Harker waved his arm toward one

of the four arched doorways in the atrium. "I'm sure that she, at least, will be delighted to see you."

John and I gazed at each other, both clearly fearing for the other's safety should we separate. I sought to reassure him by glancing down at Van Helsing's bag, the contents of which would provide my protection.

John touched his own cross, which hung around his neck, and looked down at his pocket, indicating the bottle of holy water he kept there.

He gave me a tiny nod, and I returned it.

Harker turned to John. "Let us leave your new *fiancée* to fetch Lily, while we relax in the drawing room. I'll pour you a glass of port. You look done in, dear chap."

I watched them go with great worry and uncertainty. Then I shook myself. There was no time to waste.

I made my way up into the shadows of the winding staircase. When I reached the top, I looked along the corridor. "Lily?" I called tentatively, fearful of what horrors I might awaken with my cry.

I could see nothing except the flickering shadows cast by my lamplight. "Lily!" I called again softly, but heard no reply.

I continued to creep along the corridor, holding the bag of weapons to me.

I came to a corner and spied two gnarled, scruffy figures hunched up against a closed door.

They were men, I realized. Though they appeared shriveled and undernourished.

They shuffled about, whispering to each other and listening at the keyhole. I closed my fingers round my crucifix—but as they turned, I saw from their coarse complexions and blackened, ordinary teeth that they were no vampires.

The sight of me clearly startled them.

"Is this one the master's too?" one asked the other.

"Best not touch, just in case," answered the other. "You remember what he did last time he caught us here."

"Who is out there?" the almost hysterical voice of Lily sobbed from behind the door. At the sound of it the two wraiths fled away down the corridor.

"Lily!" I called again urgently, hurrying for the door. "Lily! It is I, Mary.. . . ."

There was a loud click as a key was turned. Very slowly the door was opened, revealing the darling, tearstained face of Lily. Her eyes were huge and darkened with anguish in the lamplight.

She gave another sob, then threw the door open wide and collapsed against me. "Mary! It really is you!" she murmured.

I clasped her to me. "Has he hurt you, Lily?" I demanded, "Has he hurt you at all?"

"Who?" she asked. She drew away and looked at me, puzzled, tears streaming down her cheeks.

"Harker, of course!" I answered.

"Quincey would never hurt me, Mary," she sobbed. "But something terrible has happened, something I cannot believe! Antanasia is dead, and among her things I have discovered letters—from my mother!"

Lily moved to her desk and grasped a piece of paper. She held it out to me. I took paper and unfolded it.

Inside, there was a letter. At the bottom, a signature— Rosemary Shaw.

"She is alive!" Lily wailed. "I do not understand how it can be!"

"Have you seen her?" I asked tentatively, wondering how much Lily knew of her mother's fate.

"No." She shook her head. "There is no return address. I do not know where she is." She sat down on her bed and drew a deep breath. "But Mary, there is more. This place—this place is most distressing. I have been the victim of the most horrible nightmares. When I sleep, I dream of terrible demons. Men with sharp-pointed fangs who feed off the blood of the living. Some of the visions seem terribly real. So much so that I do not know what is dreaming and what is wakefulness anymore!"

"Oh, Lily!" I cried, my heart breaking. How could I tell her that the creatures she imagined were real? Worse, how could I explain that her fiancé and her mother *were* the monsters she feared?

I held the poor, dear girl close, my heart full of pity.

Finally, I drew gently away. "John is here," I told her, taking both her hands in mine. "He is waiting for us."

"John! Where is he?" Lily begged.

"Quincey took him to the drawing room," I answered.

Lily led the way, seeming quite fearless in her urgent desire to see her brother.

As we crossed the main hall, I searched about for the pack of vampires that had emerged from the crypt. They were nowhere to be seen.

No doubt they were already gone, I realized, seeking their evening meal.

Harker heard our footsteps on the flagstones as we approached, for he turned before we entered the room.

"Our two ladies have returned!" he announced jovially. A disquieting satisfaction filled his voice. "Do come in."

As we moved into the drawing room, I saw John sitting still and stiff on an ornate brocade couch.

Harker stood in front of a blazing fireplace, watching us. Beside him was a beautiful, immaculately dressed woman with long, dark hair. To his other side was another figure. Though her back was to us, I recognized John's mother immediately.

Finally, Rosemary Shaw turned to face us. She lifted her skinny arms outward, her face twisted into a ghoulish expression of love and anguish. "Lily, darling!" she cried. "How I've longed to see you."

Lily stared. The rose of her cheeks, inflamed by weeping, drained into deathly whiteness. "M-mother?" she whispered. Then she swayed and I saw her eyes roll back into her head. She swooned into a dead faint.

I held her up as best I could and looked to John for help, but he stared blindly through us. It was Harker who strode to my side. He scooped Lily in his arms and carried her away, back toward her room.

The dark-haired woman turned her gaze on me. The youthfulness of her skin and the sheen of wealth that enfolded her served to make John's mother appear shabby and plain by comparison. She bestowed on me a smile that froze my blood for it revealed the sharp canine teeth of a vampire.

Though I hated leaving John alone with those two creatures, I could not abandon Lily. I followed Harker's receding footsteps. By the time I caught up, Harker had reached Lily's room. A great fire burned in the grate and heavy drapes covered the windows.

Harker had laid Lily on her bed. I watched as he pulled the covers gently over her, then tenderly pushed a stray lock of hair from her face.

The gesture, though it seemed tender, had the aspect of cruelty—like enticing a rabbit into a snare with soft words of encouragement. My anger rose within me.

"How dare you touch her after all that you've done," I snapped.

He regarded me with utter contempt. "You know nothing of which you speak, Miss Seward. I have done nothing. This is Lily's destiny."

"No!" I shouted. "It is *your* destiny, and you have pulled her into it. You deceived this innocent girl, who only wanted to love you!"

He strode toward me then, his sharp teeth bared and his face twisted with rage. I backed against the wall, holding fast to my crucifix.

"It is the rest of the world that has deceived her!" Quincey raged—his face just inches from mine. "I have shown her the truth!"

I trembled at the sight of him and could not answer.

He withdrew then and headed toward the door.

"If you will excuse me, I have business to attend to downstairs. There is a wedding to plan."

I recovered my voice as Harker stepped through the doorway. "Do not hurt John," I called after him. "I warn you!"

Harker smiled strangely then. "*John . . .* is the last person I would hurt."

He left the room, closing the door softly behind him.

Lily's eyes fluttered open. "Mary?" she whispered. She held her hand out to me. I rushed over to her and took it at once.

She clung to me, half awake, half lost in nightmare. I gazed at her neck—and gasped. There were two puncture wounds there, though they appeared no larger than pin-pricks.

So, Harker had bitten her! My heart trembled, knowing what I had to do next. I took a holy wafer from Van Helsing's bag and pressed it to Lily's brow, holding my breath to see what would happen.

Lily squirmed, made uncomfortable by the wafer, but it left no mark, no burning scar on her. Tears of relief welled in my eyes. Lily was not yet a vampire. For now, her soul remained as safe as my own.

I have spent much of the night cooling Lily's fevered brow and recording here the horrors of these last hours. She continues to drift in and out of consciousness. I have had little sense from her and do not even know if she remembers what shocked her into such a state.

Meanwhile, I must believe that John remains safe. I listen with a desperate heart for his footsteps to approach, but they never come. All that breaks the silence is the crackling of the fire and the occasional unearthly howl from the wolves in the forest below.

CHAPTER 20

*Journal of
Lieutenant John Shaw*

During my voyage with Mary to this damnable place, I did not write of petty discomforts, for my love was always at my side, and it was through her that I unburdened my heart.

But even dear Mary's presence cannot dispel the living hell I now experience. My ordeal in the trenches has been replaced with a horror I could not have imagined—a torture of the mind that threatens to break me for all time.

Mother, long dead to me these many years, is no longer so. But she is not the sweet woman I grieved for. She has become an evil, parasitic vampire, feeding off the blood and the life of others.

I cannot even begin to imagine how or why she is here. My mind reels at the very idea.

Now Harker holds us captive here in this world of evil.

And there is nothing I can do about it.

Mary left me in the entrance hall to see to Lily. I followed Harker into a large drawing room. He bid me sit in one of the overstuffed brocade couches near the fireplace. I refused.

"As soon as Lily has recovered, we shall leave," I said. "You can continue whatever it is that you do here in peace. We shall not trouble you further."

I kept my voice even as my mind raced, working out how we might best make our escape—and take Mother with us too. Despite Dr. Seward's notes, I clung to the hope that somehow she could be saved once she was away from this evil place.

"What makes you think I would let Lily go after all the trouble I've taken to bring her here?" Quincey asked sardonically.

"You have no legitimate claim on her," I argued.

Anger flickered across his features. "She is my fiancée!" he raged. "And besides, who would have the courage to take her from me?"

I glared at him as he mocked me, attempting to find my voice, struggling to find words that would move him. But none came.

Staring into Harker's smug face, I felt completely and utterly outmatched.

He poured me a glass of port. "Here. This should help with the shock," he said, placing the heavy crystal glass in my hands.

I took a warming sip of its contents.

After he had poured a glass for himself, Quincey went over and stood by the fire. He stared into it for a few long moments. "Once you have heard what I have to say, John," he said, "you may not be so keen to leave this place yourself."

I waited to hear the cruel blow he was clearly preparing to deliver.

"There is a secret I have longed to share with you since we first met," Quincey went on. He stopped and drank from his glass. "We are brothers, you and I."

"Brothers in arms we might have been, Harker—but it does not, after everything else that has happened, make us friends." I glared at him, despising him. "I have no wish to be a friend to a creature such as you."

I saw his face tighten. If I thought it possible, I would have said I had hurt him.

"No, John," Quincey corrected, his own tone icy now. "I was referring to our shared parentage. We are blood brothers. We share the same father."

My mind reeled at such an absurd suggestion. A laugh exploded from my mouth. "My father was David Shaw, an English diplomat," I said. "Yours was an evil demon!"

Quincey shook his head. "No, John. Your father is Count Tepes. . . ."

My mind reeled. "This is madness!" I shouted. Pulsing with outrage, I stood up, fingering the vial of holy water in my pocket. I wished to throw it on this beast of a man. To watch his skin sizzle the way Van Helsing's notes promised.

Yet even as I railed, the memory of my mother lying in that coffin set a dark fear squirming in my belly. Could Quincey speak the truth? Is it possible that something other than mere coincidence has drawn us all together?

Quincey sighed and went to refill his glass. "I arranged for you to join my battalion in order to awaken your appetites. But you fought hard against the bloodlust I attempted to stir in you."

"The war disgusted me!" I objected.

Harker raised an eyebrow.

"Did you really feel no thrill at the scent of blood?" he asked. "No desire to sink your teeth into warm, tender flesh?"

"Of course not!" I was stunned that he could speak of his perversion so shamelessly.

He took another drink. "I promise you, John. Your body cried out for the blood and carnage that surrounded you, but your sheltered mind tried to suppress the desires that are part of your heritage."

Unwillingly, I remembered my restlessness to be out on

the battlefield with Quincey. Had part of me reveled in the
bloody reality of war? Had the gruesome dreams that
haunted me described unfulfilled fantasies stirring in my
heart? I could no longer be sure. Quincey Harker, it seemed,
knew more about me than I did.

Beads of sweat began to break out on my forehead. I
heard footsteps in the hall . . . and turned to see Mother
enter.

"John . . ." she gasped, her eyes filling with tears. "I am
overcome with joy at seeing you."

A tidal wave of emotions threatened to sweep me away.
Seeing life once more in Mother's dear, familiar face touched a
desperate, childish part of me that I thought had died with her.

But her terrible corruption sickened me. The fear in my
belly crawled up and grabbed my throat. Unable to breathe,
I sank down into the couch.

"Mother," I croaked as I held back tears. "He is lying,
isn't he? My father was David Shaw!"

Mother cast her eyes down in shame. "Quincey tells the
truth," she whispered. "Tepes, son of Dracula, is your father.
You both share his bloodline."

I trembled violently as this news seeped into my consciousness.

The other woman in the room came toward me with the
fluid grace of a snake. Her amber-colored dress stretched
across her body, gleaming in the firelight.

Quincey looked at me intently. "This is Mina, my mother. You will come to know her better."

I blinked. I could not reconcile the Mina of Dr. Seward's notes with the seductive, predatory creature in front of me. The Mina I had read of was a bright, demure woman, loved and admired by all who knew her. This *thing* before me was a monster.

"Do not be afraid, John," she murmured, stroking my cheek with slender fingers. "A great gift awaits you. Once you have embraced your life here, you will never know fear or death or the petty concerns of mortals."

I glanced at my own mother. How could this woman, whom I had loved as an infant, consort with these soulless creatures? I remembered how full of sweetness she had been. Did she revel in being one of the undead, as Mina clearly did?

Mother must have seen my confusion, for she crossed the room and knelt beside me, her eyes filled with pity and regret. "John, I am sorry. I gave in at a moment of weakness. But do not despair. What Mina says is true. If you wish, this life can bring wonderful gifts."

"You do not look as if you are thriving on it!" I pointed out bitterly.

Mother looked away in shame.

"Rosemary has not the heart for it." Mina laughed cruelly. "She is weak. She always was. I warned Tepes, but she was already part of his plan."

"Plan?" I asked.

"Just before you were born, the House of Dracul fell on difficult times," Mina explained. "The enemy stalked our lands, killing our kind as they slept."

She sat on the couch, sliding her sensuous body close to mine.

"Count Tepes's ancient soul grew weak. Our empire, once powerful, was deposed—and we were made to hide in this castle like mice."

She continued in a whisper, her mouth inches from my ear. "Like any family, we needed fresh blood to survive, but in this difficult time, we could not chance a rebellious influence. So, sensing Rosemary's docile nature, Tepes sired you. A year later, Lily was born, sired by David Shaw. Tepes became determined that Lily, your half sister, should become Quincey's bride. Thus Quincey and you—doubly united by Lily—would come to power together. And together, you would be strong enough to restore the name of Dracula to glory."

"But I am not one of you!" I argued, pushing her away. "And I will never be."

"So you say," she murmured. Her triumphant smile repelled me.

Then Mother spoke. "I made Tepes send you and Lily back to England. It was my only demand—that for as long as possible, you would not be exposed to this side of your nature."

Mina turned her scornful gaze on my mother. "He only agreed because it suited him to have John properly educated and for Lily to be raised innocent of her fate." She moved to her son's side. "How much more delicious for Quincey to seduce a creature pure of heart and thought. To turn her into a lustful beast of the night!"

Quincey gazed vacantly into the fire. "Mother," he said without emotion, "you take an unnatural interest in my affairs. You must limit yourself to your own."

At that moment, there was the sound of footsteps in the hall. Mary and Lily entered the room.

I hardly remember their presence, so drawn was I into darkness and shock. I could not stir when I saw Lily faint and watched blankly while Quincey carried her away.

I was aware only of my own thoughts and the vague shapes of Mother and Mina in the room.

CHAPTER 21

Journal of
Lieutenant John Shaw

Not long afterward, I let myself be led to a large shadowy bedroom, where I fell immediately upon the mattress.

How quickly everything has changed, I thought. My old life has been taken from me—ripped away by these fiends—and replaced by something horrible. . . .

Insurmountable.

For how can I defeat the very thing that courses through my veins?

I stared at the intricate patterns of the rich quilt beneath me. I had no idea how much time passed. A distant voice finally stirred me to move. I could not hear the words it spoke, but I could hear its desperate pleading tone.

I let myself out of the room and followed the sound along the chill hallway.

As I drew closer, I was able to distinguish the desperate Romanian words that were spoken in a rough male voice.

"Please," the voice wept, cracking as it went on. "Do not deprive me of salvation. I do not want to be cast down into the fiery pits nor share your living hell!"

I reached the door from behind which the sounds came. I opened it, not bothering to conceal my presence. Pretense seemed pointless now. Why hide from these demons when I carried their blood?

Yet for all my bravado, I was not ready for what I witnessed inside.

Before a roaring fireplace, Mina loomed above a wretched man who was crouched upon the faded rug. While he shuddered in terror, Mina circled him, reveling in her cruel power. Her eyes no longer glittered like pole stars but burned red like the devil.

Two other vampires gleefully tormented their captive prey, leering at each other each time he recoiled from their touch.

Their malice enraged me and I felt the same power rise in me that had let me command the wolves. "Leave him alone!" I ordered.

The others drew back, but Mina was no mere wolf. She looked at me and smiled with amusement, eyes scorching my soul like burning coals. "Why don't you join us?" she crooned.

I shook my head in disgust.

She shrugged, then snapped her fingers at her two cohorts. They dragged the man to his feet.

Mina's face contorted until she wore the mask of a demon. She drew back her lips to reveal long, curved fangs. Then she lunged like a snake and sank her teeth into the man's neck.

He screamed wildly—and would have collapsed if his captors had not held him fast. Mina swallowed hard and fast, gorging herself on the man's blood.

While she fed, the others watched with hungry eyes but clearly did not dare disturb her.

With a satisfied sigh, Mina straightened and took a step away. Her cohorts let the man fall twitching to the floor. They bickered, hissing and jostling over the remains of Mina's meal.

"Dear John," she murmured, her lips still smeared with blood. "Do not shun your destiny. Embrace it." She trailed her finger across my cheek. Despite my revulsion, I felt a longing rise within me that I had never experienced before.

"Think of how effortlessly you could drive off this nation's enemies," she continued. "With what ease you could enslave a fearful, grateful people! You shall gather wealth and power beyond your dreams; you will be feared and obeyed by all who are subject to your desires."

She pressed her soft body to me. I shuddered as she grazed my mouth with hers, its slick wetness staining my lips.

I pulled away, sickened, and drew my sleeve across my

face. "Do not place your stain of death upon me!" I screamed.

She smiled in response. "You will come to love it . . . in time."

I hurried back to my room, blocking the noises I heard as I passed along the corridor. I could picture now what those sounds betrayed, and the images made my mind swim.

I hoped I might exorcise some of my horror by writing down all I have witnessed, but the feeling is as strong in me as ever. My grief at discovering my heritage cripples my heart—and places it beyond all natural feeling.

As I write, the sun begins to rise over the mountaintops and I am haunted by questions:

Who am I?

What am I?

Can Mina be right? Will I become like her in time?

Journal of
Mary Seward

28TH NOVEMBER 1916

While keeping vigil at Lily's bedside, I heard the howling of the wolves growing nearer and nearer. Unnerved, I went over and drew back the drapes from the windows that over-looked the entrance.

Weak dawn light crept into the room. I opened the window and peered out, breathing in the chill morning air, damp and fragrant with pine. The sheer drop to the cobbled courtyard several flights below made my heart shudder.

Moving below me, I saw a dozen or so wolves. They prowled back and forth over the cobbles, the thick gray fur of their broad backs glistening with dew. They moved, turning and weaving around one another like smoke swirling in a hearth.

I saw the sun glint on a window of the main building a couple of floors below. Then a shape was pushed out over the sill of the open casement.

With growing horror I realized it was a man—his face pale and lifeless.

I heard an unseen voice call out from the window, and the wolves gathered below.

A moment later, the body fell, twisting in the air and smashing on the cobbles. The wolves fell upon it and I could hear their greedy snarls as they fought over the flesh.

I raised a hand to my mouth, choking back a scream, and closed the drapes so that I could see no more.

Holding Lily's frail hand in my own, I have recorded this latest abomination with my others. But now I must leave her—for I must find John—and a way for us to escape this wicked place!

Before leaving Lily alone, I fastened the crucifix John had bought her around her neck. I hung garlic around the door and windows and finally, as Van Helsing had shown in Father's notes, crumbled holy wafers into the cracks around the door frame. Though the vampires would be locked in their unnatural slumber now, I wanted to take no chances.

The passageways lay silent, still gripped by shadow, even in the day. I rattled the handles of door after door but found them either locked or empty.

Eventually, in a room off one of the corridors beyond the Great Hall, I found my love. My relief was so great I could have wept!

John was huddled upon an ornate bed. The room was chilly, the fire having died in the grate. Weak sunshine filtered in through the undraped window.

"Mary!" he gasped, stirring at my entrance.

I ran over to him, joyful at our reunion. "John! My love! Are you all right? What happened after I left you?"

A terrible look of anguish clouded his eyes. I reached out to touch him, but he drew away with such speed and force that it shocked me.

"John?" I asked. "What is it?"

"I need to speak with Lily," he muttered.

"I can take you there," I offered. He nodded and let me lead him back the way I had come.

"Is she one of them?" he asked bluntly.

"A vampire? No. She wears a crucifix now and it does not harm her. But John, tomorrow is Saint Andrew's Eve."

"We must all get away before then," he replied. "My mother too. We will find some way to cure her once she is home."

I shook my head, my heart breaking with pity for him. "John," I said gently. "There is no way to cure her but one. . . ."

He turned on me, his face growing red with anger. "You want me to kill my own mother?" he shrieked.

I felt stung by the anger in his words. "She is no longer your mother," I cried. "She is a vampire, a monster!"

My words sent a shudder through him—as though I had hammered a stake into his own heart. I immediately regretted speaking so strongly.

"John, my love . . . I am sorry we cannot save your mother. But we can fight to save ourselves and Lily!"

"If only it were so simple. . . ." John's eyes began to fill with tears. Once more I reached out to him, but he would not let me touch him.

"What happened to you last night?" I asked, suddenly unsure. "Do you still have the crucifix?" I prayed that he had not been bitten by one of those creatures and was heartily relieved when he drew Van Helsing's silver cross from his pocket.

"I cannot tell you what happened." He sighed, suddenly seeming tired and defeated. "I just want to see Lily."

I nodded, deciding it was hopeless to question him further. I led him to Lily's room.

"She's in here," I said, opening the door. "She's still in shock after meeting your mother last night. Please take care not to say anything to alarm her further."

"Do you think I would harm my own sister?" John snapped. He pushed past me and went inside, leaving me stung once more by his tone. I hesitated on the threshold before entering.

John had vexed me in his defense of his mother—but I could understand why he felt as he did.

I decided that I would have to take matters into my own hands. I could not rely on John to kill Rosemary. But as long as Rosemary remained alive, John would be held here—or worse, he might carry out his threat to take her back to England.

Yes, I had to act. Saint Andrew's Eve was only one day away. With the sun high in the sky, it was the perfect opportunity to carry out my plan.

I left John watching over Lily and turned toward the coffin room, Van Helsing's bag in hand.

Trepidation gripped me once more. Images from Father's

notes flashed through my mind: the screaming and writhing of the vampire, blood frothing from its mouth. . . .

But other words from the notes came to me too:

> When this now undead is made to rest as true dead, then the soul of the poor lady whom we love shall again be free. . . . She shall take her place with the other angels.

In killing Rosemary, I consoled myself, I would be releasing her soul. I would be freeing her from her living death.

Taking courage from this thought, I stepped up my pace. I made it across the entrance hall and down the dark stairway to the coffin rooms. With a racing heart, I turned the handle of the door to Rosemary's tomb.

It was locked.

How naive of me! Of course such precautions would now be taken.

John and I had tried, and failed, to kill these vampires yesterday; they would be fools to let us try again.

Perhaps the only way was to leave here—and brave the forest.

I wandered the castle, hunting for a suitable window or door through which we might gain freedom. I discovered no door save the front entrance—where snarling wolves gathered to greet me.

Of the windows, there were only two kinds—small gaps for battlements, too small for a body to fit through, or wide casements that fronted the cliff's very edge. One slip and we would all be dashed by the rocks below.

I hurried back to Lily's room. John lay on the bed beside his sister. They slept together like babes in the wood. I decided to let them rest.

Now I must get some sleep myself before sunset, when we shall again be at our most vulnerable.

Pray God I find a way to escape from this place—before it is too late.

Journal of Lieutenant John Shaw

28TH NOVEMBER 1916

I have just awoken beside dear Lily. Mary sleeps on a chair before the fire. How happy I would once have been just to be among them, watching the two I hold most dear, happy in peaceful slumber.

Now that I know of my dark heritage, I can hardly bear to look at them. Fate seems to have woven a noose around our necks. My hope that we might escape this remote hellhole feels little more than an impossible dream.

Mary stirs and shifts in her seat. Her angelic face catches the sunlight. In that moment, her beauty was so intense, it seemed enough to break my heart.

As I gaze at Lily she seems so innocent, so in need of someone's care.

I must shake myself from my despair and reverie. I cannot give up hope!

We must escape. For Lily and Mary's sakes—I must try.

Tonight, I shall challenge Quincey.

I will defeat him—and we will be gone from this place by sunrise.

Journal of
Mary Seward

28TH NOVEMBER 1916

I was awoken after sunset by a knock on the door. I saw that John had gone. Why did he not rouse me? Lily slept on. I think she must now find solace in unconsciousness.

I opened the door to find Rosemary standing outside.

She saw the garlic strung around the inside of the door

frame and stepped away from it, a hiss of discomfort escaping her pale lips. I felt relief at seeing its effectiveness—but it was not enough to drive her away.

"Please let me see my daughter," she begged, her eyes pleading.

"No," I refused. "How do I know you do not want to make her into a monster like yourself?"

I found it easy to be bold with this creature; she frightened me less than the others, for I sensed a weakness in her that the rest do not disclose.

A look of horror froze Rosemary's face. "I may not be the virtuous woman my children remember, but I could not corrupt one of my own!"

Her emotion seemed genuine. I decided to trust that Rosemary meant Lily no harm.

I unhooked the garlic from the door and stepped out of the way so she might enter. Still, I felt in my pocket for the bottle of holy water, reassured by its presence.

Rosemary stood over her daughter. Hesitantly she reached toward Lily's face. I could see by her trembling hand and by the disgust that curled her lip that the presence of Lily's crucifix disturbed her, but she forced herself to touch Lily's brow. "She has a fever," she said anxiously.

I nodded and fetched the cloth beside Lily's basin. I wet it and held it out for Rosemary.

"Thank you," she murmured, taking it from me. She began to gently dab Lily's burning face with it.

"How unbearable it is, this burden of guilt," she said heavily. "How could I have brought this sweet child into the world to face such a fate?"

"What do you mean?" I asked, filled with a sense of foreboding.

"Lily was chosen at birth to be Quincey's bride," Rosemary told me.

"Chosen?" I asked. "By whom?"

"By Count Tepes, son of Dracula," Rosemary explained. "Twenty years ago I was seduced by him. I bore him a child—a boy."

I could hardly breathe. *John—my own love?* He carries the Tepes blood?

"Afterward, I bore the child of my husband, a daughter. Tepes determined that she would be a mate for his first son, Quincey."

For a few seconds the horror of what I had just learned rendered me speechless. I understood now what Quincey Harker had meant by destiny.

John was sired by one of these monsters—and Lily surrounded by them her whole life.

Then I shook my head. "How could you have given your son and daughter to these vile creatures?" I asked, the abhorrence clear in my voice.

Rosemary looked away in shame. "The same thing that brings Lily here ensnared me too."

"Love?" I asked.

"Desire," Rosemary answered. "When Quincey enthralled my daughter, he awoke something in her she will not be able to ignore—until it is satisfied."

With a pounding heart, I believed her, for I had seen with my own eyes the quivering state to which Quincey was able to reduce poor sweet Lily. I staggered over to one of the windows and opened it, gulping desperately at the cold night air.

After a moment, I felt Rosemary's cold hand on my arm. "You should not lean out so; it is a long way to fall."

I sat back on my chair and Rosemary took my hand. "Lily *must* be saved from the same fate as mine," she said.

"But how?" I asked. "There is no way to escape."

"I know of a secret tunnel down to the valley. It comes out not far from the village." Rosemary's eyes glistened as she spoke.

I leaned forward in my chair, my heart hammering with hope. I gazed deep into Rosemary's red-rimmed eyes and wondered if we could trust her.

"Come, I will show you the entrance," she told me, rising. I followed her out of the bedroom to the huge studded front door.

With some difficulty, she turned the great handle. It opened with a yawning clunk. I looked toward the great staircase, fearful that we had been heard by the vampires within the house. But there was no sign of movement. I crept after Rosemary into the cobbled courtyard.

"Here," she whispered. She hurried toward a great flagstone in the middle of the cobblestone drive. It was weathered and smooth at the edges and I could see a huge iron ring had been bolted in—a handle to lift it, no doubt.

"The entrance is beneath this stone . . ." Rosemary began.

A flutter of wings high overhead startled me. Swooping down toward the castle was a huge black bat. As it flew lower, I heard a squalling, crying sound, like that of a lamb separated from its mother.

Something dangled from the bat's claws—a cloth bag, which squirmed as though some creature struggled inside it.

Rosemary gazed up, a sorrowful look creasing her face. "It is an infant for Tepes," she murmured sorrowfully. "Babe's blood—the most powerful rejuvenator—for him to consume at sundown tomorrow. It will give him strength to attend the wedding ceremony."

I gasped, horrified. "But—we can't let them kill it. We must stop them!"

"And steal from Tepes?" Rosemary's eyes widened with fear. "No. Let us return to Lily, who needs us more."

And so, I am recording these horrors here at Lily's bedside, while she continues her uneasy slumber and Rosemary bathes her fevered brow.

It seems I cannot dispute that John is Tepes's son and Quincey Harker's half brother. It is no matter. John's nature is good and true. He will resist the evil influence of his bloodline and join us in our attempt to escape.

Journal of
Lieutenant John Shaw

28TH NOVEMBER (CONTINUED)

Full of resolve, I rose and slipped from Lily's bedroom, where Mary and my sister still slept. I found Quincey in the drawing room. He sat in one of the ornate armchairs.

"Good evening, brother," he said.

"You cannot hold us here," I told him.

"You cannot escape your destiny," he replied calmly.

"We are leaving. Tonight," I stated.

Quincey stood and whirled on me. "If you try it, you will be killed! You and Lily and your precious fiancée! Is that what you want?"

"I will kill you *first*," I threatened. My collar felt tight around me as my neck throbbed with rage "I will come while you sleep and knock down any door that stands in my way. I will hammer stakes through your heart, you unnatural monster!"

Quincey reared his hand back and struck me across the face.

It was merely a slap, yet the force of the blow threw me backward. I flew through the air and crashed into the far wall of the room. I landed hard and scrambled to my knees.

Quincey strode over and stared down at me impassively. "This urge to destroy your own kind will not last long," he promised. He turned and left the room.

"I despise you!" I screamed. Quincey paid me no mind.

"There is no other way than this, John," he called over his shoulder. "You will see."

I swore at Quincey's back. But my threat echoed back to me—empty and hollow—in the great room.

I sank down and began to weep with anger and despair.

A moment later, I turned at the rustle of satin beside me. Mina stood before the fire.

"You are a fool to weep," her voice said smoothly.

"Why?" I spat the word at her. "Why am I a fool? I am impotent here—powerless over my destiny. I am prey, an insignificant life, toyed with by all of you—until the appointed hour."

Mina smiled. Her sharp teeth glinted in the firelight. "But John," she said. "You are not one of the prey; you are a predator. You will only be weak so long as you fight against your true nature."

A wickedly playful look glittered in her eye. "Accept your destiny. Then you may challenge Quincey—and beat him."

"No!" I shouted. "No!"

I ran from the drawing room. Perhaps there was still a chance for me to save what is good and true.

*Journal of
Mary Seward*

28TH NOVEMBER (CONTINUED)

John returned near midnight, hammering wildly on our door. "We must leave this place right now!" he exclaimed. He strode over to the bed, threw back Lily's covers, and scooped her in his arms. "You will come too, Mother," he said.

Rosemary turned her eyes away. "If only I could, John. But what happens when sunrise comes?" She looked at him then. "I was lost to you years ago. Take Lily and Mary. There is still a chance for you." She gently kissed them both, then drifted over to the door to return to her dark resting place.

"Your mother has told me of a secret passage," I told John, grabbing Van Helsing's bag. "Follow me."

Nothing stood in our way as we made our way to the front door. I turned the heavy handle and pulled it open. The courtyard beyond was shrouded in mist, but I could see the flagstone entrance to the tunnel ahead of us. We were close to freedom!

"Come! We are nearly there," I called out.

"Yes, but you would be wiser to return."

Quincey Harker's voice behind us struck horror once more into my heart. I took the bottle of holy water from my pocket, swung round, and held it up toward him. "You cannot stop us!" I shouted, refusing to be dominated by the fear that rose inside me.

He raised a sardonic eyebrow. "Is that so?" he said coolly. But I saw his eyes, tinged red with fury at my audacity. He looked out at the forests beyond.

A great howl rose in the misty night air.

The wolves.

"The wolves will not harm me," John said in a voice as calm as Harker's. I looked at him, unnerved by the similarity.

"They will do as I command them to," Harker told him quietly. "They might recognize your bloodline, but they observe my leadership."

Into the courtyard came the wolves, saliva dripping from their sharp white fangs. My heart sank as I saw them creep forward, their rippling pelts obscuring the flagstone that was to have been our gateway to safety.

Quincey stared at John. "I told you. They will sooner rip you all to shreds. There is no escaping your fate."

I gazed at John—at Lily hanging limply in his arms. It was more than I could bear. We were trapped between two terrible ends.

John stared back at me, his eyes wild with indecision.

I grasped his arm and led him back inside.

Seeing their sport retreat, the wolves rushed up to the doorway, but Harker held up his hand. "No," he growled.

Immediately the wolves halted and sank to the ground.

As Harker shut the door on them, I turned and led John back up to Lily's room.

Our latest failure seems to have broken John. He has stormed out. I cannot bear to think what will happen now.

As I write, I can see the wolves milling around the courtyard. A feeling of claustrophobia threatens to overwhelm me.

We are utterly at Quincey Harker's mercy.

*Journal of
Lieutenant John Seward*

28TH NOVEMBER (CONTINUED)

All hope is gone now. I am but a waste of a man, unable to protect myself—or those I love—from the darkness.

After our attempt at escape, I placed Lily back in her bed and installed Mary at her side. I could not look at either of them—I had failed them so miserably.

I left to wander the halls of the castle.

These dank walls will contain me for the rest of my days, I thought. I shall never see England again, and my dear Mary will never have her wedding in the sunshine.

I cursed myself then—and cursed Quincey all the more. I would damn him to hell for dragging us all into this nightmare, but it seemed that he, and all of us, already resided there.

Come . . . Come to me . . .

I heard a whisper, echoing softly in the corridor.

Come to me, my sweet . . .

Whose voice was it that beckoned?

Was it Mary's? Was she in danger?

I followed the sound. It drew me down a dimly lit passageway toward a door. Behind the heavy wood, I could hear someone whimpering.

I turned the knob and entered silently.

Inside the room was a huge four-poster bed, its heavy canopy draped in purple velvet. A red-haired young woman was curled up on one side of it, sobbing quietly.

Mina Harker stood on the other side. She gazed at the girl, her eyes smoldering. "Come to me, my pet. I swear you will feel no pain."

The girl's tear-reddened eyes grew wide with fear as Mina lay down beside her.

"Come, my innocent," Mina crooned. "Turn to me."

The girl turned. Immediately her face took on the aspect

of one mesmerized. She was enthralled by Mina's stare. Her sobbing ceased.

She embraced Mina then, and my eyes were drawn to the lines of her body, showing through her flimsy undergown.

"Do not be afraid," Mina cooed. "You shall feel more pleasure than pain."

The girl shuddered, yet continued to lie in the arms of this temptress. I stood and watched, enthralled by the tension that filled the room.

Mina stroked the girl's flushed cheek. She let her fingers trail on down the girl's neck and along her shoulder. She pushed away the thin fabric to expose the curve of a breast. I swallowed, my mouth suddenly dry.

Mina looked up at me then, her mouth curled into a knowing smile. "Is she not splendid?" she purred.

I could not answer. A stirring began in my belly I had never felt before.

"Such soft skin," Mina whispered. She leaned over and pressed a chaste kiss on the girl's forehead. Then she lowered her lips to the girl's mouth and then her neck. She kissed the girl again and again, moving lower with each touch of her lips toward the girl's now heaving bosom. I felt my own passion stirring. It grew as I heard the girl groan with pleasure.

I drew closer to the bed, eager to see what Mina would do next.

The girl lay back against the lilac bedding, her eyes closed. As Mina continued to caress her, I could see a pulse flickering at the base of her creamy throat. A tiny moan escaped me at the sight of it.

Mina licked her lips, then drew them back to reveal her sharp fangs. In a swift movement she lunged down and sank her teeth into the girl's arched, willing flesh.

Her eyes jerked open in panic and fluttered unseeingly as she flailed against Mina's hold. But Mina clung on, pressing the girl down. Twitching with pleasure, she sucked the lifeblood from her.

Though I shuddered in horror at the sight, my body throbbed with a rapture I could not control. When Mina was done, she lifted her head to watch me. Seeing my excitement, she left the dazed and gasping girl on the bed and wrapped herself around me.

She kissed me then with lips still warm and wet with blood. The iron tang of it exhilarated me—consumed me. I surrendered, pulling Mina closer, relishing the softness of her body beneath my hands. Her lips dragged away from mine and pressed their way along my jaw toward my neck.

I knew what she intended to do.

I heard myself whisper, "No . . ." But my body overruled me. It arched forward, desperate for that final kiss, the one that would sink me into darkness forever. We sank, entwined to the floor. And when the sweet agony of her piercing bite gripped me, I convulsed with an ecstasy I could never have imagined.

I awoke in the room sometime later to find myself alone.

I was not dead, and for a brief moment I hoped against all reason that the dark activities had been a product of my tormented mind. But as I heaved myself from the rug, I felt tenderness in my neck, then saw drops of blood on the ruffled lilac sheets.

I remembered Dr. Seward's notes.

Mina's kiss has begun my transformation from mortal to immortal.

What have I done?

*Journal of
Mary Seward*

29TH NOVEMBER 1916

Lily awoke just before dawn. The fire in the grate cast a rosy glow over her pale skin. "Mary?" she whispered.

I gave her water to drink and stroked her hair as she gradually roused into full wakefulness.

"I dreamt I saw my mother again," she murmured, creasing her brow as she tried to remember.

I took her hand in mine. "Lily, there is so much you should know," I began. "I think it is best if I tell you everything."

"Everything?" she repeated tremulously.

With a heavy heart I began. "You have been deceived, Lily, most terribly deceived."

I told her of Harker's true nature, of the plan that had deprived Lily of her mother and father, and how she had been raised by Antanasia in preparation to be a demon's wife.

With every revelation I waited for her to scream or cry or swoon away, but she only stared at me blankly until I wondered if she were really awake or merely in another state of stupor.

"Lily, do you understand?" I asked her when I'd finished.

Her eyes searched mine and she nodded slowly.

I put my arms around her. "Why do you not cry?" I implored, my own eyes filling with tears of frustration and pity.

She did not answer but gently drew away from me and climbed from her bed. I watched as she made her way to the white gown hanging from a dressing screen in the corner.

Someone had placed the gown here—in her room—while we attempted our escape. It was to be her wedding gown. And this, St. Andrew's Eve, her wedding night.

She fingered the fabric delicately, admiring it with a melancholy expression. "Quincey made me happier than I'd ever thought possible," she said quietly. "To have felt that, for even a short while, is more than I'd expected of this life."

"But you *will* reject him now," I responded. "Won't you?"

She remained silent.

"Lily," I implored her. "Tell me you'll reject him."

After several long moments she turned to me. "Where is John?" she asked.

"He's resting," I lied. I did not want to add to her distress. The truth was, I had no idea where her brother might be.

"You must rest too," Lily replied.

I nodded.

It is true, my limbs grow heavy now with sleep. When I awaken, I shall take my courage in both hands and search the castle to find out where Harker sleeps. I *cannot* give up and must keep on looking for a chink in his armor.

CHAPTER 22

Journal of
Lieutenant John Shaw

Early this morning, Mary came to find me. She fixed me in a sorrowful gaze.

I lifted a hand to my neck, hoping that my collar covered the marks Mina left there.

Shame engulfed me like flames. I could barely meet her eyes.

"What do you want?" I demanded. "Why do you look upon me so?"

"Tonight is Saint Andrews' Eve," she said. "I only wonder how we might comfort one another in this dreadful hour."

I bristled at her soothing tone, convinced that she was patronizing me—that she knew I had yielded to Mina's cruel seduction.

"You are lying!" I yelled.

Mary stood her ground, betraying only faint shock at my attack.

"I have failed to save you and Lily!" I shouted at her. "I have failed to save myself. I should not have brought you here. You hate me for doing so."

"I do not blame you," Mary said softly. "It was I who volunteered to come."

"And I agreed—because I was too weak to face this alone." I flexed my fists, trying to contain my fury. "I am *still* too weak, and you stand there and stare at me like I am a child to be pitied!"

"John, I understand. We are the victims of a plot more terrible than we had imagined. We must continue to think about our escape—and not give in to despair." Mary's voice was sweetness itself, but the more she tried to pacify me, the more I felt her distance.

She began to pace the room, her face set in deep concentration.

As I watched her, my temper flared higher. She still had hope, the foolish girl! She refused to give up!

Then another thought entered my mind and filled me with a shame I could not bear.

My resolve was so weak, it could not even match a woman's!

I could bear to look at Mary no longer. The sight of her

repulsed me. I stormed out of the room, leaving her in her confusion.

Dawn was still nearly an hour away. I did not welcome its coming, wanting instead for the darkness to linger. Dismayed by this alien sensation, I went in search of liquor, thinking it might ease my emotions.

As I entered the drawing room, Mina was standing before the fireplace, her dress illuminated by the flames. She smiled knowingly at me.

I flashed her a look of disgust and strode over to the cabinet to pour myself a whiskey.

"You will not quench your thirst that way," she observed in silken tones.

Her voice stung like salt rubbed in a wound. I flung my glass into the fireplace. It shattered on the grate before her feet. "Shut up!" I yelled.

She did not flinch, only smiled again, her eyes beginning to glow red as she fixed her gaze on mine.

I felt my fury begin to melt into desire.

Mina walked slowly across to me. "That's better," she said. She began stroking my cheek.

It was as though my flesh remembered her caress and welcomed its return. She kissed my lips and I grasped her and pulled her to me.

This was not like before; I was not overwhelmed by my

passion, but felt a growing power in me to control it. I kissed her hard, hating her as much as I desired her, wanting to make her feel the power that was awakening in me.

"That's right, John," she breathed between kisses. "Accept your destiny, revel in the pleasure it can bring you."

I silenced her with another kiss, not wanting to hear her gloating sermons. "I cannot live as I did before," I told her, "weak and afraid."

"Once more," she whispered, "and you will have all the power you need."

I felt her lips on my mouth, on my cheek, on my throat. There was no place left for me in the world I'd left behind, but here I could have all the power and pleasure I desired.

Better still, I could finally defeat Harker and punish him for his ruination of everything I loved.

"Finish it!" I ordered, shaking her.

I shuddered with satisfaction as I felt her teeth pierce my neck.

There are no words to describe the draining of my life. I do not even know if I lost consciousness. I only remember Mina's glowing eyes, the image of which seemed to burn on when dawn drove her back to her resting place.

I climbed the stairs toward the peace and seclusion of my bed.

Drapes covered the windows of my room when I reached

it. I welcomed the gloom, safe from the hateful daylight outside.

I feel a languorous fatigue creeping through my bones.
And now that I have recorded this momentous passing, I
shall sleep a long and dreamless sleep, my heart calm at last.

*Journal of
Lily Shaw*

29TH NOVEMBER 1916

How pretty the wedding gown looked on me. Though I had
no mirror, dawn had hardly yet lightened the sky outside and
I was still able to view my reflection in the windows. I'd
slipped the gown on as soon as Mary had left, and the sight
of it made me long for Quincey so!

I had promised Mary I would not stray, but I could not
help myself.

I stole from my room and went in search of my beloved, calling for him as I wandered the shadowy corridors. My calls
echoed along the stone walls, sometimes coming back to me—
making me wonder who else could be calling out so desperately.

And suddenly he was there . . . coming to me from out of
the shadows.

I fell against him, desperate to feel his solid chest against my own.

He held me for a moment. Then spoke with a curious concern in his voice. "Lily, why is Mary not with you? Let me take you back to your room."

I gazed up at Quincey's beautiful face. "My love . . ." I whispered, reaching out to touch his smooth cheek. "Do you like the gown on me?"

With a deep, fathomless expression in his eyes, he ran his fingertips gently along the lace-edged neck of my wedding gown. He nodded. "You are beautiful," he told me softly. "The most beautiful creature to ever walk in this place. But Lily, you must know by now . . . you must realize what sort of monster it is that you love."

"So . . . it is all true . . ." I said brokenly.

Quincey nodded. "I'm sorry, Lily. . . ."

His apology—the confirmation from his own lips—nearly undid me. But he cradled me so tenderly in his arms, wiping my tears as I wept. God help me, my heart remained his. . . .

"Hush, my dearest." He spoke soothingly. "Please, don't cry."

"How can I dry my eyes?" I asked, gasping out the words. "You have never loved me. You merely carried out your father's wishes."

He took my chin in his hand and gently turned my face toward his. "I may not have told you the truth. But in my affection I did not deceive you. I did not think it possible for a heart as black as mine, but I have fallen for you, Lily. Your very presence brings me a joy I have not felt since I was a boy."

"Then how can you ask me to be a part of this life—of these horrors I cannot bear to imagine?" I asked.

Sadness played upon his face. "There can be no other way. But I promise you this—I will protect you from all that offends you. You will be safe and comfortable with me here. And when your transformation is complete, we can truly live together for all eternity." He paused. "I promise you, Lily. I will do everything in my power to ensure that you are happy."

I gazed at him—my beloved. His words were so sweet. In that moment, I felt that I could believe him.

"Lily, will you be my bride?" Quincey asked.

I nodded, and he held me so tightly I felt the true force of his affection for me.

"Dawn is coming," he said when the embrace was through. "I must go. Tonight will be the beginning for us, my darling. Do not be afraid. I will be by your side."

He kissed my hand, turned, and strode off to I know not where. I stood in the empty corridor—struggling with my wild emotions.

I had asked for an eternity by Quincey's side—and now I could truly have it. But at what price?

I wish I had never awoken from my innocent slumber to

this unbearable reality. When I leaf through earlier pages in this journal, it is as though I wrote from another life. Every hope has since been dashed.

And yet I long to feel Quincey's embrace once more. I love him still, though I know what he is. I cannot let go of the tenderness I have seen in his eyes. I cannot believe he does not love me.

Enough. As Quincey said, there is no other way. I will go and prepare for what must be done.

*Journal of
Mary Seward*

29TH NOVEMBER 1916

I awoke to find the day almost gone! The sun was setting. Lily sat at the window, motionless, lost in her own thoughts.

I was furious with myself for sleeping through the hours of safety, but nothing would be gained from regret. Taking garlic and a bottle of holy water with me, I left the room, telling Lily to lock the door behind me.

I made my way down the staircase and crossed the entrance hall to the wing opposite ours. The layout of the wing was a mirror of the one Lily and I inhabited. I tried each of the doors. All were locked, save the last.

I pushed the door open, and my breath stopped in my throat. It was a large, opulent bedroom. A British Army captain's uniform hung on the side of a massive wardrobe. I'd found Harker's lair.

Relief and suspicion rose in me at once, as he had not locked his door. Heart thumping, I looked around, ready to flee if I had to.

The large bed was empty. I wondered if Harker ever slept there or if he, like his grandfather, needed the sanctuary of a coffin in which to rest. Perhaps now, returned to his home, he had embraced the vampire custom and chose to lie in one of the coffin rooms. I hoped so—I hoped he was far from here.

I stepped inside. A huge desk sat before one of the windows, cluttered with papers. Along one wall were rows of books, a lifetime's reading. Not knowing when he might return, I hastily rummaged through Harker's possessions, desperately looking for something that might provide a key to our escape.

The contents of his bookshelves ranged from classics I had read myself to darkly titled books on the occult that I feared even to touch.

I came upon a collection of journals. With trembling fingers I plucked the most recent one from the shelf and began to scan its pages.

Journal of
Captain Quincey Harker

I wish I had not brought that poor sweet creature here. She is like a lamb among lions. Why couldn't Father have chosen a less gentle and innocent mate for me?

Now that I am returned to the bosom of my family, I feel my destiny pressing on me as never before. The weight seems, at times, more than I can bear. Out in the fields of France, where my victims were also my enemies, it was easy to slake my bloodlust. But remorse pricks at my heart when I am compelled to ruin those I have grown to know.

Do I really want this dynasty of gore and darkness that has been planned for me?

Perhaps, if Lily Shaw is at my side . . .

So gentle and yielding is she that she begs for me to take her.

I want only to ease her fears. But she is right to be afraid. The life that Father has determined for her will change her forever—as it changed my mother, as it changed Rosemary Shaw.

As it now changes her son.

Like Lily, John Shaw must be transformed by St.

Andrew's Eve, and no doubt Mother is making quick work
of it. Shaw is so weak-willed and impressionable that it will
barely be a challenge for her.

When I look at Shaw, I wonder what Father sees in him. What makes him believe that John is suitable to restore our bloodline?

It does not matter.

It is truly out of my hands. And by tomorrow night, Father's wishes will be fulfilled. I will have completed my destiny.

*Journal of
Mary Seward*

29TH NOVEMBER (CONTINUED)

The journal slipped from my fingers. Could Quincey's suspicions be true? Was Mina Harker seducing John? Turning him into a vampire?

My heart railed against doubting my love. Yet his demeanor was so changed, so hateful since arriving here. . . .

I shook my head.

No, no. It could not be. John loved me. He could not be lost to me forever!

My mind whirled, thinking of all that had happened. I was not aware of the time that passed.

Then I heard footsteps approaching in the hallway outside. I stood and faced the door, realizing that I stood in almost total darkness.

I gasped. Night had fallen! How could I have been so careless?

I reached for the bottle of holy water in my pocket just as Quincey entered.

The look of surprise on his face gave way to cold rage.

"So we are alone," he muttered. I gripped my bottle of holy water harder, taking strength in its presence. But I was determined I should not reveal my fear and so faced Harker boldly.

"I know of your doubts," I challenged him.

Quincey's eyes glittered as he returned my unflinching gaze.

"Even *you* cannot bring yourself to spoil such an innocent," I pressed on.

"I must honor the house of Tepes," Quincey replied. "Lily can not escape her destiny."

"I will do everything in my power to ensure that she does," I warned him.

He raised an eyebrow, as though my threat intrigued but did not worry him. "I shall enjoy watching you try," he said.

Legs trembling, I crossed the room, my heart stopping

for a moment as I passed him, and went through the open door.

I looked back and saw him just standing there, still as a statue.

I turned a corner and began to run as fast as I could, back toward the haven that I shared with Lily.

What relief I felt when I saw John outside Lily's door. "John—thank goodness! I was so worried!" I called. He looked so strong and healthy that I thought Harker's suspicions about him could not possibly be true.

But then he turned to look at me. I saw his eyes were as hard as glass.

Then, out of the shadows, stepped Mina.

I faltered, dreading what this might mean. As I drew nearer I noticed, with repulsion, the familiar way Mina rested her hand on John's shoulder.

"John," I pleaded, "do not give up the fight. It's not over yet. I've seen Quincey's journal—"

John cut me off with a contemptuous laugh. "Have you been reading other people's diaries again, Mary?"

I flinched at the malice in his tone, but he continued to accuse me.

"She likes to pry, you know," he told Mina. "In fact, the first thing she did when I was brought to the sanatorium was steal my journal. She delighted in my private thoughts while I lay helpless in a hospital bed."

"Please, John, don't talk so," I begged him. "You love me. We are to be wed. . . ."

Mina glared at me scornfully. "I don't understand what you ever saw in a creature like her," she sneered.

"She took advantage of me when I was weak," he muttered, turning to her.

A stab of pain seared my heart at his wicked, cruel words—but I felt it crack when I saw the two large puncture wounds on his neck. They were just as Father described them in his notes. The same wounds suffered by Lucy Westenra.

My stomach lurched as if the floor had suddenly dropped out from under me. John was now a vampire. He truly was lost to me.

I took the cork from my bottle of holy water. "Get away from the door," I screamed. "Leave Lily the last few hours of peace she will have—until your evil ceremony destroys all that is good in her!"

As I waved the bottle at them a few drops scattered in their direction. Mina hissed in pain as a drop caught her hand. The acrid smell of burning flesh filled the damp air and her skin turned as black as if it bore a bullet wound.

She clasped her hand and glared at me, her eyes burning red. "Enjoy your peace while you can," she hissed. "The ceremony is tonight. And once Lily is one of us, she'll have no further want of you—except, perhaps, as dessert."

I fell, weeping, into Lily's room. Mina said nothing as I took every sacred thing in our possession and shielded the entrance.

As I regained my breath, I opened my eyes—and realized that Lily was not there. A letter sat on the bed, addressed in Lily's own hand. I picked it up and read the contents.

Letter from Miss Lily Shaw to Miss Mary Seward

Dear Mary,

Forgive me, my dear friend, for leaving you, but I can do nothing else.

Though I know the terrible truth—Quincey has confirmed it to me himself—I shall be drawn to him for as long as I live. Every fiber of me yearns for him. How tempting it is to take him as he is, to join him and spend eternity in his company. But I cannot live a life filled with evil and death—and I cannot live without him.

And so, I must end it.

Take care of John, Mary. Be happy in his genuine love. I pray your strength and goodness are enough to overcome the dangers you will face.

Do not weep for my passing. I tasted happiness once, and that must be enough.

Your eternal friend,

Lily

My heart, already hammering, lurched in fear. I glanced toward the open window, its heavy drapes billowed outward into the chill air.

A piece of white lace hung from the latch. "No!" I cried.

I rushed over and forced myself to look down to the jagged rocks below.

In my heart, I already knew what adorned them.

Lily had freed herself from this wretched place.

I sobbed with such passion then that I thought I would not stop.

I cannot help but believe that once restored to her home in England, she would have learned to forget Harker. I pray God forgives her for this, her final sin, and takes her sweet soul to where it may be safe from evil and misery.

I smiled bitterly. At least she was spared the knowledge of John's corruption. How acutely I feel the irony of her words. *Be happy in his love.*

That was impossible now.

But I would not succumb to this evil plot.

I would not believe, as Harker did, that this was a destiny I could not escape.

No, I would fight my way out, or I would die in my attempt to be free.

CHAPTER 23

Journal of
Captain Quincey Harker

29TH NOVEMBER 1916

I strode through the great entrance hall and gazed at the bustle around me. The ceremony my father had planned was only hours away. Frenzied arrangements were taking place.

As I watched the preparations, I considered the weight of what the next few hours would bring. Inevitably, my thoughts wandered to Lily.

Was she dressing right now? Was she frightened? Confused? I wanted to ease her fears if I could—to convince her of the efforts I would make to ensure her happiness.

I decided to speak with her and walked swiftly her room. I knocked gently on the door and called out her name.

There was no answer from within. Clearly Miss Seward was occupied elsewhere—and so much the better. Lily and I could speak without interruption.

"Lily, are you asleep?" I called when still no answer came.

Finally, I pressed down on the handle. The door opened and I glanced around the room. It was empty, but I did not think it odd.

I turned and saw the open window, the wind whipping the curtains like great black wings. I moved to close it—and glanced down.

There, on the rocks below, I noticed a figure illuminated in the lights from the castle. Bright red slashes stained the lace of its white gown. Its position on the jagged cliff was twisted and unnatural. Mahogany hair billowed around its skull.

I looked closer, and my breath stopped in my chest. I felt a pain so intense, I could not remain standing. I fell awkwardly into a chair facing the bed.

It was Lily—my dear Lily—dead on the ground below.

I needed no one to tell me what had happened. My bride, my love, had preferred death to joining me in eternal life.

I raised my head to the sky and cried out in anguish. I would never see her face again. Never know her passionate kiss. Then the tears came—a strange sensation I had not experienced since my transformation.

What of our destiny? I wondered. What of Father's plans?

All these years of preparation made them seem like an absolute certainty—an end that no one could alter or escape.

Lily had proved that notion wrong with one final act.

Perhaps . . . I thought. Perhaps I have been wrong about my destiny.

Perhaps there is another way. . . .

I shook my head.

I could not think of that now. Instead, I would go to Rosemary.

I was the reason her daughter's life had ended. I must be the one to deliver the horrible news.

Journal of
Mary Seward

29TH NOVEMBER (CONTINUED)

I crept from our tower into the depths of the castle, toward the vampires' crypt. Such preparations were going on for the wedding ceremony that I was hardly noticed. I snuck to Rosemary Shaw's resting place.

In one hand I held the lamp, and in the other I gripped Van Helsing's bag. Knowing I was protected by his weapons gave no ease to my breast. My heart hammered with fear as I descended the final staircase that led to the coffin room.

I knew I must leave tonight—before Lily's body was discovered. And I hoped that Rosemary could help me. There was information I needed from her—and something I must do before I made my escape.

I pushed open the heavy oak door, remembering the last time I had been there, with John at my side. The memory jabbed at me, filling me with grief, but I forced it away.

I could see the shape of an unlit lamp ensconced in the wall ahead. I hurried to light it and another beside. Rosemary lay in her coffin, the cover open. Mina's coffin was, I noticed with relief, empty.

How gaunt Rosemary looked compared with the rosy bloom I'd seen in Mina's cheeks. I could not help but feel pity for her. She was like a beggar among the others, unable to relish this life, but driven by a hunger she could not resist.

I used my crucifix then, holding it over Rosemary to rouse her from her slumber. She woke with a violent start.

"I am sorry," I apologized, placing the cross in my pocket. "I did not know how else to wake you."

"Mary, what is it?" Rosemary asked.

"It is Lily," I told her. "She is dead."

Rosemary searched my face, her brow knit in fear and confusion. "But how?" she asked. "She is Quincey's. The others here would not dare . . ."

"She left this," I said, handing her Lily's suicide note.

Rosemary read her daughter's words. As she neared the

end, her face twisted in pain. For a long time, she simply stared at the paper. Then, finally, she spoke.

"How different from me my daughter became," she whispered, tears forming at the corners of her eyes. "This life was meant to be an escape from pain and death; Lily embraces death rather than remain."

"I am sorry," I repeated.

"Do not be," Rosemary said. "She is free. And in that, I envy her."

"I cannot be here any longer," I said, anxious to make my intentions known. "Lily is gone, and John has become—"

"One of us," Rosemary interrupted. "I know."

"If I stay, I will surely be killed," I continued, "but I need your help."

"What can *I* possibly do?" Rosemary asked. "I am too weak to fight the rest of the demons here."

"I do not wish for you to fight. Only to tell me where the child is."

"The child?" Rosemary asked.

"The babe we saw brought to the castle," I clarified. "I will take her when I make my escape."

"Mary, no," Rosemary argued. "The babe is Tepes's. It is too dangerous for—"

"Something pure and innocent must emerge from all this wickedness!" I yelled, interrupting her. "I will not leave that child behind. Now please, tell me where she is."

Rosemary revealed the place where the babe was being kept. They would be taking it to Tepes soon, she said. I must hurry.

I turned to go but could not leave, for Rosemary asked one favor of me in return. . . .

"Please, do what I ask with a clear conscience," she begged.

I agreed. She lay back, and I waited for her to once again fall into slumber.

After a few moments, I removed a stake from my bag, then lifted out the hammer. Resting the wooden tip on Rosemary's breast, I pointed it at her heart. Her garment dimpled where the stake rested.

Steeling my soul, I raised the hammer and aimed a blow so fierce with intent that, as I write now, I am still amazed at my own strength.

The stake pierced clothing, then skin, to the flesh beneath. Rosemary writhed in the coffin, screeching with such terror that the chamber reverberated with the noise. Blood spat from the wound, spraying my face. It frothed from her nose, her mouth.

I hit the stake again and hammered it through to her heart.

Finally, she fell still.

I wiped my face on my sleeve. I heaved, wanting to vomit. But I could not fall apart. Not now. I forced myself to take deep breaths.

I turned to make my way from the crypt—and saw Harker in the open doorway.

"Rosemary," he whispered. His face held a stunned expression.

Frenzied with terror, I felt for the glass bottle in my pocket. "I will never forgive you for what you have done to John and Lily!" I cried as I uncorked the bottle with my thumb. "I am leaving this place!"

I sprayed the contents of the bottle at Harker's face.

He ducked, but some drops caught his cheek. He yelled in pain as his flesh burned with a hissing sound. He gasped and stumbled, but I did not wait to see what injuries I had inflicted.

I ran as fast as I could through the door and up a back staircase to the north wing. As I climbed the steps, I heard a whimpering cry.

I tracked the noise to a small arched doorway set back from the second-floor corridor. My heart racing, I pushed the door open and peered inside.

It was a plain room, furnished with an ancient cot, an old nursing chair, and a crib. A tall angular woman was stooped over the fireplace, prodding the coals with a poker. She turned and at the sight of me hissed in anger. She bared her sharp fangs and lunged toward me.

I took the final bottle of holy water, uncorked it, and flung its contents at the woman. She screamed in horror as the water hit its mark. Flesh dripped from her face and hands, revealing first muscle, then ancient, yellowed bone.

She staggered backward toward the fireplace, clutching her face in agony. The flames from the fire seemed to reach out and catch her long skirts—racing upward, greedily consuming them. She fell to the floor, writhing like a soul in hell.

I flung the vial away and grabbed the baby from the crib. A quick glance told me that the child was frightened but physically sound. I slung the screaming infant onto my hip and ran from the stinking, smoking place.

I held it close, pressing it to my hammering heart.

I ran with all my might down the stairs again and into the courtyard toward the tunnel shown to me by Rosemary. It was our last hope.

My heart pounded with such ferocity it seemed to hammer against my breastbone. I glanced nervously up at the castle windows and I pulled the iron ring to lift the great flagstone.

My heart froze in panic. I hadn't the strength to lift the heavy stone. I crouched and pulled again, cursing my weakness.

I heard a shuffling behind me as someone approached. I looked up to see Quincey Harker towering over us.

I made no move as he leaned down toward us, his chiseled jaw almost grazing my cheek. I shuddered as I smelled Lily's faint perfume still upon him.

My life was over, I was certain. I said a quick prayer as Harker's demon eyes gazed into mine.

He placed his hand over my own as I held the ring. I felt his iron grip tighten and I yelped in pain.

He pulled and lifted the great flagstone, and I saw the passage beneath. I stared up at him in utter confusion.

"Go," he said, letting my hand slide from under his. I felt rooted to the spot by my bewilderment.

"I will fight you to the end," I warned him.

"I know," he answered softly.

Then, without another word, I hurried down the stone steps. I was only a few paces into the tunnel when I heard the flagstone lowered back into place.

CHAPTER 24

*Journal of
Captain Quincey Harker*

Lily is dead. There is little I can do for her now.

But I have protected Miss Seward and helped her to leave this hellish place.

I believe that Lily would approve.

Afterward, I sat in my room, numbed with pain. My cheek smarted where the holy water had blistered it.

Near dawn, something was thrown up at my window. I heard John's voice calling me from below, over and over. His taunting tone filled me with foreboding and I moved quickly from my bed to see what excited him.

Shading my eyes, I drew back the drapes.

John stood below, recklessly exposed. Seeing my shadow move to the window, he began to laugh. "Look, dear brother!" he called. "I'm about to pay you in kind!"

I peered through the repellent rays to where John's already reddened hand was pointing. Against a long-dead tree trunk rested a black shape.

"I was careful to shield her as I carried her out here, for I would hate for you to miss the full glory of her destruction," John sneered.

I stared on at the strange form attached to the tree. A sickening realization gripped my belly.

"You taught me well, Captain Harker," he sneered. "Perhaps you remember Private Smith?" John pulled away the cloak that covered what I now already knew to be there.

It was Mother. John left her there and quickly made his way into the safety of the castle.

In moments, the sun rose, awaking her with a start. For the first time in my life I saw her eyes widen in fear. She writhed against her bindings as her face began to blister and bubble like pork on a spit. I imagined the flesh sizzling and crackling, though I could hear nothing but her agonized screams. Smoke poured through the satin of her dress.

I watched helplessly as her body crumbled away, charred to ashes. Then a wild rage possessed me.

I turned and ran from my room, taking the stairs three at a time. John was waiting for me in the crypt. "I did not realize what a dry old stick she was!" he gloated.

I grabbed him by the throat. "Why did you do it?" I spat, struck by how little fear he betrayed as I began squeezing the breath out of him. His blue eyes had grown as icy as my mother's used to be.

His lips drew back in a grimace that showed teeth long and sharp. He gripped my wrists with a strength that, disconcertingly, almost matched my own. "You should not have killed *my* mother." He gulped, dragging my hands from his throat.

So that was it.

"You are mistaken," I said, struggling against his grip. "I had nothing to do with Rosemary's death."

"I saw you coming from the coffin room, and then I found her body!" John accused. "You drove a stake into her heart. Who else could have done it?"

"Who was it that brought stakes into this place?" I asked.

John let go of my arms. His hands fell away. "Mary," he whispered. His face hardened as shock turned to anger. "Mary!" He grasped his head in his hands as though it might split in two and roared with an uncontrolled rage. "I'll kill her."

I struggled to mask my shock. "Too late," I told him lightly. "She is gone. And so is Lily. Dead. She threw herself from her window." I waited to see how this news would move him. But no sign of grief broke through the expression of rage that gripped his face.

"So she chose to die rather than marry you," he sneered.

I flinched at his words. "Are you not at all sorry?" I demanded.

He shrugged. "She has proved herself weak. We are stronger without her."

I stared at him. Though I had spent many more days in the shadows than him, my soul had never been as black as his.

"Enough!" I snapped. And I strode back into the castle.

At sundown, my destination will be a place never before visited without invitation.

LATER

As the sun was setting I fetched the key that would give me access to the tower of the north wing. I yanked the door open and made my way up the narrow spiral staircase.

I reached the studded door at the top, lifted the latch, and entered.

"Father!" I shouted.

Tepes stepped out from the shadows; his body, though stooped, still hinted at the great strength it once harnessed. "Quincey . . ." he breathed. "Why have we not begun the wedding celebrations?" Concern lit his rheumy eyes.

"There will be no celebrations," I told him shortly. "The bride you chose for me preferred death to becoming one of us."

Father's hands dropped to his sides. "How could you have let her get away?" he demanded.

"Surely 'how' does not matter," I snapped. "Rosemary is

dead. And I am leaving this place. John may have it all. I want no part of my inheritance. I no longer have the stomach for it."

Father's expression changed to one of icy threat. In an instant, he no longer looked frail. "Whatever has happened, you will stay! It is your duty!" he bellowed at me.

"All I have done is *your* duty!" I spat back. "I will do it no longer. This future you've planned for me—this *destiny,* Father, is not glory. It is ruination. I will go now to find my own way."

I turned toward the door.

With a great roar, Father leapt at me, hurling me against the wall.

He lunged again, but this time I was prepared. I grabbed him by the shoulders and flung him away.

With a crash, he fell upon his ancient desk. Ink pots and pens clattered to the floor.

"Let me go, Father," I growled. "I do not want to hurt you."

"I will kill you first," Father hissed, utter hatred in his eyes. A thin trail of dead, blackened blood leaked down his temple.

I shook my head, disgusted by the pathetic sight. I turned again toward the door. A second later, I felt something crash down onto my back. As I reeled round, I saw Father had hit me with the wooden chair from the desk.

I watched as he picked up a splintered chair leg, its end split into a sharp and deadly point.

I did not have time to think as I deflected his next blow, just grabbed the leg and used it as he had intended on me. I gripped it tightly in my fist and plunged it into his chest. I felt the bone of his breastplate shatter and the stake lodge deep into his dark heart.

Screaming and writhing, he grasped the stake between his hands; his contorted face reflected his dreadful realization.

I heard a loud gasp from the doorway and found John there.

I let Father's impaled body drop to the floor. It had already begun to degrade, but he hung on like the demon he was.

"John!" he gasped. "Regard your true sire . . ." Black blood welled up in his mouth and he swallowed it back.

John's face was a mask of revulsion and horror as he took in Father's face.

Then, with a final sigh, Father gave up his damned and blackened ghost.

For a final time, I turned and walked to the door, passing John without a glance.

As I reached the top of the stairs, John's cold, hard voice came to me.

"You brought me here. You helped unleash my true nature. And now you are abandoning me?"

I bowed my head, unable to deny it. "I am sorry," I replied. "I gave you what was rightfully yours. It is up to you what you do with it."

Before I leave, I shall fetch Lily's broken body from the rocks and bury it away from here. A true innocent claimed my heart—yet died because of me. Lily's death must be the beginning of my salvation.

Journal of Mary Seward

30TH NOVEMBER 1916

I pushed through the vegetation that disguised the tunnel's entrance and we emerged into soft morning light. The child roused and looked around her, wide-eyed, as though thankful as I for the cool fresh air and sight of the village ahead.

I turned back to look at the castle, bathed in the bloodred glow of the sunrise on its mountain perch.

How startled the villagers were to see us. The innkeeper took us in and his wife fed the baby warm milk. Villagers crowded at the doorway, jostling to see the woman who had returned from the castle—in daylight, and with one of their own.

When I had finished eating, the innkeeper brought the infant to me and placed her back in my arms. I looked at him in surprise, having expected her family to come and claim her once word of our arrival had reached them. I gestured to the child, then to the houses beyond.

The innkeeper shook his head and motioned to me to stand and follow him. He led me down through the village to the churchyard. There, he showed me a series of gravestones—one that looked newly placed. Carved on it were two names. The innkeeper looked sorrowfully at the infant and crossed himself.

I understood. The child's parents had recently been taken. She had no family left here.

That night, the child and I slept side by side in a great soft bed. For the first time in days I felt safe, secure behind the wreaths of garlic blossom that hang at the window, as they do around every door and window in the village.

8TH DECEMBER 1916

It seems we shall be home in time for Christmas. I sent a telegraph to Father this morning.

The ship rocks gently beneath me as I write. The captain

says the weather will remain fair for us all the way to England.

Here in my cabin the infant sleeps peacefully in her cot. No one from the village offered to take her. I think they were frightened, as she had been so long in the castle. I have named her Grace.

I pray daily that God will protect us both from the darkness we have left behind—and that somehow, my heart shall heal from the grief that afflicts it.

Beyond the watery horizon lies England, where I shall make a home for Grace. A safe haven where God, and peace, shall dwell.

THE STORY OF DRACULA'S
LEGACY CONTINUES . . .
TURN THE PAGE FOR A SNEAK
PEEK AT THE THRILING SEQUEL

BLOODLINE

BOOK TWO
RECKONING

Journal of Mary Seward

I visited Grace today. Her parents were holding a small party to celebrate her second birthday. Today is the date we chose for her, knowing she was around three months old when I rescued her and brought her to England a year and nine months ago.

The maid showed me into the Edwardses' parlor, bright with the afternoon sun. I smiled at the balloons and streamers put up for Grace, who was running happily around the room, her face lit up with excitement. Her adoptive mother and father gazed on fondly.

On seeing me enter, Andrew and Jane immediately came over.

"Look who it is, Gracie! Aunt Mary has come to see you!" Her father called to her.

Grace came running and flung her arms around my legs. I

swept her up and kissed her, then swung her round. She laughed gleefully and the sound filled me with joy.

To me, it still seems like a gift from God that I found a local Purfleet couple to adopt Grace, and so soon after I escaped from Transylvania with her. There had been times in Castle Dracula when I believed I would never see home again. The horrors of that place will haunt me forever, but Grace, being just a babe of three months when she was imprisoned there, will have escaped unscathed in mind as well as body, God willing.

Seeing Grace today, now two years old, beloved and safe, brought me such joy. Jane asked me to stay for dinner and part of me longed to linger within the warmth and cheeriness of the Edwardses' home. But I had to refuse, of course, in order to get home before dark. For since my return from Transylvania, the darkness frightens me more than it did when I was a child. Back then, I only suspected monsters lurked there. Now I know they truly do.

As it was, the sun was already a low fiery ball in the sky as I set off along the empty lane. My heart began to quicken. I despise the restless anxiety I now feel as twilight approaches. I cling to the symbols of religion like a drowning man clings to driftwood, keeping both my crucifix and a small vial of holy water worn as a pendant on chains around my neck.

I gripped them both now as dusk enveloped me, only the

horizon retaining its pale light as the sun swiftly began to set. Dead leaves swirled about my feet as I hurried along, their noise becoming the swish of vampire wings in my mind. A menacing outline seemed to lurk in every shadow, sending fresh terror coursing through me like electricity as I passed by.

I heard a twig snap behind me, and my alarm spiraled into panic. I broke into a run, my coat fluttering behind me. I had only to turn the corner and I would be in view of home—but my breathing was so fast I felt light-headed. Sparks of light began to flash before me. I feared I would faint before I got there.

Sucking in great gulps of air, I battled to outrun my panic and reach the gate. I burst through, leaving it swinging on its hinges. My feet sent the gravel flying as I raced along the path to the door, fumbling in my bag for my key.

What was that noise behind me? I could not look. My heart felt it would burst as my shaking fingers tried to fit the key into the lock. At last they found purchase. I flung open the door and fell inside, slamming it behind me.

Leaning against it, I drew the bolt, relief making me weak. I slid into the chair beside the coat stand. My chest heaved with sobbing and I fought to stifle it, lest Father hear me.

Eventually, I gathered myself and forced myself to look

out of the hallway window. The garden stood quiet and empty in its darkness.

Once more, fear and anxiety have misled my senses. I have seen or heard nothing of John or of Quincey Harker since returning to England. And yet, even now, as I write in the safety of my room, I am governed by my fear of them.

I pray that I shall one day be free from the tyranny of it.

Clyst Abbey, Devon

The Daybook of
Father Michael, Abbot of Clyst

13TH NOVEMBER 1917
3.05 A.M.

Thanks be to God that we have made it through another night.

My sleep has been fitful, disturbed again by the unearthly noises coming from the prisoner's cell. Lord have mercy on us all if he should break loose while the bloodlust is upon him. Though I know that his chains are strong and the lock on his cell door heavy, fear clutches my throat when I am caught in his fiery gaze.

When the moon is at its highest, his tortured groans echo down the stone hallways—normally so still with the silence kept by our Cistercian brotherhood—until the whole abbey seems to ring with his torment.

He howls for blood, of course—craving it to nourish the darkness within him. Our keeping him from it strikes hard at his blackened heart.

As I write he howls still—but less fiercely now, with dawn coming. The daylight shall quieten his vampire soul.

By starving him—chaining him so that he cannot indulge his bloodlust—I pray that the evil that possesses him might eventually shrivel and die.

Shall the mortal remains of Quincey Harker survive such trial?

That, I do not know. I have come across no record of such an exorcism being embarked upon before.

I must hasten to the chapel. Prayers will be soon. The early morning vigil calms me, now more than it has ever done—warm candlelight flickering on the smooth stone pillars, white robes swishing against the gleaming wood of the pews as the brothers lower themselves to kneel alongside me to pray.

Afterwards will come the blessed light of dawn. And Harker will be still again . . .

I fear that sleep is proving impossible tonight. The presence of our prisoner, locked below, has truly unsettled our community.

As I entered the refectory for supper this evening, the room hummed with whispering. The brothers, seated at the rows of long wooden tables, glanced up, eyeing me anxiously before returning to their hushed conversations.

"Good evening, brothers," I said. "Is all well with you?"

Brother Sebastian glanced uneasily across at Brother Stephen, but ventured nothing.

I took my place at table, said Grace, and then helped myself to stew and a hunk of bread, freshly made that morning in the abbey's bakery.

And then Brother Sebastian began to speak. "Father, how can we be well, when we harbor Evil beneath our roof?" he asked quietly.

"Harker was more unsettled than ever last night," Brother Stephen added. He gazed at me, his blue eyes earnest in his gaunt face. "He seems to be making no improvement."

I understood their concerns. Even I, in the darkest hours before dawn, have questioned whether we really have any hope at all of redeeming Quincey Harker's twisted soul. But there must *always* be hope. "I beseech you brothers, keep your faith. We must not abandon this work," I insisted.

"With no fresh blood to sustain it, the Evil in Harker must surely be weakening."

"That may be, but his will remains fearsome," whispered Brother Sebastian.

"Maybe we should take our cue from the old lunatic asylums," grunted Brother Matthew, breaking a hunk of bread with his rough, stout fingers. "They'd 'ave beaten the Devil out of Quincey Harker. Flogged 'im and purged 'im with emetics." He pushed a piece of the bread into his mouth and began to chew.

I shook my head. "Brother Matthew, this is 1917 and we are men of God. I hope we have left such barbarism behind."

"We may have," Brother Stephen said. "But Quincey Harker hasn't!"

I stared at him, surprised at the harshness of his tone. His voice dropped to a whisper. "Harker is a *vampire!*" he spat. "There is *no* saving him. His soul is irredeemably lost. Surely it would be safer for all if he were destroyed in the traditional way."

"A stake through the heart!" I exclaimed. "Brother, we are not murderers!"

All but Brother Stephen looked away. "It would not be murder," he argued. "We would be freeing his soul at last, and ridding the world of a great evil."

"Brother Stephen," I sighed, "do you have so little faith in prayer left? And what of God's mercy? Our Lord Jesus spoke of love—it is the most powerful weapon. We can weaken the Evil that grips Harker's soul by depriving it of the blood it craves. And once it is weakened we must trust that God will show mercy and cleanse the darkness from Harker once and for all. Remember the words of Saint Paul: *'God's strength manifests itself when I am weak.'*"

Now Brother Stephen looked away too.

"We *must* believe that God's love has the power to save Quincey Harker," I went on. "And we must be his vessels."

As I write, moonlight floods my desk, brighter than the candle flickering beside the page. I can hear Harker beginning his own midnight vigil—his mournful, agonized howls piercing though the thick stone walls to ring out into the night.

29 NOVEMBER 1917

After prayers and breaking fast this morning, I visited Harker in his cell.

I entered the dank, stone chamber, closing its iron door behind me. The heaviness of the earthy-smelling air made it hard to breathe.

Harker was resting in the shadiest corner, away from the weak shaft of sunlight filtering through the tiny barred window high up on one of the walls. He was sitting on the floor, his head leaning wearily against the wall. But his eyes glinted watchfully. He reminded me of a caged panther I had once seen at London Zoo.

"You should sleep," I advised. "You must be tired."

"I have no wish to sleep," he growled, staring in disgust at his narrow blanketed bunk.

"But is it not in the nature of your kind to sleep through the day?" I asked.

Harker sprang to his feet, the heavy chains that bound his wrists clanking in protest. "I may hide from the flesh-burning sun, but I am not such a slave to the vampire nature as most of my kind," he hissed, his eyes flashing.

I took a stumbling step back, a hand sliding to my crucifix. His sudden anger alarmed me. Even though it was daytime, I feared I might glimpse that fiery glow that rages in his eyes when the hunger for prey grips him.

His gaze retained its dark intensity, however. Harker pushed a lock of black hair away from his forehead and then, to my surprise, he smiled. "It is you who should get some sleep," he warned. "For tonight is Saint Andrew's Eve—when all the world's evils are at their strongest." He drew in a long breath. "My hunger is sure to be at its . . . most disturbing."

I fought the icy fear that chilled my blood at his words, thinking instead of his howls of anguish ringing out each night. "I'm sorry your hunger torments you so," I told him. "But we keep you here in your best interests. And tonight we shall pray for you."

Harker lifted his chin and let out a harsh laugh. "Do you believe God will listen?" he mocked.

"God is always listening," I assured him.

"But does he always *hear*?" Harker asked.

I returned his gaze uncertainly. Was he taunting me?

"I pray that some day you will know his mercy," I murmured, and stepped towards the heavy iron door.

As I turned the key in the lock from the other side of it, I saw Harker still watching me through its small barred window. I looked away.

What am I to make of our prisoner? After listening to him curse and struggle against his captivity each night, I hardly expected to find his conversation still so lucid. But can I believe it is Harker with whom I speak? Am I conversing with a man or with the evil that possesses him? I pray that the Lord in His infinite wisdom will give us the strength to bring this tormented soul back into the light.

The moon is rising—and, I fear, a storm is too. The dark crags and rolling heathland beyond the abbey walls are now brushed by glowering skies. Though the seasons here in the West Country are known for their mildness, Dartmoor seems to have a climate of its own—as if the moor itself draws down the worst of the elements, and conjures up squalls and tempests like some ancient storm-bringer. On nights like this, staring out into that bleak landscape beyond, one feels very far from civilization. It is hard to believe that the busy cathedral city of Exeter is but a few miles away.

I shall now join the brothers for a night of prayer. For on tonight of all nights, we must do all that we can to protect Harker from the evil within him

30 NOVEMBER 1917

I must record the horrors I have seen.

Last night, as I led the brothers in prayer for Harker, terrible groans of torment began to rise from his cell below. And then, just before midnight, a terrible, tortured scream rang out from the cell—a scream so chilling that it seemed to choke me into silence.

I picked up an altar candle and, signaling Brother Sebastian to do the same and follow me, I hurried down towards the vaults.

Harker's cell door stood ajar.

Brother Sebastian looked at me, his customarily ruddy cheeks stricken white with terror.

The most monstrous howling could not have filled me with more trepidation than the heavy silence that came from within the cell. Was Harker somehow escaped, and at large?

I prayed for strength to stop my hand from shaking as I reached out and pushed the door wider open.

Harker was there. His chains still hung upon his wrists, shackling him to the wall. But he seemed insensible to our arrival—his attention entirely focused on the white-robed figure slumped in his strong grasp. For long moments I could neither move nor speak, watching him convulse in rhythmic shudders as he sucked the life blood from his victim's throat, thick groans of gratification rumbling up from his own. And then, in one swift movement, Harker twisted his prey's neck and I heard the cracking of bone.

The victim's head lolled back unnaturally, neck clearly broken. His face was contorted like that of a gargoyle, the dead whites of his eyes like marble in the cold moonlight that sliced through the tiny barred window above.

It was Brother Stephen.

I found my voice. "No!" My cry echoed around the cell.

Harker raised his head, his lips and chin gleaming wet with blood. His eyes glowed like embers as he met my stricken gaze. He let Brother Stephen fall to the cold flagstones. Blood oozed from Brother Stephen's throat like that of a slaughtered lamb, staining the white wool of his robe.

I sank to my knees beside Brother Stephen's body. "Why

did you come here, Brother?" I sobbed, though I knew he could no longer hear me.

And then I saw the long, sharpened wooden stake and mallet, lying in the corner of the cell as though flung there. Brother Stephen had decided to take matters into his own hands. He had come here to kill Harker—to hammer a stake through his evil heart—God rest his poor, impetuous soul. "Oh, Brother Stephen . . . why couldn't you have put your faith in prayer?" I murmured brokenly.

"Father Michael, come away!" Brother Sebastian had followed me in, and was pulling at my robe. "The prisoner is still possessed! You must come out of his reach!"

But God must have entered my soul like iron, for I felt no fear within me as I looked up and met Harker's fiery stare. Only sorrow.

I lifted my crucifix and, holding it out in front of me walked slowly toward Harker. He roared at the sight of it and tugged at his chains, his face frenzied. A superhuman strength seemed to possess him. With an almighty heave, he wrenched the iron wristbands, and snapped them from the chains that held him. The chains clattered on the floor, dangling useless now from the fastenings in the wall. He was free!

Harker lunged forward, pushing me out of his way. My fall was broken by the still-warm body of Brother Stephen. Drawing in a sharp breath, I turned to see Harker charge past a cowering Brother Sebastian and through the open cell door.

"We must stop him," I gasped, as Brother Sebastian helped me to my feet.

"Father Michael, I fear he is unstoppable . . ." Brother Sebastian whispered.

"Then we must return to the brothers in the chapel and pray for Brother Stephen's safe passage to heaven—and for any poor souls caught out on the fog-wrapped moors. For now, no creature is safe. Having hungered for blood for so long, I dare not imagine how much it will take to slake his thirst."

Dawn is lighting the sky. I have returned to my cell to rest after our vigils, but I cannot sleep. Some of the brothers are still praying. It is a mercy, at least, that Brother Stephen died of a broken neck, and not from being sucked dry of his blood. His body will not rise as one of the vampire undead.

Despite his crimes, we pray for Quincey Harker too. For who can save his blackened soul now?